EVERYDAY, MONSTERS

EVERYDAY, MONSTERS

BY

C. M. CHAPMAN

&

LARRY D. THACKER

EVERYDAY, MONSTERS

"The Unimaginable" was originally published in the summer 2016 issue of *Dime Show Review* ; "Big Buddy" was originally published in the Fall 2016 issue of *Unlikely Stories Mark V* ; "Gertrude's War" was originally published in the spring 2018 issue of *K'in Literary Journal*.

Attention schools and businesses: for discounted copies on large orders, please contact the publisher directly.

This book is a work of fiction. Names, characters, businesses, organizations, places, events and incidents either are the product of the author's imagination or are used fictitiously. Any resemblance to actual persons, living or dead, events, or locales is entirely coincidental.

Unsolicited Press
Portland, Oregon
www.unsolicitedpress.com
orders@unsolicitedpress.com

Cover design: Kathryn Gerhardt
Editor: Kay Grey; S.R. Stewart

ISBN 978-1-950730-88-9

CONTENTS

HOLY ROLLER

Larry D. Thacker

Wilma didn't think. She acted.

It was a reaction driven by pure adrenaline.

She would have defended herself with a rolled up Sunday newspaper if she'd been on the front porch reading one when Jake came after her, not that it would have done her any good. Lucky for Wilma though, come to find out a frozen roll of chocolate chip cookie dough is about the same size and striking strength as a wooden rolling pin. She'd just pulled the package out of the freezer to let it thaw a bit when Jake stumbled from the living room for another beer, bumped into the kitchen table, and knocked the fresh lemonade Wilma'd been squeezing on all over his clean, pressed jeans.

"I was gonna preach in these tomorrow night, woman!"

The accident was somehow Wilma's fault, which meant she'd get it upside the head at least once if he could catch her, which he did, but not as hard as it could have been and not as lightly as she might have hoped, but on this occasion something deep in her head clicked in a different direction than usual, she saw red, and she swung back. Again, it could have been a frozen bean burrito or a hot iron. The iron skillet Jake's momma gave her or the six-pound, three-generation family Bible they kept on the coffee table. But it was a rock solid, thirteen-inch-long, two-inch-thick roll of cookie dough that might as well have been cast iron. His fist grazed her cheek. She countered with a two-fisted swing that would have put his head across the street into the neighbor's lot if it hadn't been connected to his neck. He crumpled like a winter sack of potatoes, his temple split wide open. He started bleeding in such a way as Wilma'd never seen anyone bleed, like the water hose was left on and it was the bloody Nile during the plagues running from her husband's ear and the long dark gash across the left side of his head. Jake loved preaching about Moses and children of Israel and the Great Exodus into the wilderness for forty long years.

There was a little lemonade left in the pitcher. She turned it upright and poured what was left into the morning's coffee cup and sipped it. Her cheek hurt a little. He'd mostly missed, but it might still bruise. She hoped not.

When life got tough, whether with him and Wilma, or at the Copper Creek Temple, Jake laid it at the Lord's feet, as he'd say.

Lay it at the Lord's feet. God's will's got a plan for everything. If he didn't want something to happen, it wouldn't now, would it?

It was one of those catch-all phrases that fit most any bad situation. While most church members took solace in that sentiment and it even helped Wilma feel better most of the time, she wasn't convinced when "Preacher" Jake started beating on her after a six-pack and some shots on a Friday night. She'd asked him once if God wanted him hitting her all the time and he'd threatened to send her to heaven to ask the Lord in person.

And now there Jake was, piled up on the kitchen floor, having breathed his last, a pool of blood growing like a scarlet halo around his two-faced, drunk-assed head.

"Shame he fell and hit his head on the countertop like that," she muttered out loud, sipping the last of the lemonade. "I swear, he must have slipped. He'd been drinking, again. He fell all the time."

God's will and all. Lay it at the Lord's feet.

Wilma looked around the kitchen, the one room of the house she felt safest, though that obviously wasn't always the case all the time. She still held the roll of dough. There was the slightest dent toward the end. A spot of red marking the spot. Her hands still trembled. The area under her intense grip was thawing now. Her whole arm throbbed up into her arthritic shoulder.

She set the dough roll down, at about where she was rehearsing in her mind the side of Jake's head smacked the gray and white streaked marble countertop, sort of near the corner. She practiced the sound in her head. What it sounded like from the back porch pantry where she'd say she was at that terrible moment, when she was head first in the deepfreeze digging for frozen catfish fillets for supper. Would it have been more of a *whack* or a *thump* or a sort of wet *smack*? Would he have let out a holler? A moan or groan? Yes, more like a *ka-thwack* and a *yelp*. Then the *thump* of his heavy body.

She lifted the hems of her denim skirt and stepped quietly over the dark pool setting up on the linoleum, reaching for an oven dial. She'd made these cookies so often for the grandkids she knew the proper temperature – 350-degrees. She prepped a baking sheet with some wax paper. She could have done it blindfolded, this act of baking love for the young'uns. Pulled a knife from the utensils drawer and split the spine of the package open exposing the tannish and speckled dough. It felt like cutting through flesh. A bit tough, but giving with enough pressure, the plastic snapping through. She cut little rounds off the roll just as if she were slicing up an apple, filling the sheet up. Her hands were still shaking. She had to be careful. But what about blood on the plastic?

She eyed the end of her thumb as the knife swept by with each slice. Another. Another. Then an icy pain hit. Her own blood rushed forth. Like water from the rock. The sin of Moses. It dripped on the countertop. She turned, letting some drip to the floor to mingle with Jake's dying lifeblood. She wondered if his blood was still flowing. If there was any life at all left in the body. She thought of Lazarus coming back to life and wondered if even the Lord had been surprised.

The oven dinged, signaling it was preheated and ready. The blast of superheated air shocked her when it struck her face and neck and upper chest. The twisting elements glowed, always reminding her of what the tiniest percent of damnation must be like. Is that just the smallest inkling of the devil's hell? The lake of fire? A sinner's destination for the ultimate transgression? Even if they were defending themself?

She shoved the pan of cookies in with a metallic rattle and slammed the door and set the timer for fifteen minutes and went to the living room to think. Jake not laying stretched back in his beat-up recliner was awfully odd. That he wouldn't ever be there again seemed odder. Five empty beer cans set around the chair. Another one on the edge of the coffee table leaving a circle. She couldn't wait to drag that chair out back to the burn pile.

Things would change, wouldn't they? Right quick like. What would the church do? Would the Temple keep on going? Find another preacher? He'd started Copper Creek, hadn't he? Would they want someone else? Too many questions. Did any of it matter? It'd work out.

God's will and all.

The oven dinged. Cookies. Didn't they smell good.

Wilma got up from the couch and went back to the kitchen. Something hung in the kitchen air besides the thick aroma of warm cookies and melted chocolate. The essence of aging, coagulating blood. Like someone had left hamburger out all day. Along with the rancidness of urine. Jake had pissed himself come to find out. But thank goodness it was mostly cookies she smelled now. She'd had bouts of a weak stomach in the past and now wasn't the time for a relapse.

She grabbed the sheet of cookies from the oven with her best oven mitt, the one she kept hanging on the wall for special occasions, the one that said: *Lord, Bless This Mess.* She slid the cookies onto the countertop, wishing the grandchildren were around to enjoy them.

The cookies made a perfect little pyramid on the large plate she chose from the cabinet. The Dollywood one with Dolly singing into an old style microphone and playing a big guitar. She didn't want to be alone eating all of these cookies.

The evidence.

God's will and all.

She grabbed her diabetes meds and swallowed one down. Maybe that would balance out the task ahead. There were twenty five good sized cookies. At least they were warm. They melted in your mouth when they were fresh out of the oven.

She poured herself a cold glass of whole milk. She walked out to the porch with the plate of cookies, grabbing the cordless phone along the way, and sat on the metal sled rocker with the plate on her lap. It looked like it might rain. The grass needed cutting.

She picked a single cookie from the top of the pile, pushed it full into her mouth and chewed the sugary warmth with a smile and swallowed.

Then she dialed 911.

SIXTEEN HUNDRED MONKEYS

C.M. Chapman

The captain's desperate, nocturnal walks had persisted for a year now. Martin Cooke didn't understand the insomnia which drove him from his cabin nightly, like an animal released from a cage, out onto the deck of the *Sea Mule*, where his pacing found the larger venue for which it yearned. Again, tonight, as he stepped out of his quarters on the O3 deck, he questioned his sleeplessness. Was it some sort of precognition? For everything else, his life was secure. He had forty years on the waves, first with the US Navy, and then working his way up with one of the larger shipping companies in the merchant marine fleet, Mason-Jennings International. After fifteen years, he made captain like his father, Eli Cooke.

Some nights, he would run into one of the bridge crew, down from the O4 to use the head, but not tonight. It didn't matter. They knew better than to question his night walks at this point. Cooke supposed they accepted it as normal behavior by now. In any case, he didn't try to conceal his movements as he headed into the ladder well. When his father passed away with cancer, Martin, the only survivor, inherited the entire estate. That, along with his own savings, had given him the collateral he needed to start his own company, Cooke Shipping. What the crew thought about his dark journeys didn't matter.

Captain Martin Cooke no longer sailed for any other man.

On his way down the ladder well he passed the O2, which housed the officer's quarters and showers, as well as two guest compartments for those times when passengers would book passage on the *Sea Mule*. It wasn't uncommon to have a passenger or two, but there were none on this particular voyage. The O deck, which he passed through at ship level, was split in two. The infirmary and radio room took up one half, and the other half contained the commons area and a workout facility.

The *Sea Mule*, a dark green, general cargo vessel, was Cooke Shipping's first purchase for just under a half million dollars. At a hundred sixty meters long, the majority of the *Sea Mule's* deck was comprised of the long, flat, mid-ship area where the cargo containers were stacked, sometimes five high. At her bow, the foremast stood fifteen meters high, next to the anchor winches.

After his descent, Cooke emerged from the hatch at her stern, below the white superstructure which rose four decks high and was topped by the conning tower. The bridge, surrounded by glass, reflected the cargo corridors stretching into the dark, looking down on the ship like an airport control tower.

She was the only vessel in the Cooke Shipping fleet.

The *Sea Mule* currently glided over calm seas, on the return side of the Mumbai run, a voyage they made twice a year, in spring and fall. The run included a drop-off of logistical supplies for the military in Dubai. Then, the *Sea Mule* would continue east to Mumbai, where they took on a variety of cargo, most of which consisted of various Indian food products for an Asian grocery wholesaler in New York.

The Mumbai run also offered a chance to transport another lucrative cargo, rhesus macaques for a bio-tech company called Gen-Op, who paid top dollar for the monkeys. The live cargo came with a lot more red tape and necessitated the hiring of a handler for the voyage, but the profit far exceeded the extra cost. This was the *Sea Mule's* seventeenth monkey haul. Cooke never gave the creatures a second thought, except to occasionally make sure the handler kept that area of the ship clean and sanitary. As time passed, he liked more and more for his ship to be clean.

The captain followed his regular routine, checking in with the watches, and quietly contemplating the echo of his footsteps through the corridors of orange and gray shipping containers that towered above him like a dead city. On some nights those alleyways were black as death and he would have to feel his way along. Eventually, he found his way to the foremast, where he lingered at the bow, looking out at a sea that contained a light all its own.

Cooke still carried his sidearm with him even though the *Sea Mule* was past Gibraltar and long past any likelihood of pirate attack. Once past the Suez, that particular threat diminished greatly but, even so, he still always breathed a sigh of relief to be back in the Atlantic. The Atlantic felt like home.

He was not overly afraid of pirates. An arms locker on board held several M-14 rifles which could be used to defend the *Sea Mule* and he kept his night watch armed with 9mm's as well. But vigilance was prudent, and so, once out to sea, he carried his at all times. It was his way of keeping the crew on their toes. Cooke did not take the safety of his ship lightly, but he knew that none of the other merchant marine captains did either.

After finishing a lap of the main deck, the captain entered a hatch next to the superstructure and descended the ladder to the tween deck where he poked his head through the hatch and took a look toward the galley. He intended to do a round of the passageways below-decks, check in with the black gang on the status of the engines, and maybe grab himself a glass of milk on his way back to his cabin. Below decks, the galley was the closest compartment to the superstructure above. Most of the crew ate here except the Captain and the officers who ate on the O3, in the ward room. The galley was dark and silent as he stepped out of the ladder well. Cookie would be up in a few hours, prepping for breakfast.

The last compartment at the end of the tween deck was the space they used for live cargo like the macaques. It was large, encompassing two entire ship sections. And it was enclosed, providing a certain amount of insulation from the noises of the ship. He didn't intend to tour the tween deck, but as he turned back to the ladder well to go below, he heard one of the monkeys shriek.

He paused as it occurred to him that here he was, with his own private zoo- they'd once even carried a herd of alpacas- and he'd not once taken advantage of it. He never really paid any attention to the monkeys and there had been many of those aboard. Considering their likely fate, it was probably best, he supposed. Gen-Op did neuro-ophthalmological research aimed toward developing an artificial eye. He wasn't sure what that might entail or if he even wanted to know. He continued through the hatch and down the ladder.

After a brief exchange with the junior engineer standing watch in the engine room, Cooke made his way forward again, toward the lower hold, where he traversed the stacks of cargo containers and considered the state of the *Sea Mule*. The lower hold was full up and the ship was running fore-heavy on the return. He was glad the seas had been calm. He hoped they stayed that way.

He returned aft through the starboard passageway, his sights set on the galley.

Cooke left the galley port-side with a carton of milk, a couple packs of cheese crackers, and every intention to head back up to his cabin. But the walk had not left him ready to sleep and he'd already seen all the new movies brought on board this trip. On a whim, he turned up the tween deck's port passage, toward the live cargo compartment. On his right, he passed the quarters of the animal handler, Burgess. He couldn't remember the kid's first name.

The live cargo compartment wasn't completely dark despite the fact that the main overhead lights were off. One small fluorescent bulb was lit on the far wall above the metal sink and counter. Cooke entered, shutting the hatch behind him.

The cages were stacked four-high, aluminum squares secured to each other and against the port bulkhead, a hundred monkeys in all. He did not venture into the darkened rows, but walked along the outside, peering into the outer cages which were dimly illuminated by the utility light.

One of the macaques took an interest in him immediately, approaching the bars of the cage.

Cooke had no experience with animals. His father would not suffer them when he was a child. Once, in grade school, his class had taken a field trip to the zoo, but the only part of the trip he remembered was the aquarium. From the time he was a small child it was all ships, sea monsters, and the stern judgment of the ocean.

Now, face to face with the monkey, he was stunned by human characteristics that he'd never before considered. This macaque had a light blond, thin, mustache and goatee that contrasted with his reddish skin. His ears were pointed, and his beautiful light fur radiated around them like peacock feathers as it did around his jawline. His eyes were an orangish-brown, curious, and intelligent. To Cooke, he looked like a miniature Chinese philosopher, a tiny Confucius. As he considered the similarities, he felt a completely alien urge come over him.

"How you doing, little fella?" he said, chewing on a cracker. It was the first time he'd ever spoken to any animal and it felt less ridiculous than he might have imagined.

The macaque sank into a squat, his hands on the bars of the cage, his attention fully on the captain. He thrust a furry arm through the bars and held his hand out, palm up.

Cooke looked at the little fingers, the little palm with its dark, etched surface and laughed. "You want one, eh?"

The monkey flexed his fingers.

The captain laughed again. These animals were supposedly from a farm. This one was obviously used to begging and had probably eaten worse. He held out half a cracker. The monkey snatched it back into the cage and leaned against the side while he examined it. After a couple tentative nibbles, he wolfed it down, checking afterward for crumbs. Then, still leaning, he rested his head against the side of the cage as if he were cozying up to his mother and looked at Captain Cooke.

"So, Marty," said the macaque in a soft, mellifluous voice, "You look tired."

#

Leonard Stubb was worried. He hadn't seen the monkey yet, but the whole crew was laughing and talking about it. The First Mate of the *Sea Mule* was worried because he always took it upon himself to learn about the cargo that they carried. One of the things he'd learned a long time ago about rhesus macaques was they were known to carry a virus deadly to humans. And, while that was worrisome in itself, this situation was really just the latest in a long line of strange behavior from the captain.

Stubb had been worried about *him* much longer than the monkey.

Ever since Cooke's divorce from Lucy three years ago, and especially since word had come that she had remarried within two months, the captain had become more and more withdrawn. Stubb had been with him for nearly fifteen years, since the Mason-Jennings days, and could remember when Cooke took an active role on the ship. Now, aside from the midnight strolls, his appearances seemed to be more formalities than anything else. The few times that they'd gone through bad weather, he'd been on the bridge, doing his part, but mostly, his appearances were brief. Even those midnight strolls were odd, and Stubb knew that some of the men had started referring to him as the "night stalker."

On top of that, normal company policy did not allow for too many consecutive runs. It was well-known that one could go stir-crazy from too little time ashore. Duties shifted and schedules were juggled to make sure every seaman had significant leave time. But the captain hadn't skipped a trip in three years. He seldom left the ship while in port, not even home port in Norfolk. But how do you tell the company owner that he's violating company rules?

And now, thought Stubb, he'd turned a possibly diseased monkey loose on the ship.

The crew was having all kinds of fun with the idea of it, their stern captain with a monkey riding around on his shoulder. Still, Stubb was going to have to say something, he was sure. He remembered the day when he and Cooke had been friends. He could have said something to him then, but now?

He had two hours left on his watch. Then he had some rounds. After rounds he would find Captain Cooke and scope the situation out himself. He hoped the monkey would stay away from him.

His plan was interrupted an hour into his rounds when he got the news that Cookie was dead.

#

The monkey's soothing voice was like a balm to his unraveled nerves. The beast was so sympathetic that it didn't take long before Cooke spilled out everything about his divorce, the ten childless years together, the revelation that he was sterile, her unwillingness to adopt, and, of course, the bitch's almost immediate betrayal.

The monkey stuck out his hand for another cracker. "Sounds like a real mess," he said.

"I'll never have any of that now," said Cooke, his voice cracking. "I wanted to pass my legacy to a son. I'm fifty-eight years old. It'll never happen now."

"Then again," said the macaque, eating his cracker, "You could have my lot in life. Living in a cage, likely to have your brain sliced open soon."

Cooke looked around at the other cages. Some of the macaques were watching but none gave any indication they could talk. Most weren't paying any attention at all. It was just this one, little Confucius, as though some magical communication bubble surrounded them, separating them from the rest of the world. It felt *good*, somehow. For the first time in a long time, something actually felt *good* and *right*.

"I could let you out," said Cooke.

"Well," said the furry philosopher, "that would be mighty sporting of you,"

Cooke opened the cage and the macaque came out into his arms, probing his shirt pocket for another cracker. Cook took hold of his miniature hand and marveled again at the dark little fingers and nails, with their sparse, light fur. So human, he thought, no wonder he could talk.

The overhead lights came on. The handler had arrived for his morning routine.

"Captain! Sir! What are you doing?"

Cooke heard disapproval in that voice, a reprimand he didn't like. "Don't worry, Burgess, everything's fine. I'll take care of this one."

"But sir-."

"In fact, I believe I'll keep him." said the captain. "Don't give me that look. This is my ship. Gen-Op will just get ninety-nine monkeys this time."

"No sir, you don't understand. This animal hasn't been screened! He could be carrying the Herpes B virus. That can be deadly when it crosses over to humans. Have you been scratched?"

Burgess scrutinized Cooke's arms and face. "Please, put him back and wash yourself good in the sink over there."

"No need, Burgess, this animal's fine. I'll hear no more of it."

Cooke turned to go, and Burgess would have sworn he heard him whisper, "Sorry, no offense," as he was headed out the hatch.

#

Cooke left the live cargo compartment with the macaque on his shoulder. He turned aft and stopped off into the galley for a cup of coffee and a couple more packs of crackers, since the monkey seemed to like them so well. Cookie was prepping for breakfast. Soon the bacon or sausage would be on the stoves and filling the air through the lower hold, drawing in the crew from all points.

"Got yourself a new friend there, skipper?" asked Cookie.

"Yeah, Cookie, whaddya think?"

Cookie seemed amused, if unfazed. "Just don't let him near my food or counters, skip." He laughed, an old, sea cook cackle as he went back to peeling potatoes.

There were men in the passageway now. Everyone he met seemed to be in a great mood, smiling and saying, "Morning Skipper," or "Morning Cap'n." He went up to the main deck to catch the sunrise over the sea. Still, to this day, he thought there was no more beautiful sight and he wanted to share it with his newly found friend. On deck he made his way toward the bow, once again talking to the macaque about his marriage.

"Yes, I was gone a lot, but I tried to make up for it when I was home."

"You're telling me you gave it to her pretty good, huh?" asked the monkey.

"Oh, come on now- why would you say that?" asked the captain.

"Well, it's what *I'd* do." said the macaque.

"Well, you're not me."

"Hmm…how about a cracker?"

"Here you go."

The sun came up. It was warm, the sea was calm, and Cooke spent most of the morning walking around between the stacks of containers, deep in conversation with a rhesus macaque. He was prudent enough to stay out of sight as much as possible. Mostly the monkey rode around on his shoulder, but occasionally it would jump off and climb the cargo containers as Captain Cooke laughed.

As morning wore on, the monkey said, "So let me get this straight. You were trying to *have* a kid, but you weren't putting it to her at every opportunity?"

"Well, some…"

"Cause speaking from experience Marty, at least from the perspective of us *animals,* the more you put it to her-"

"Yes, I know." said the captain impatiently. "But remember, the doctor said-"

"Oh, don't fall back on that! You didn't know that then, did you?" said the monkey. "I mean, a nubile, young female who wants to participate in the miracle of life it's a wonder she wasn't all over you all the time."

"You seemed a lot cuter before."

"How about a cracker?"

"Here you go. Now, what are you trying to say?"

"Well, not to speak out of turn, but maybe somebody else was putting it to her, you know?" The monkey raised his eyebrows.

It was a thought that Cooke had been fighting since he'd first married the young beauty who had worked for his young company in their Norfolk port office.

"I bet it was even someone on this ship," said the monkey, reaching down to grab his breast pocket and leaning down to sniff it. "You know, I can smell her on you."

"No, you can't. It's been over three years."

"Super smell power, my friend. And if I can smell her on you, I can smell her on anyone." The macaque raised his nose and sniffed the air. "*Somebody* on this ship was banging your wife."

Cooke clenched his fists. "Who? Tell me now, damn it!"

"Put me down. I'll show you."

Cooke set the macaque down and it took off running. He had to run to come even close to keeping up and he was far behind when he saw the monkey go below decks. He was huffing and puffing by the time he hit the bottom of the ladder on the tween deck. He looked up and down the passageway but couldn't see the macaque. Then he heard a shriek and some crashing from the galley.

As he came around the corner through the doorway, he saw Cookie laying on the deck, the monkey beside him, nibbling on a piece of sliced apple.

"Here he is," said the monkey, "the dirty bastard who was banging your wife."

"Cookie!" the captain blurted out, almost in protest. "But he's so old!"

"You're no spring chicken yourself, Marty. Apparently, your gal liked her men a little more experienced, hmmm?"

Suddenly, the captain realized that Cookie was motionless on the floor and didn't appear to be breathing.

"Shit! Oh Shit! Cookie!" He ran over to check for a pulse.

"Yeah, I killed him for you," said the monkey.

No pulse. Captain Cooke looked around quickly, toward the passageway and up at the clock. 1400 hours, which was fortunate. This was a dull part of the ship at that time.

"You see what I will do for you?" asked the monkey.

"Why?" asked Cooke, almost pleading.

"Cause you saved me from the brain slicers, Marty."

"I've got to get you out of here," Cooke said, "back to my cabin. Before someone finds out what happened here."

The monkey pointed. "Hey, grab some of those apple slices, would ya?"

#

"What he die of, Doc?" asked Stubb.

"I dunno," said Doc. "If I had to guess… heart attack. But natural causes in any case. Ole' Cookie's made his last voyage."

"Could it be a virus?"

"Virus!"

"Yes, humor me." Stubb looked up as Second Engineer Perkins thundered into the galley.

"OH FUCK!" said Perkins, a large, bearded man. "And I'll bet there's not one limp-dicked asshole on this whole boat who could cook his way out of a paper bag."

"Not now, Perkins," said Stubb.

"Man, I don't wanna be eatin' fruit, nuts, and crackers for the next week and a half."

"Shut the fuck up, Perkins!"

"Sir?" A seaman had just come through the door.

"What is it, Reynolds? Did you notify the Captain?"

"Yes sir, but I don't think he's coming. He never came out and it sounded like he was yelling at someone in there." He paused, expectantly, looking at Cookie laying on the deck.

"When I told him Cookie was dead, he just said, 'Well, Cookie was old.' You believe that? He said that he was trying to get some sleep and that you would take care of everything."

"Okay then, get back to your watch, Reynolds."

"Right away, sir."

"Well Doc?" Stubb turned back to the doctor.

"Well? What? - oh, a virus? I suppose it could be. I'll have to get him up to the infirmary and my resources are limited, of course."

"Well, see what you can figure out, okay?"

The doctor shrugged his shoulders and gestured to two men who carried Cookie's body out on a stretcher.

"Lenny! I've been looking for you for an hour." It was the animal handler, Burgess, looking around as if confused, "What happened here?"

"Cookie's dead," said Stubb, "and I already know about the captain and the monkey."

"Bummer. How'd Cookie die?"

"We're not sure."

"Yeah, and what is *up* with the monkey? That thing shouldn't be running loose."

"I don't know, Burgess," Stubb almost whined. "I haven't been able to talk to the Captain about it yet."

"Well, it shouldn't be running loose."

Perkins voice came from back near the prep counter. "Aw, he was makin' apple pie- fuuuuck me!"

"Cookie was awesome, for sure," Burgess said to Stubb. "What are we gonna do there?"

"Burgess." Stubb turned to him.

Burgess put his hands up. "I see you're busy. Let me know about the monkey thing. I'd like to get it back into its cage."

Stubb turned back into the galley. "Perkins, get the fuck out of here. You'll eat what you eat. Don't bug me about it now."

Perkins left and Stubb looked down at the scattered pile of apple slices. One of the slices on the floor caught his eye and he picked it up to find it gnawed on one end.

Something was definitely fishy here. He didn't like where he thought this was going. He went to the sink and washed his hands.

#

The monkey told a sordid tale. Captain Cooke fumed, and yelled, and argued with him for three hours, pacing back and forth in his cabin, before finally coming to the conclusion that Confucius was right.

"You saw them as well as I did," said the macaque.

Every single crewman he'd seen that day had been laughing at him, Cookie included. It was really the final proof.

All those years she'd worked the desk at the docks, flirting with everyone like she did. They had *all* slept with her. Every last one of them had the opportunity at one time or another. There was always somebody on leave, someone ashore, while he was out to sea.

"It explains why I can smell her everywhere," said Confucius.

The captain was well involved in this conversation when someone had rapped on his cabin door to tell him about Cookie. Reynolds, he thought, maybe. He put the seaman off, elbow-nudging the monkey and winking when he said, "Well, Cookie was old."

Confucius had killed Cookie and Cooke had covered it up. Would they figure it out? Surely not, he thought. He didn't care now. Confucius had made it all clear to him.

The second knock came later. "Captain, sir?" It was Stubb, his "friend," perhaps the most poisonous of them all, he thought.

"What do you want?"

There was a moment's hesitation before Stubb said, "Sir, Burgess is concerned about the monkey."

Yeah, thought Cooke, he should be concerned, and so should you, Stubb.

"Monkey's fine, Stubb." he said through the door.

"Doc's trying to figure out how Cookie died." Stubb called back after a moment.

"Keep me appraised then." The captain could feel his throat constricting and a corner approaching in which he would be trapped. Maybe they did know, after all. Did someone see him?

"They're going to try to use it against you," whispered Confucius.

"You feel alright, sir?"

"Fine- trying to get some sleep."

"Uh, alright, well, I'll update you later, then," said Stubb.

When Cooke was reasonably sure that Stubb was gone, he turned back to the monkey.

"Did he?"

"That one fucked her more than all the others." said Confucius. "She's all over him. She must have licked him *everywhere…*"

"Enough!" Cooke clenched his fists and his jaw. "And now they plan to take over my ship? I won't give up my ship, Confucius!"

"Whaddya say we try a little experiment?" said the macaque.

"What kind of experiment?"

"First," said Confucius, leaping into his arms, "gimme some more of that apple."

#

Stubb was finished throwing up.

Behind him, he could still hear Third Mate Carlson blubbering. Carlson woke him twenty minutes earlier, sobbing the inconceivable words, "They're all dead, Lenny! All of 'em! All of 'em!" Stubb ran up to the bridge and only needed to look a foot into the room before he turned around and ran down to the O deck to check the weapons locker. It was empty. This was not the work of pirates or they would all be dead or captured.

Second Mate Teddy Sims was dead, as was Helmsman Nick Fine, Quartermaster Dick Williamson, and Seaman Henry Jones, who'd been standing Lookout. Stubb felt it necessary to go over all their names in his mind. It was 0445 and the sun would soon be rising on a blood-soaked bridge and it was hard to tell where one man ended and another began.

The communications panel was destroyed, presumably by the same implement used on the crew, a fire-ax, by the look of it. The radio room three decks down was smashed as well.

The Captain, last known to be in his quarters one deck below, was nowhere to be found and neither was his monkey.

Doc was doing his best on the bridge, trying to put the right pieces in the right places. A couple men with strong stomachs were helping him and starting to clean up some of the blood. Stubb's head was still spinning. He hated sending anyone in there. He gestured to Carlson, who approached, tears still streaming out of his eyes.

"It should have been me Lenny. If Cookie hadn't died and Teddy and I hadn't traded watches, it would have been me."

"Paulie, I need you to get yourself together. Once they get it cleaned up, get in there and assess the situation. Then report back to me"

"You want me to bring us to a stop?"

"God, no. Keep us at full steam, just make sure we're on course. The sooner we get back to port the better. In fact, figure out the closest US port to our present position and put us on course."

"Where's the Captain, Lenny?"

"Until we can find him, I'm the Captain. Is that clear?"

"Yes, sir."

"And listen Paulie, part of me thinks, well, I mean, you've noticed his behavior lately, right?"

"What?" Carlson looked precariously close to the edge. "Don't say that, Lenny."

"Just watch your back, okay?"

At that moment Seaman Reynolds burst through the hatch, breathless. "Some of the guys just came running up from below—said there's gunfire down there."

#

Confucius had bounced around, screaming, "Kill! Kill!" as Cooke methodically worked his way through the bridge crew. They barely put up a fight. By the time their senses rallied it was too late. First, they were too distracted by the monkey to notice the fire-ax behind his back and two of them, Williamson and Jones, were dead before Sims could even comprehend his need to escape. In the end, it was easier than he expected, just like the monkey said it would be.

But ever since he'd open fire on the black gang, Confucius was nowhere to be seen. He stepped over the bodies of the engine crew to look up and down the passageways on both sides of the engine room. Cooke's head was ringing and he was seeing through a haze, but on the port side, he heard the voice of the macaque, echoing from the shadows.

"I'm here, Marty. You'll forgive me my fear of ricochets."

He had two M-14s and his sidearm, as well as plenty of extra clips. He knew that some of those bastards were armed, but they wouldn't be able to hold out against him long. He laughed to himself as he thought about them checking the arms locker. Confucius was one forward-thinking macaque. Those weapons were safely stowed in a ballast tank now.

He prowled the lower storage hold like a shark, merciless, hungry. Confucius stayed out of sight, afraid of the gunfire. Somehow the men down in the hold had gotten past him. He would have to make his way aft again. His way up the starboard passage was interrupted by a gunshot that rang off the overhead. He didn't think. He sprayed gunfire down through the corridor without heed.

"Captain Cooke! Captain, listen, please!"

It was Stubb. Goddamn Stubb. He'd probably led the way the first time his wife was gang-banged. He was leading the mutinous conspiracy to seize Cooke's ship. It would be a pleasure to kill him.

"I'm coming for you, Stubb!"

"Marty, please. Something's gone wrong here. We can talk this out."

"Too late, Stubb!" Cooke sprayed more gunfire down the corridor and began advancing.

#

The members of the crew still alive were already gathered on the deck as Stubb and the two men with him tumbled out of the hatch.

"He's coming! Take cover!" yelled Stubb, and the crew split into every direction, most running into the avenues of storage containers. Stubb hid around the side of the hatch, hoping to catch Cooke unaware as he came through, but he never came. When the sound of gunfire rang out, The *Sea Mule's* First Mate looked toward the bridge in time to see four or five muzzle flashes and realized his mistake.

Carlson and Doc were dead. Shit. Who was up there with them? He couldn't remember.

Cooke had control of the bridge, as well as an eagle eye view of the deck. Stubb turned and fled into the containers. Eventually, the 12 surviving crew members found each other.

"Fuck this," said Stubb. "Perkins, take Curly and Reynolds and get the motor whale boat prepped."

"Life rafts would be a lot easier, sir. From up there, he'll be able to see us prepping the boat. Life rafts, we could go over anywhere…"

"Yeah, but the boat at least gives us a little fuel if we need to move quickly and we can all get in it. Do what you can from out of sight. I'm going to try to draw him off the bridge. Watch for it and get that boat ready."

"Not going to be an easy launch, Cap," said Perkins. "We're under full steam. It could be tricky."

"Which would you rather take your chances with," asked Stubb, "a rough launch or an armed maniac?"

"I see your point, sir."

"Watch your back. You three come with me. The rest of you, wait two minutes and then follow Perkins in two groups that go within 30 seconds of each other. Got that? Don't all go at once! Perkins, don't fucking leave without us, you hear?"

Stubb took a deep breath. One of the guys with him, Harrelson, had a pistol. He must have been on watch when everything started. Two pistols against a crazy man armed with

M-14's. If he had his way, it wouldn't matter. They wouldn't have to shoot at all.

Stubb gestured to the three men and headed to starboard, as far from the lifeboat as possible, making sure that Cooke could see them periodically as they moved between the stacks.

#

"I see you assholes," Cooke muttered. There were two groups, one moving up each side of the ship. They were trying to sneak around and enter the superstructure from behind. He'd lost track of the group on the port-side. When he finally got a glimpse of movement on that side, they were much further back than he thought. The starboard group was much closer. He fired at them, slowing their advance and then ran quickly from the bridge. He would get down the ladder and be waiting for them at the hatch.

From the deck, Stubb saw Cooke's silhouette disappear and held his breath. If the captain went up, to the conning tower, they would be screwed. He hadn't thought about that possibility before. When Cooke didn't appear up there, he exhaled. He had taken the bait. Stubb turned to the men with him. "Go now! Run! Straight for the boat!"

The four ran across the small area of open deck in front of the superstructure as fast as they could. If Stubb had figured right, Cooke couldn't see them at all right now. He wasn't a religious man, but he was definitely talking to *something* as they ran across the deck.

Perkins had the boat ready. It was indeed a tricky launch and they didn't have time to be careful. Stubb hoped that the captain wouldn't figure out what was going on until it was too late. The calm seas helped and with the exception of some disturbing lurches, they got the boat in the water and everyone made it. They cranked the engine, pulling away from the ship and the perils of the backwash as quickly as possible.

On the ship, Captain Cooke crouched behind a crate outside the hatch, waiting for his victims to round the corner, when something caught the edge of his sight. It was the boat, already 100 yards back.

"NO!" he screamed and began spraying gunfire out toward the ocean. He thought maybe he got someone, hoped at least he'd put some holes in the boat. "Burn in hell, you adulterous whores! That's what happens to mutineers!"

They were already beginning to fade from view.

Cooke turned and looked around for Confucius.

#

The ship became a distant spec on the horizon. Stubb half expected Cooke to turn around and try to sink them, but it didn't happen.

"Well, now we're in a helluva place," said Perkins.

"We'll be alright," said Stubb. "We're right on the main lines. Hell, the *Miskito* is just a day behind us.

"If the current doesn't move us too far," said Burgess. "Lenny, what the hell happened back there?"

"I don't know Burgess… Cap went over the edge."

"Yeah, no shit, but wow! What put him over like that?"

"I dunno, could he have caught a virus from that monkey?"

"What? Herpes? No, I don't think Herpes does that." said Burgess.

"Well," said Stubb, "I think that damn monkey had something to do with it."

"I hated that monkey," said Perkins. "Looked like an evil imp."

"Yeah, well, it wasn't the monkey that killed all those guys." said Burgess.

Perkins harrumphed an acknowledgment.

"It was guilt."

Everyone turned to look at Reynolds.

"All those monkeys he took to be experimented on."

Perkins snorted. "When did you turn hippie, Reynolds?"

"Look around you, Chief. The day you quit respecting that, out there, is the day that it will kill you."

"And your hippie point?"

"It's life, Chief. Look at it." Reynolds looked disgusted and dismissed Perkins with a wave of his hand.

"All I see out there is intense boredom in a little boat with a bunch of assholes. And now I find out they're hippie assholes. *Guilt-* pshh!"

"No," said Stubb, "Cooke got squirrely a while back, right after all that shit with Lucy."

"Lucy," said Perkins lustily, and most of the men on the boat murmured a lusty agreement.

"What's that look for, Burgess?" asked Stubb. "You got something to add?"

"Nah."

"Come on, there's something."

"No, really."

"Too late, man. You're stuck with me on this boat. I saw that. Out with it."

Burgess appeared to struggle to speak. "I never told anyone about this, but I guess it doesn't matter now…"

"Well, get on with it, monkey man," said Perkins.

Burgess flipped him the bird and continued, looking down through the bottom of the boat into the great sea of reminiscence. "A couple weeks after I was first hired, I went down to the office to fill out some papers and find out when the ship would be back in port. Well, she came on to me. Asked me what kind of animals I handled." Burgess laughed. "We hooked up. I had no idea then who she was. Later, I was terrified Cooke would find out."

"Well, Burgess," said Stubb, "I doubt the Captain went crazy 'cause you fucked his wife six years ago, so relax."

"Was she an animal?" asked Perkins. Burgess nodded sheepishly. Perkins moaned.

"So," said Stubb, "How we fixed on provisions?"

"We got water, Cap." said Reynolds. "The watch had a few cases stashed deck-side that we were able to grab. We should be alright for a little while. Might shed a few pounds if it takes a while."

"Aw shit," said Perkins, "was I complaining about fruit and crackers? Fuck."

#

Cooke was alone. He still hadn't seen Confucius, but occasionally the monkey's voice would come from inside a hatch, or behind a crate.

"You know what you have to do, Martin."

The monkey's plan was simple enough. Say the ship was attacked by pirates. But for authenticity, he needed to be wounded, preferably by rifle fire.

Cooke had learned, from the DVD copies of *M*A*S*H* on board, that most self-inflicted wounds were in the leg or foot. He felt it needed to be elsewhere, ultimately deciding the shoulder would be the least dangerous. Wedging the rifle at an upright angle in a conveniently sized rectangular depression on a shipping container, he leaned forward until the rifle's muzzle nestled into a spot he hoped was the least damaging. He hesitated.

Right when he thought he was getting up the courage, he felt something hit his shoulder from above. It was Confucius. Cooke was completely unprepared for the weight of the monkey and lost his balance, the point of the rifle sliding up under his chin as his right arm, seeking balance and security, unfortunately sought it by pressing down on the surface with which it was in contact.

The trigger.

#

The monkey was no stranger to humans. The first 4 years of its life were spent on the streets of a village in central India where it became well acquainted with scavenging, begging, and stealing. It was his penchant for begging that got him captured by a group of teenage boys and sold to the black market. From there, it was on to the "legitimate" farm and sale for bio-medical research.

These initial stages of captivity were terrifying to the macaque. He had never existed inside a cage. As he was transferred from one place to another, moved from truck to truck to warehouse to ship, he slowly calmed down and gave up, a kind of shock settling in on him.

The first time he saw Captain Cooke, his instincts and experience told him the man was weak, a good mark for begging. Once the captain had freed him, the crackers seemed as good a reason to stay with him as anything. The ship was a strange and alien environment and the captain was as close to security as anything else he'd seen in a month and a half.

The monkey took olfactory note of the galley when Cooke obtained more crackers. There were lots of good smells in there. When it became obvious that Cooke's supply of crackers was diminished, he ran straight back there and straight to the man with the fruit. This man was hostile, and the macaque had to dodge his flailing arms, leaping from counter to shelf and back again, scattering pots and containers. When the man fell over and quit making harsh noises, the monkey knew it was safe to eat.

The first man came along and scooped him up, shoving some of the fruit in his pockets. The macaque would have preferred to stay at the source of the food, but the man carried him off. The ample supply of apple slices contented him.

In the glass room, he was not content at all.

The macaque understood violent death when he saw it. He panicked, shrieking, trying to find a place to hide, but there was no escape from it. When it was over, the man held out an apple slice. The monkey understood it as a gesture of dominance and submitted to him, slowly.

The gunfire below decks, though, proved too much for him. He fled blindly into the ship, hiding amongst cargo containers, behind ballast tanks. Every shot drove him from his hiding place. He found his way back to the galley, but there was no food laying where he could see, and the gunfire drove him on to the ladder and open sky, where he fled into the strange, windowless village. He hid in between the containers until the shots rang out again, driving him onward to a new hiding spot.

At one point, beneath him, a group of men gathered. He could smell the fear coming off of them. He was familiar with one, another man who had given him food. He almost approached but was still too spooked to venture from his hiding spot. More gunfire rang out and he climbed deeper within the crates where he trembled.

The shots finally ceased long enough for the monkey to calm down and he worked up the courage to look around, approaching the task like his brethren would, by climbing up high and surveying the landscape from the top of the containers. The group of men was gone. The wind shifted, and the macaque caught the scent of Captain Cooke. Cooke was now the closest thing to an alpha male he knew, the only familiarity. He set off across the tops of the containers in that direction.

He found Cooke bent over below him. From his angle above he could see into the captain's breast pocket which hung slightly open, revealing one brown apple slice inside.

The monkey looked at Cooke's shoulder. He'd been there before, and it seemed solid. On the figurative fruit tree of Captain Cooke, it was a branch he trusted. He did not hesitate before he leaped.

It was some time before he reemerged from the deep recesses of the containers.

Hunger drove him out of hiding as the sun was setting. He headed back to where he knew there was food. It didn't take him long to figure out the cabinets and drawers in the galley. He was lucky. The produce walk-in hadn't latched when the apples were retrieved earlier and stood slightly ajar. As he munched on a banana, he heard the shriek of one of the other monkeys and followed it back to the live cargo room where there was yet another ample supply of food, easily obtained.

At first, he shared food with his caged brothers, becoming their caretaker, so to speak. It's common for many species to show compassion in this way. However, it didn't take him long to figure out the latch mechanism on the cages. After that, everyone fed themselves.

For about a week, it could be said that monkeys ran the *Sea Mule,* not quite as cleanly as Captain Cooke would have probably liked.

#

It was five days before the crew on the lifeboat was found. No one had any idea what the *Sea Mule's* last heading had been, complicating matters. So, the ship had plenty of time to run aground on an island off the southeastern coast of the United States.

The *Sea Mule* was stopped short of the island by a sandbar, which she hit at full steam with an ungodly noise and a jolt that sent every un-anchored object on the ship flying. She immediately began to list. The monkeys unharmed by the crash were all driven out onto the deck, seeking the open air as their new world slowly fell over. They climbed to the top of the containers and the superstructure, but the containers began sliding off the side. As the stacks toppled and the superstructure listed further, many of the monkeys were thrown into the rough water. Fortunately, some of the containers floated reasonably well and many of the monkeys managed to climb onto them for the wild ride to shore.

Of the 100 monkeys on the ship, 60 or so, including the macaque briefly known as Confucius, made it ashore, some of them perishing later from taking too much water into their lungs. A few of the shipping containers broke open on the rocks, providing plastic bags of dried dates, figs, and other Indian food stuffs that the monkeys were able to eat as they transitioned to the nutrition provided by the island, which, as it turned out, was sufficient to support a growing population of rhesus macaques and continues to support them to this day.

Standing on the beach as half of the *Sea Mule* sank beneath the waves behind him, Confucius was no longer the defeated animal of mere days before. His fear was gone, even if he *was* still in a high state of wariness. Land beneath his feet was reassuring. He had his eyes on a young female macaque and was already thinking about exploring the strange looking trees. A bug scurried across the sand in front of him. He snatched the insect, popped it into his mouth, and it was good.

PRODUCT

Larry D. Thacker

A shower was all she wanted. For God's sake, just a shower. Hell, a splash bath if nothing else, a little water on the pits and privates would have improved Amy's mood immensely, and Gil's as well. They were past intolerable by now, both the ripeness of their moods and bodies. But the water was off. Had been for almost four full days. And it wasn't coming back on. Ever. This much they knew but hadn't talked about. What little they'd stored and managed not to drink was nearly evaporated in the heat.

Amy knew they'd reached a certain line in the sand when Gil said, "Ya know, you'd be a might more tolerable if I could stand to be next to you." They'd been arguing about something she'd already forgotten. She was beyond hungry. Faint from it, and memory was suffering.

"You stink to high heaven."

She wasn't too faint for her usual biting sarcasm, though. She leaned closer to him, flaring her nostrils. "You smell about the same, Gil. But I was used to it before all this shit hit the fan."

And that was it. End of argument. She'd won, as usual, with a final dashing blow of cleverness, accurate and searing. He went silent and she figured he was asleep again. It's about all they did now. Argue for a little about nothing. Then sleep in

"

their fatigue. And watch the street through the small circles they'd cleaned on the dirty windows.

When you're free to roam about never worrying about a thing, four days seems like a short time. What's four days out of a whole life? A blink, underappreciated and forgotten. But when you're trapped in a two-room music store with your husband, and dying, it's a newly discovered crowded black closet in hell she didn't think she'd ever earned.

She checked Gil. Yep. Asleep again. Too tired to snore, which was a relief. She leaned in, hovering her nose near his chest, then smelled her own pits, her days old blouse. *Pretty ripe. But he's worse,* she betted. There was no mirror in the place, thank God. She'd have broken it by the second day. It surprised her that her own odor fought through the fumes stewing in the bucket of waste in the back room closet. At least after a few days of no food and water you quit pissing and shitting.

Amy tip-toed, barefoot, to the front windows, a rusty evening light just sneaking through the streaks and crusts of grit. She had her own little circle, eye level, quarter-sized, just enough to see out but not be seen. Gil's was a bit higher. She let her eyes focus with the change of light. It was so dark inside.

There was movement here and there, mostly in the shadows. She could see one of her sandals laying on the asphalt near where they'd laid down the motorcycle before tearing off into this awful place for what looked like quick safety. She shook her head in disgust, remembering the frustration of begging Gil to try the store next door, the coffee shop, The Super Bean Café and Karaoke Bar. But no, he had to drag her into his buddy's music store, The Last Note. A place he felt safe. She swore she could almost smell the coffee through the foot-thick, hundred-year-old brick and mortar wall. When the hallucinations came on, she could hear a party over there, the espresso grinder vibrating the wall, the milk steamer hissing enticement just to remind them what could have been. To be so close to the possibility of food was maddening, even if most of it was going to hell by now. They'd just ended up in this guitar, dulcimer, and fiddle store, with the power out, surrounded by useless, inedible mountain instruments Gil and his buddies loved so much. Well, he could choke on them now for all she cared. Fuck bluegrass. Shit, this wasn't even Kentucky.

A few days back, when they could still stand each other, they'd stewed up a plan of getting over to the café. This store had luckily been open. It was hard to tell about next door. It might have been locked, barricaded from inside by someone. Guarded. Already infested. Taking a chance might have been trading a bad safe spot for a terrible demise, caught in the street, trapped and unable to turn around. The end.

"Why," Amy pleaded, "did you drag my ass into this worthless place? With the possibility of cold coffee and stale desserts within reach! Should have just went without you!"

Their screams grew. They forgot their predicament, where they were. Like it was old times, back home for a good old knock down, drag out.

"I wish you had!"

And then the light banging on the front door started, the scrapes and slides of fingertips and palms, faces even, wet and weak fists against the glass panes, moans and gurgles. Blood and spittle. Crazed, slow eyes, dying ears, seeking out the noise, the look of the blood hunger. After that, their arguing had been fierce but in whispered screams. Their forced quiet saying more than any yelling and fighting.

Now, hungry near to passing out most of the day, on the verge of maybe dying of thirst soon, baking in the building's sealed up summer heat, all she wanted was to clean up. Maybe die without looking and feeling such a wreck. It was so embarrassing. At least she wasn't cooped up with a friend who cared how she looked.

But past a charred car frame, past Gil's mangled Harley, across the two-lane avenue, was a paradise she desired just once more, before it was too late. A Dollar World Store. In all its beautiful, unsullied glory, the store waited there just for her, calling a bit more each day. Tempting its fresh wares just past arm's reach. Guarded by the hungry, walking dead.

In front of its long strip of pane windows, near the automatic double doors now dead without power, stumbled a figure out of the shadows. And another. This was the problem. They were everywhere. Wandering through downtown in singles, in small groups, led by some remaining hellish sense pointing them in the direction of fresh flesh. Was it scent? Sound, sight? Spirit? Zombies everywhere. The only thing keeping her from some temporary relief.

To hell with food. Water. She wanted to clean up.

There was bound to be water left in the pipes. Maybe a sink. Bottled water, too. Gallons of it, unopened. Smelly soaps. Bubble bath. Shampoo and conditioner. Hair brushes.

Her mouth watered. She wouldn't use it all for a bath. She could drink some. But they'd have some pops in there, too, so she didn't have to use all the water to bathe in and drink. Good God it was hot. Her eyes nearly crossed looking through the circle.

Makeup, eyeliner, mascara, blush. Umm, lipstick. Eyebrow pencils even. Hairspray. Cheap fresh clothes. Mouthwash. Toothpaste. Floss.

She checked Gil. Still asleep, his breathing almost too shallow to make out. Was he dying faster than her? There was so little light she couldn't tell. She brushed a fly off his cheek with the back of her hand. It was almost love she felt, but mostly shame and pity.

Back at the window, she scanned the scene again, planning.

Tanning spray. Deodorant. Cheap perfume. Room deodorizer. Stacks of bagged chocolate, the imported dark kind she craved and would go out of her way to sneak and buy and pick up from this very store and have eaten by the time she got home.

By God, she had to get over there.

Two stumbling forms, ragged and ruinous, shirtless, loitered close to the store entrance. With power the auto-doors would have opened, inviting them in. They stayed shut. It was all safe. Unless, she thought, one of them stumbled into the doors, pushing them open. Could they? Might they be locked? What then? She couldn't think of it, how awful that would be. She was already there in her scattered hallucinations, taking her time roaming the aisles, feet in new bunny-eared house slippers, savoring each choice as she filled the shopping buggy, taking in the cleaner air, Gil's stench out of her nose, feeling safer, anticipating the ecstasy of cleanliness as she collected up a day spa's worth of products.

She knew it wasn't exactly in the Bible, but the phrase "Cleanliness is next to Godliness" crossed her mind. Gil was such a slob. Her mother was right after all, had warned her plenty enough times before they'd run off to Pineville to marry in such a damned hurry. "That man ain't clean like you need, baby. You need a neat and clean man in your life, like I raised you." Amy mouthed the mantra, *Cleanliness is next to Godliness*. It was her mother's voice coming out, fogging the glass.

One staggered clumsy and clueless over a motionless body lying twisted on the sidewalk in its own decomposing filth, thumping its shoulder into the store's pane glass, bowing it, the last remnants of evening sun glinting with the rhythmic impacts.

Don't you dare bust that glass, motherfucker, she whispered.

If she was going to do it she had to act. She'd lie down soon, too tired for much of anything else, and not wake up. Maybe like Gil now.

It would have to be fast. Faster than them, which wasn't difficult, but even dodging slow-movers could trip her up. There were so many. If she went down they'd be on her like a pack of starved pit bulls, and it wouldn't be slow. It wasn't like they went for the kill or a favorite spot. It's just mindless feasting on the closest *whatever*, ignoring the struggle. Gil and her had witnessed evidence of that too many times already.

How her friend Thelma sounded when they'd caught up to her was impossible to shake. They'd been crossing a field. Thelma fell behind, limping. Three of the monsters pulled her down and commenced with their only purpose for existing. Her screams and moans and begs echoed clear across the field for ten long, guilt-ridden minutes. They'd listened and watched, horrified by their own curiosity. Amy promised herself that wouldn't happen. It was funny how they always quit eating once the screaming and struggling stopped, like that triggered them. As if only something moving and trying to get away, out from under them, activated their need to feed.

Clearing a larger swipe of the window with her nasty blouse sleeve, she tried getting a decent peripheral view. The street was nearly clear, a few of them dotting along the way, but spread out and unorganized, not that they organized. One was face first through the passenger window of a burning car, its legs twitching and peddling. What looked like a prior businessman slowly passed by the music store now, a crusted brown stump swinging from his shoulder, his neck dark and torn, a laptop case slung over his shoulder. Down the way was what was left of a woman, still stuck in her vehicle, barely clawing at the windows and doors, baking for days, decomposing in motion. Amy could see what was left of sunset shining off the woman's exposed skull. The one that had stumbled into the store's glass was half a block down now, weaving a mindless trail through the obstacle laden street and sidewalks, bumping off abandoned cars, over its own kind now too decomposed to support their weight against the elements and gravity.

Gil stirred, his head pounding, throat seized dry and straining his breath, his innards pained in a hollowed out twist like it was lined with breaking glass. He'd slept eleven hours, barely moving, feeling like a statue moaning itself out of achiness as he finally committed to sitting up.

He cracked his crusty eyes open a bit. He could tell what time of day it was by where the sun hit in the front end of the store. It was morning. The shock of the place's fetid scent shook him fully awake. It smelled like death, unmistakable, like something left along the road for days but invisible over in the high weeds. But it was from outside, cooking and creeping into what little breathable air was left in this oven.

His thoughts finally wandered to Amy.

"Baby." He listened, struggled to turn from his seated position on the grime of the floor.

"*Baby*." A little louder, but still barely a scratchy whisper.

There was a shuffling from somewhere back in the storage room. She could be in the back, he thought, now trying to stand, his head swimming. He expected to find her sitting on the bucket, stinking the place up some more.

But she wasn't there. Not between the racks of instruments and equipment in the dark, not in the little closet area on the bucket. He limped out to the front, figuring she was snoozing in the corner. She liked the light in the morning, didn't she? Nothing. Under the front desk? No. Again to the back room, the warmth of panic and dread filling him up. A low thud sounded on the opposite side of the back door. Had she gone out there?

He leaned his head near the wooden door and whispered. "Honey?"

Another thud and a smearing sound traveled along the outside. The smallest sliver of light was bolting through near the top hinge. Something moved on the other side, blocking the light for an instant. The hinge was separating, breaking apart with each heavied smack on the other side. *She's not out there, she can't be*, he tried convincing himself, backing away. If she is, it doesn't matter anymore, does it?

Gil collapsed in an office chair and stared across the room, confused and defeated, exhausted so quickly. Then he noticed the front door, the missing bar they'd pried across the knob, the desk scooted away just enough to open it. Amy was out there. With them. Not here. With him.

A wash of terror and relief spread through him, bloody images of what they'd done to her, the guilty pleasure of being rid of her nagging, her sharp tongue. Maybe they'd torn it from her mouth. But all that imagery just made him feel guilty.

He plied himself up from the seat and tiptoed to the front glass. Looking through the newly cleared swath Amy had made, he scanned the street, only his eyes darting around and excited, the morning light straining his vision with a burn. A crowd of those things were in a clump across the street, wandering, bumping into each other, their backs to him. Then their heads slowly swiveled, shoulders turning, their blank gazes following something in unison. Then across the inside of the glass panes of the store across the street clearly strolled Amy. The crowd crept behind, drawn to her movement. Another one walked up and joined the mass.

All he could do was stare. Something was different. Her hair was what he noticed first, all done up, like a big helmet. He could almost feel the hairspray thickness, the toxic smell she'd be trailing. The cherry red lipstick stood out, her eyes darkened with liner and mascara, all her features clear from across the street. She was smiling big, drawing a last long puff on a cigarette, mouth ratcheting on a candy bar at the same time. Her clothes were clean, a bright pink blouse and white knee length skirt, reminding him of when they'd first met that time at Billy's Rib Pit. She'd never been so pretty since. He watched her pace along the inside of the windows, seemingly oblivious of the interested horde growing on the other side of the glass.

She didn't see him watching. How could she? He was tempted to yell out. He tried wiping the window clean with his sleeve so he could get her attention, waving his arms, only whispering her name. Then she was tearing open a bag of Red Vines, stomping her smoke out on the store floor, a tallboy pop

can in the other hand. He was jealous, acutely aware of how near
to dying of thirst he now was. She stopped and stared at the
growing crowd on the other side of the glass. Then she must
have saw Gil's face. She gave a little wave, propping her hand
on her hip like a pose and twirling. He knew what she was
asking.

What do you think, Gil?

This pissed him off to no end. How dare she snub him like
this, with her protective gaggle of undead between them. She
flipped a few of the dead horde the bird, looking them in the
eyes. He could see her cussing them, one-by-one.

He screamed her name, the escaping scratch of voice
louder than anything he'd uttered in days, not in a warning way,
but in searing hatred for the woman. He didn't care. Finally,
what mattered? All the anger pent up over the last five days,
from being cooped up in this disgusting place with her, her
criticism, surrounded by the dead, all the death, him starving to
death and her over there now prancing about stuffing her throat
with both hands, clean and gleeful, happy for a time.

He was livid.

Gil screamed Amy's name. Again. And again. It wasn't
enough through the glass or over the din of accumulating
grumbling dead.

He turned and grabbed the fiddle he'd been eyeing for
months. A 1930s dark wooded fiddle priced at a now worthless
$1,100. He unbolted the store's door and cracked it open a
piece with his foot and laid the instrument's rest to his jaw and
shoulder, clamping it there as he screwed the bow up and
rosined it nicely from the dryness.

A few staccatoed test chirps across the fiddle's strings and
it was clear the fine instrument held its last tuning well in these

first days of the apocalypse. Since him and the boys had played a few tunes those days back. Then Gil was whining out the song he'd learned recently through the crack of the door right over the empty heads of the stumbling dead, tapping his free foot on the off beats, giving it all he had left in his starving state. The old bluegrass tune "Cumberland Gap" echoed off the bricks and walls of Ailor Avenue, perhaps for the last time in history, fine and true.

This they reacted to, one sensing this foreign pitch, then another, the group seeming to work in slow single-mindedness, pivoting their fragmented bodies in unison, searching Gil's noise. This music, once familiar, now only a calling racket to dead, but instinctual hearing.

A ghoulish dance of fumbling ragdolls commenced, one splintered leg catching another, a snapping arm, a body stumbling, the smacking together of heads and limbs, clumsy and mindless, and, like flaccid dominoes, the wave of bodies shifts left, tangles, drifting right, the combined dead and crawling weight smearing a wet-black trail across windows only inches from where Amy stood, mortified in sudden realization she is no longer safe and happy as the dance falls by.

The glass panes bow once. Again. Buckle. Snap with that sound only shattering glass gives out. Gil hears it from across the street over his music. He smiles, ramping up his tune as the chorus comes on strong. Glass caves as half the bodies fall into the Dollar World, bodies buried, bodies in slow scramble, bodies of one mind: to consume.

Amy's huge bun of freshly sprayed hair and one high reaching hand with drying crimson nail polish sinking into the massed attack is all Gil sees as he quietly sneaks from the store into the street.

The evening sunlight feels good on his dirty face. The fiddle case feels good nicely strapped to his back.

Amy gives up screaming under the weight of the horde, only whimpering. Amidst the twisted smash of riot squirm, she thinks she hears the cranked rumble and then fade of a Harley V-Twin before all goes dark in the Dollar World.

THE EGG

C. M. Chapman

The Captain of the Night Watch awoke drenched and terrified. It took a long minute to pull himself together, only to find he was still shaking. Of all the nightmares that had plagued him every night over the last few weeks, last night's was the worst.

Last night, of course, was technically a misnomer since he had retired to bed in the early dawn, but the captain was still having some trouble with that distinction. Sleeping was properly a night-time activity in his mind. But the promotion to Captain of the Night Watch had come with the change in shift. Night was his day and day was his night now.

He stayed in bed for several minutes, trying to slow his heartbeat, trying to fool himself into believing that waking life would bring relief, and failing on both counts. He stared at the ceiling and wished that he could blame all of this on his change in work pattern. After all, he was coming off twenty years of humping a daytime beat through the Shell Heights market district, breaking up arguments, keeping disreputable merchants in check, and chasing pickpockets or children with stolen bread. It would be so much easier to think that the change in lifestyle had unhinged him and that none of it was real.

But that was not the case. Doom wasn't just in his dreams. It awaited him, tonight, on the watch.

He had deserved that promotion, by the gods he had. And he'd needed it badly, with three children now to feed. Things were just starting to get easier and then-- this. He looked at the empty side of the down mattress. Mary would have been up for several hours now. The sky must have been overcast because the usual shadows of time were absent from the walls. He guessed it was well before midday, hardly a rest for a man on the edge. He sighed and rolled himself from the bed. There would be no more sleeping after that dream. As he slipped into his britches he wondered which was worse, the impending horror of his shift tonight, slowly creeping toward him like some putrid, carnivorous worm, or the impending horror of his dreams, ready to spring on him like a wolf to his throat.

After last night, he figured it was a toss-up.

He shuffled into the house's living area. This home was much nicer than their previous one, thanks to his promotion. The walls were of smooth clay and stone and the roof was nicely thatched. They still had to live with a dirt floor but at least it was level and didn't get wet when it rained.

Mary had already fetched the water, effectively ruining the captain's plan to make himself useful. She was nowhere to be seen, which meant she was probably at the market. The captain altered his plan and decided to go out for some extra firewood instead. Jonah Simms and his boys regularly cut in the forest beyond the city walls and sold the wood on this side of the city.

The forest. He shuddered. He didn't think there was a promotion in the world that could make him go in there.

That was where it began. It was from those woods, or at least the space once occupied by those woods, that he first heard the three accursed words which now plagued his existence. If only it had ended there. If only he hadn't seen anything.

The King's High Necromancer would be waiting for him tonight as he had been every night since the first incident. The wizened old man would be lurking at the entrance to the tunnel stairs as he passed through the garrison muster hall.

"Good evening, Captain," he would say with that disconcerting lick of the lips, "Did you dream again?"

The thought of it made him uneasy. Would he confess his dream of this morning? He didn't know. His willingness to share them had diminished as they'd become increasingly more bizarre and disturbing.

In the beginning, he would have talked to anyone, *anyone*, who would have displayed the tiniest amount of empathy. The shock of that first encounter had left him shaken and shattered. His men had looked at him like he was crazy. The Garrison Commander had even threatened to demote him. The High Necromancer had intervened, pulled him aside, and spoken to him in soft, reassuring tones.

"What did you see?" the ashen-skinned, wraith of a man had asked.

"I don't know," the captain had said, still blubbering, "It was as if the forest suddenly melted into one thing- or part of a thing- and that thing- oh gods- it reached into me--."

"Try to calm yourself, Captain. What sort of thing? What did you see?"

And so the Captain had related, for the first time, how the forest morphed into sinister, seemingly formless black in front of his eyes, emitting waves of what could only be called sickness, seeping from it like heat, making him want to vomit, sucking the life from his soul, and robbing his legs of their ability to stand. He told the necromancer of the slow comprehension that the massive thing in front of him was only part of something vastly bigger, and how after what seemed like eternity transfixed by the thing, he'd finally understood that he was staring into a monstrous, pitch-black eye, unblinking, stretching nearly the entire length of the southern forest.

Once it began spilling from him, it all came. The eye was unfeeling, uncaring, detached from human concerns and obliviously destructive. It seemed like the eye of a giant bird, no bird of beautiful plumage, but one ancient and flightless, lying in a festering heap just behind the illusion of the forest, its consciousness probing the captain's mind like the tentacles of a man-o-war. He told the necromancer about the three words, unbidden, forced like rape, words which he knew were not just for him, but for the whole world.

The necromancer had smiled, a kind smile that seemed completely alien. "Don't worry, Captain," he said softly, "Open yourself. You are the herald of a new age. Soon, all of King Humphrey's enemies shall fall and we will enter a golden age of unparalleled knowledge. This is a good thing. Rejoice in your heart."

But it did not feel like a good thing. It felt about as far away from good as possible, farther even, than the laws of nature allowed.

One step out of his door informed him of why it was so difficult to judge the time. The world had obviously changed and, from the looks of it, not for the better. The captain found Jonah Simms in his usual spot but not his usual mood, which was hardly surprising under the circumstances. Simms looked at the captain like the harbinger of death, not the look of a man who is afraid of it, but one who recognizes an inevitability. There were no words spoken. The captain handed over his money and took his small stack of wood, conscious of the fact that these actions seemed futile and meaningless. He turned to go home. It was true, then. They were all going to die. If not tonight, then very, very soon.

"Planning to burn down the city?"

He turned toward Mary's voice to find her behind him, their wooden cart in tow, loaded down with firewood, turnips, onions, and several loaves of bread. Even in the fluorescing light of doom she was caring for her family, planning for a future, if only in the form of next week's meals. There was humor in her eyes attached to the question, but it was a dark joke. He was overwhelmed by his feelings for her.

"Well," he said, smiling, "I guess it's an option." He added his stack of firewood to the cart and leaned over to kiss his wife. He hadn't been able to see her enough lately. She had a lovely face that touched him as deeply as ever, and even though three births had left her with an egg-like figure, in his mind she was still the slender beauty he had wed many years ago. He wished (hoped) that the strength of his love for her could be enough to turn back whatever was coming, but he wasn't strong enough to believe it.

The captain took the handles of the cart from her and they walked in silence toward home.

"You didn't sleep well again," she said after a few moments.

"No."

"Anything you want to share?"

"No." He smiled and kissed her on the forehead.

She knew. Just like Jonah Simms. Just like everyone by now. It was no secret. The morbid nature of the royal family had been public knowledge for generations. The necromancer order was the most powerful order in the city, more powerful than the City Watch, by far. It was even said the elaborate and massive city walls, which encompassed all the disparate districts of the city, were constructed in the shape of some arcane symbol.

And more and more people had seen the thing as time went on. Not all perceived it as an eye. Two of his men had perceived a great, black egg, seeping putrescence from many cracks, about to hatch.

His duty-honed observational skills told him everything he needed to know as they walked. Everyone knew death was near. It was obvious, if only in the unnaturally pale green sky laced with slender, silken tendrils of silent lightning that pulsed above them. The captain walked along with his wife, conscious of the fact that there were things he should probably be saying to her, thankful to her and loving her more for not having to say them.

At home, Mary fried some sweetbread for lunch. Her husband helped her by brewing some mint tea, not something he would have usually done. A couple times they got in each other's way and those were times of lingering touches, sad smiles.

"Are you sure you don't want to talk about it?" she asked at the table, "I would share your burden."

"I am sure," he said, "and I know. You are too good to me."

"I am your wife."

He had not burdened her with any of the dreams. The first time that he'd been able to sleep after seeing the eye, he dreamed of floating, suspended in blackness, the same three words he'd heard earlier, coming from everywhere and nowhere at once. Those three words were never to stop. They would be present from then on, except during those waking hours when he wasn't on duty and could shut them out. But even then, they echoed.

The dreams escalated in horror, both physical and existential, and each one, he knew, was a message from that abomination outside of the city. Some were incredibly bizarre, including one where he looked down at himself to find he was fat, with legs not big enough for his body. He was dressed in a strange outfit with half-pants and suspenders, the words swirling around him like a whirlwind of sound, making the world spin out from under him.

In another, a slobbering demon peeled his hardened skin from him in chunks and ate him. They grew stranger and stranger, worse and worse, but the dream of that morning had an air of finality to it that seemed incontrovertible.

In it, he was being ripped to shreds. He was in pieces, lying upon the blackness that he now knew to be the eye, like he was held by gravity. Over and over, the three words bombarded, pierced him, in all inflections and dialects, all languages, none of which the captain knew and yet which he understood clearly. He heard them from without and within, even in languages dead for millennia. A thin silver strand held his disparate pieces from floating away from each other but it was being gnawed upon by greasy flightless, shambling birds and each peck was an agony to his scrambled soul. In the dream, he knew the end had come at last.

He was not going to share that with his wife.

In time, the children were home. Too soon, he thought, or not soon enough. Time seemed to have slipped loose of its moors. In what seemed only a brief moment, Mary was setting the table for dinner. His shift was approaching.

He helped his wife get the children ready for bed, lingering to touch each child's face a moment longer and exacting a kiss from each. As his youngest, Tessa, kissed him gently on the cheek, an involuntary spasm of breath forced its way through his nostrils. He held it at bay.

Part of him wanted to stay, but the captain was, in the end, a man of duty.

So he left home with the fleeing daylight, such as it was, knowing deep in his heart that tonight would be the end of all things. There was no sound of frog or cricket in the air, no evening swallows diving and swooping above the rooftops. All nature seemed to have fled this place. Nevertheless, the captain kept a slow pace. He was in no hurry and, in fact, was fighting a primordial urge to flee blindly in any direction. An easy enough urge to fight. No direction held safety.

In the muster hall it appeared that many of his men had not come tonight. The garrison commander was still there, at his table in the side chamber off the main hall. He glared as the captain passed his view. Those men who had shown up were gathered in a corner of the hall. All had the look of the woodcutter. He passed them, avoiding contact.

The necromancer was waiting with his hungry smile.

"Good evening, Captain," he said, bowing, "Do you dream still?"

The captain had decided not to tell him. Let him be surprised.

"I try to remember, Holiness, but they are hidden from me."

"Ah, so it is, then." He bowed again and the captain returned the bow as he slipped past him into the wall's inner passageways. He followed the torchlit tunnel until he came to the stairway to the southern guard tower.

At the top of the stairs, the Captain of the Day Watch was waiting, looking most relieved to see him.

"Captain Ernst, I present myself as your relief," he said, with a crisp salute.

"Captain Dumpty," Ernst replied, returning the salute, "the wall is yours." And then he was gone.

The captain stepped out onto the ramparts and looked toward the forest. There was the ancient, avian eye, locking on to him, sucking at his very essence. He thought maybe he was beginning to perceive the rest of the thing, or at least the potential of its existence. The air around the eye was shimmering as if it were ready to dissolve into form. The words, unheard during the time he'd been able to concentrate on his wife and children, renewed their assault on his mind.

"You. Will. Fall."

Perhaps, tonight, he would.

FEUDING WITH BIGFOOT

Larry D. Thacker

"You say something big took a runnin' jump off your back porch, do ya?"

Bless her heart, not even Sheriff Randy would risk the next election telling Mabel she couldn't dispatch after twenty-seven years, even if she was seven years past retirement and refusing to wear her hearing aid because she claimed it got in the way of the dispatch headset.

"No, Mabel, honey. I said bigfoot has gone and taken a *runny dump on* my *front* porch."

"Well, it's that time of year, I reckon."

She hung up. I was on my own to deal with it.

Have you ever smelled something so retched it woke you up? Well, that's what this did. And I'm pretty sure it wasn't just the little gift left on my front porch, it was the creature's trailing mythological stench to boot. I thought it was me at first, like I'd sharted myself in the middle of a worse than usual nightmare.

I'd have preferred that, to tell the truth.

I shook off the initial shock to the senses and searched the house for a source but couldn't find anything in the fridge or the trash or the toilet. I had, after all, put in a late Mexicano Monday night at Pickle's Pool Hall, so it was very possible I'd neglected to flush.

Then I heard it. An unsettling grunt. Then another. Like a terribly uncomfortable groan, out front.

Damn that bear, I thought. He'd been tearing through my trash bins this time of year for as long as I could remember. I imagined him dreaming in his hidey-hole up the mountain for good weather to break so he could get down to my property as quick as he could and wreck my trash. I was surprised he was this ripe, though.

I snuck over and spied through the blinds, still half asleep and not a little intoxicated, I admit. I expected to see the old boy head and shoulders deep in one of the bright red city trash cans they provide, and if not him, maybe a pissed off skunk or an overly stinky opossum.

But no, it wasn't that bear. It was something much, much worse.

It was some gigantic, shadowing thing, crouched over the top step up to the porch deck of my trailer, letting loose a bowel movement you'd have to see to believe. And I've got the pictures of the end result, so don't worry. The more it cut loose the more the stench burnt through the night and infiltrated the thin walls of my abode. I watched best I could, surprised I hadn't startled the thing with my lurching sounds.

You ever smelled something so strong you tasted it. Well this was burning the back of my throat like I'd bitten into something very, very wrong I'd blindly taste-tested from back of the fridge. Like I'd upended a bottle of Uncle Nate's Carolina Reaper Poison Sauce from the county fair. Like a mix of bad stink cheese and three-day summer roadkill had fallen in love and had litter of spoiled kids.

The thing's long stringy hair reminded me of Spanish tree moss in the swamp. Its eyes were like orange-red coals when it turned just right in the porch light. The porch isn't that big. It squatting there took up most of it.

The creature let out a long straining grunt. It sounded awfully painful, like it was in bad need of a dose of salts, as my granny used to say. Nevertheless, it was managing pretty well.

I was so confused and scared by the whole scene, I was questioning my recent transition to agnosticism as I realized I was trapped in my own domicile. What if the thing didn't leave? How much food did I have? How long could I last? Would it break in on me? Were these things murderous? Cannibalistic?

After a sufficient assault on my senses and safety, I'd had enough and decided to run it off no matter what might come of me. I commenced to stomping as hard as I could which vibrated the whole trailer like the ground was opening up.

It worked. You ever been scared and entertained at the same time? Well, I was both horrified and borderline giggling as this thing hopped up from its private business, smashing its head on the two-by-four rafter of the porch tin roof, gave out the scariest screech of a howl I've ever heard in God's creation (I've since converted back to the Baptist faith, mind you), sort of twisted its ankle on the top step as it spun around searching for where the rumbling disturbance was coming from, gave out another painful howl, righted itself, hauled off with both fists and punched a big dent in my metal front door, and bounded down the steps (six of them) with one jump, whereupon it ran/limped its way across my yard into the night, screaming hell the whole way.

I didn't dare go outside. I ain't crazy.

That's when I called Mabel at the 911. Of course, it didn't do any good.

I didn't fall asleep until around four, afraid the thing would return for vengeance and that I'd accidently wing myself since I was so tightly hugged up to my 12-guage. The sun couldn't come up fast enough.

Lucky for me I'm a prepper. I had an Israeli gas mask and some US military NBC (nuclear, biological, chemical) gloves handy. I strapped on the mask to breathe clear and snapped on the gloves for obvious sanitary reasons and broke the seal on my damaged door, very possibly taking my life in my own hands.

After a quick security check of the perimeter I figured it was safe. My yard is an eighth of an acre butting up against a swampy field stretching out for a quarter mile before there's much to hide in. But there's one spot not too far past my property line, a small patch of woods no bigger than a dozen trees maybe, some cypress and live oaks and scrub, a lot of shadow. If something was hiding, especially if it was gimpy, it'd be out there. That's where I'd be. I could feel it out there, watching me then, the rank thing.

It had left my porch a t-total mess. That creature had stomped in its own poo and slipped, probably hurting itself pretty good. I felt vindicated in a way. Its humongous footprint was smack-dab in the center of this pile of freshness along with some major splatter and a slide of the material across the decking like you wouldn't believe (but again, I've got photos). I think it was the heel that slid, preserving most of the footprint.

Now I'd tried reserving full judgement on what I'd seen (and smelled) that early morning but being up close and personal now I knew what I was up against. This was a Squatch print if ever I'd seen one. But I'd only seen them on TV, the Internet at the library, and at the one Bigfoot hunting conference I'd attended in Montana years ago, and those were plaster casts. What I had here was obvious, pressed clearly into at least a gallon of poop. I could see that even through the fogging goggle eyes of the gas mask.

I glanced out at the expanse of available bathroom availability for such a creature.

I yelled out, "What'd I ever do to you!?" but I don't think it probably understood me through the mask.

My natural instincts for the investigative kicked in. I retrieved my insta-camera, got shots from several angles of the imprint, of the porch as a whole, and the dented door. Down where the creature impacted the ground was an indentation but no distinct footprints. I was disappointed. Neither were there any distinguishing footprints stabbing out across the yard, only a few spots of smashed grass at a long limpy gait. There was no scat or hair. At least I had an idea of what direction the thing had retreated. And guess what? It was out toward that little stand of trees.

I removed the mask, braving the air. I knew what I had to do. I had to get into town for some concrete mix. I figured by the time I got back the poop would have dried enough to set a cast. I'd have in hand all the evidence I'd need.

The boys at the hardware just about didn't let me in the store.

"Barry. Um. You been havin' it out with a skunk out there at your place?"

I think it was in my clothes and hair at that point.

"You got water out there, don't you?"

"That don't smell like skunk to me," offered Renfro, the oldest of the old-timers. "That there's skunk ape, fellers. I'd know that ripeness from a mile down the road on the hard end of a hundred-year hurricane."

"Make it quick, Barry," Ray the owner demanded, curling his nose. "I got other customers, too, ya know."

"Y'all won't believe the night I had," I offered, ordering some quik-crete from Ray.

A bunch whooped it up at my expense, pinching their noses and going on like they've never needed water tossed on them before.

"Smells like Barry's been adopted as one of 'em."

"Maybe one's taken a shine to 'em."

"Bet I believe ya," Renfro shot back loud enough to hush most of the boys. "I saw that booger last month in my headlights crossin' the road down at Gator Ford Park. Oh yeah. It's for real." You could have heard a fart in a storm.

"Well, I'll have proof for every one of you come tomorrow."

Ray handed me a five-pound bag of quik-crete powder.

"Well, take a bath beforehand, ok?" Ray requested.

I can't say Linda at Linda's One-Hour Photo and Snack Bar wasn't much happier with me as a customer that warm afternoon. Her eyes were real big and watering as I stood at her counter and she seemed like she was hurrying me up.

"When you need these?" she asked.

"Tomorrow OK?"

"That'd be fine, Barry," she said, sounding relieved, reaching over to turn on a fan. "I'm closing early anyway, I think."

I leaned in. "Now Linda, these photos are of a sensitive nature," I whispered.

"It's only us in here," she reminded me. Everyone else had left.

"I'm not going to ask."

The ruthless August heat had cooked that Bigfoot poop to a fine and cooperative crust when I got back with the casting material. The creature's footprint was clear as the noonday Florida sun, nice and deep. He'd splatted his own foot – a good fourteen inches long – real good in his own mess. I bet he'd regretted that mistake all night, walking around with a turned ankle covered in your own awfulness. Of course, on the other hand, the way these creature's smelled, truth be told, they might have a habit of rolling in their own waste just to keep us away. But that wasn't working on me. No sir. If it was still around, I was finding it.

I got down to business and mixed up the quik-crete. I poured it into the crevices of the footprint. Now my dad's principle of leaving cow patties alone came in handy at this point. He'd always told me, "Son, if you leave a cow patty alone, it'll dry up and go away, but if you mess with it, it'll crack back open and you've got to deal with shit again." He claimed it was a metaphor, but in this case it was a literal application to the situation. As long as I was careful, I wouldn't crack this Bigfoot patty back open and be dealing with half the stink it bore into the world earlier. He was a wise man, indeed.

I went inside for a PBR and came back out. I paced the yard. I couldn't wait to see how the cast turned out. I was walking the perimeter where the swamp grass starts when I noticed a division in the taller grass. It resembled an animal trail and not straight toward the clump of trees I reckoned my visitor had taken the night before. It was a winding route.

A few feet into the trail and I could feel the squash of the turf. I sunk to my ankles in muck. Every other step sunk me another inch until I was slopping my feet out of suction. I stood there for a long while with water running into my boots wondering if the muck leveled out solid enough to walk through.

Then I felt it. I was being watched.

You ever had that feeling of being watched? Whether you saw anybody watching you or not? Well I had it. The hairs along my neck vibrated. It was like a laser zapping through my head, though I knew Squatches didn't have any such technology.

Plus I detected that thing fresh again. I was downwind.

My heart jumped to my throat with a hop. I froze, scanned the long field, the little copse of woods. Some nervous beach crows and a pelican were vacating the higher limbs. Something was in there.

Watching me.

I squinted into the sun, sweat rolling into my eyes, my feet were pruning, my body still as a piece of driftwood. Was that it, there maybe, in the shadows of that tree branch? Or there, half hidden behind that tree trunk, spying on me? Or was it down in the grass just over there, only a stone's throw away, within pouncing distance. It could hide out there all day, unaffected by the swamp muck and mosquitoes. I couldn't. I was vulnerable.

Defeated, paranoid, I turned back. I'd watched that documentary on preserved bog men they'd found in Europe. I wasn't about to end up one.

While most castings of Bigfoot feet have been whitish, mine ended up a little brown and green stained for obvious reasons. I'd have painted it, but being the natural born investigator I am, I didn't want to interfere with any evidence. All in all it was a fine cast, though. Solid, in one piece, with good formation of the toes, heel, and instep. It was obviously a Squatch print. Who could deny it?

I flecked off some particles and clipped away a few blades of grass that must have been in the original material, wrapped it in a two-gallon freezer storage bag, and stored it in the trunk of my Suzuki for safe keeping.

The next day was going to be something else.

A bang rattled me up that early morning. Then another. I guessed it was rocks popping against the side of my trailer. Then a whooping.

Guess who was back? And angry. At least I figured it was mad. Why would anyone holler and go on throwing rocks if they weren't pissed off at somebody? The rocks got bigger. One smashed and skidded across the flat roof. There was a crash in the living room from the shock. I wondered how close he was.

I grabbed the shotgun and leaned on the inside of the front door with my ear against the cold aluminum listening. I heard it, out there rustling around, pacing, kicking stuff around. Mumbling to itself. Rocks smacked the door. Then there was a crash of glass, but it wasn't a window of the trailer.

The you-know-what just smashed my Suzuki windshield, I thought. I ran to the bedroom window and snapped the blinds up, not caring if it saw me. I wanted eye contact now. Sure enough, there it was. And it was squatting again. On the hood of my car! Taking aim at the hole in the windshield it'd just made. What had I ever done to this thing?

That was it. I saw red. I'd had it with this bully.

Before I could even question myself I was busting out the front door, charging my shotgun, and lighting up the front yard air with as many rounds as I could before I lost my nerve. It was like a late 4th of July celebration. This scared the daylights out of Bigfoot. Between its turned ankle and a good layer of night dew on the newly waxed hood of my car, mixed with the calamitous racket I'd mustered, the creature lost its footing and fell ass first into what was left of my windshield. It howled awful from the pain of glass shards, rolled off my car, and rather than coming at me to tear me limb from limb as I fully expected, and probably deserved, it ran, with a harder limp than before, not out into the field or to the little woods, but down the main road toward civilization.

All I could think of was having to walk that same route in the morning with the casting to show it off and to get my photos from Linda since I sure as hell wasn't ever going to be driving that car again.

It's a two-mile hike into town. I was resting on the front porch of the hardware that next morning when Renfro hobbled up. I hadn't gone in yet. I was bathing in the pre-light of glory. My casting was unwrapped and airing out.

"That there your proof you were talkin' about, Barry?"

I nodded to it, proudly. "Indeed, sir."

He eyed it over his glasses, reached and gave the casting a sizing up against the length of his hand, grunting approval.

"Renfro, I had some time to think this morning as I was walking into town. How about you and me putting together a little to-do with this creature in mind?"

Renfro spit. "Tell me more."

The wind shifted and Renfro hiked his nose to the air and sniffed. No telling how long that casting was going stay that ripe.

"You smell that?" he asked, knowing what it was.

"Yeah, I do," I answered. "You know what it is," I asked him with a smile. "That's the smell of money, my friend."

I was pretty confident by then I was going have the last word when it came to this feud between me and my Bigfoot intruder.

"You don't say?" Renfro laughed.

"Pull ya up a chair."

Come hell or high swamp flood, Renfro Holmes and I'd be inaugurating our first Bigfoot Conference in Watchacal County come the next summer.

BIG BUDDY

C.M. Chapman

"The Wild still lingered in him and the wolf in him merely slept."

-- Jack London, *White Fang*

Everyone around the neighborhood agreed. Tommy was a bright boy. From the time he first ventured forth beyond the confines of his picket fence on his red tricycle, he was recognized as a friendly, outgoing child, inquisitive and unafraid to ask questions.

Why do you give the car a bath?

Why do you plant the flowers?

Why do you feed the birds?

Why do you trim the bushes?

The Laurel Lane development was populated by upper middle-class households, most of them older with children already in college, or moved out, or, in some cases, moved back in as adults. Consequently, Tommy was the only young child in the neighborhood and the sight of that little red tricycle, tooling down the concrete, soon taught everyone that questions trailed a few feet behind, like a close companion.

In an upscale neighborhood like Laurel Lane, the Peyne family was respected. Raymond, the father, was an oral surgeon with a partnership. His wife Lydia, in her mid-thirties, some fifteen years younger than Ray, was an outstanding homemaker, an active member of the homeowner association, and never failed to attend a Rotary event, where she was always a bright and vivacious presence. Lydia's father, prone to dementia, stayed with them in the tastefully large colonial-style dwelling with a reasonable number of columns on the front, and what would one day be two large, stately oaks flanking a Japanese maple.

Laurel Lane was still a reasonably new neighborhood, the first homes, like the Peynes,' barely ten years old and a few lots still in various stages of development. The lane itself gently curved and looped around a couple square miles of lots with two different accesses from Route 10. In the center of the loop, a five square acre park was maintained by the Laurel Lane Homeowners Association.

As for little Tommy himself, well, he was a cute kid and no one really minded his questions. There was something about that inquisitive face that could involve anyone and, for every answer- which were different in many cases, as Tommy loved to point out- his lips would purse in such a delightful way and his brow would crinkle just so as to make anyone laugh, tousle his hair, and have the honest feeling that they had perpetuated knowledge in the world. For the selfishly affluent, a sense of giving back was important.

Of course, the tricycle on the sidewalk was soon replaced by a bicycle on the lane, a big yellow whip flag announcing the arrival of the inquisitive one. Tommy began going to school, and those in the neighborhood used to seeing him all the time felt a little poorer, a little guiltier, like maybe now they weren't giving enough back to civilization. Summer vacation brought the boy again, and all was well. But now the questions reflected Tommy's life in school, his assimilation into the outside world.

Why do people have different color skin?

Why do we walk through a metal detector at school?

Why do some people have so much and others have so little?

He must have asked that last question to everyone in the neighborhood.

It's just the luck of the draw, said one.

Some people just handle their money better, said another.

Because we live in a free market system, said Norman Walsh, a retired investment banker. That means those of us who work harder end up having a little more than others.

Each answer was greeted with Tommy's usual scrunch-faced scrutiny.

It was Norman Walsh, though, coming home from the golf course a few days later, who completely missed seeing the high-flying triangular flag of inquisition, and nearly ran Tommy over. The boy had stopped and was straddling his bicycle in the middle of Laurel Lane. Walsh's cellular reception had dropped out on him, and he had been fiddling with his phone as he drove. He didn't see Tommy in the street, staring up at the sky, until it was almost too late and his no lock brakes shook him to a stop just feet from the boy.

Say here, Tommy boy! What are you up to?

The seven-year-old didn't even acknowledge his presence, gazing into the sky. Come down here! Tommy yelled, gesturing to the air.

Norman Walsh peeked toward the sky, but the twelve pack he'd consumed through the course of the afternoon did not allow for a steady enough view to distinguish just what young Tommy might be seeing up there, or a good golf game for that matter.

Escaped canary, Norman thought, and drove around him.

But Tommy, even after that incident, could still be seen watching the sky, calling for something to come down, day in and day out, and the neighbors soon began to wonder what was going on here.

It was Lydia who first spotted it.

I'm telling you Ray, it was some kind of UFO or something, and when I saw it, it was like it just disappeared, like it ducked down behind the trees over in the park!

The wife thinks the boy is talking to aliens, Ray said to the neighborhood menfolk at one of their Saturday afternoon driveway gatherings and the menfolk all had a good laugh. By this time the sight of the boy waving to the sky was three weeks old and the neighborhood just shrugged and went on with fences, lawns, and rotary events, occasionally pausing to wonder what the curious boy was looking at.

Well, I don't know, said Pete, owner of a regional chain of restaurants who lived across the street. I thought I saw something the other day, a glint, or something.

The occasion prompted all four men to glance up toward the sky at once, like syncopated rock stars in a music video, an illusion partially dispelled when all of their heads jerked back an inch, their eyes widened, and their jaws fell open.

Hey now, what's that? asked Sherm, his eyes wide.

I think it *is* a UFO, said Pete, his eyes wide.

I don't know, said Ray, suddenly reconsidering Lydia's blond observations, but I don't think I like it.

At that instant, the shape began to grow quickly. A high whine, not immediately discernible, began to fill the air.

It's coming! cried Pete, stepping back.

Oh shit! yelled Sherm and took off running down the street, holding the rear of his pants.

Ray started toward his house leaving Pete and Jerry standing there gawking. Whatever it was, it approached rapidly and Ray had to break into a run to try to get to his son in time. He didn't. It swooped down from above, and as he reached the edge of his lawn, he found himself face to face with an MRX-12 Spectre military drone, hovering in his path.

There was an explosive menace about it when seen head-on, a deadly giant insect, everywhere protrusion. It's wings, perfectly straight, stretched some thirty feet from side to side. The two tail wings jutted upward in a V, abutted on the rear by a whirling propeller. The rear landing gear, in its reversed V nearly made a perfect X with the tailwings. The front double-wheeled landing gear obscured the lower tail piece with the vertical flap and seemed to pop right out of the domed, wide lens surveillance camera on the underside of the nose which panned up and down, scrutinizing Ray.

Ray could see Lydia out on the porch, her hand over her mouth. Tommy stood in the yard, yelling, Come here, boy! Come here, boy!

Lydia, get Tommy in the house! I think this thing is dangerous! His eyes darted over the various rocket-like devices which dangled below the wings. Lydia started across the yard toward the boy and the MRX-12 Spectre shot skyward and swooped over the yard, cutting off her path. She froze.

Ray ran for his driveway and his open garage door. He grabbed a garden shovel and ran back out toward the thing with no clear idea of how idiotic this gesture truly was. Later, he would have a dream in which he jousted with it, mounted on his lawn tractor, garden shovel held in front of him, speeding toward the hovering beast at five miles per hour.

The drone simply turned toward him as he approached. Ray heard a loud *clitch* and a short burst of escaping air, as if something had released, come open, and it stopped him in his tracks once again. He experienced a powerful sense of imminent death and this feeling was completely new to the oral surgeon.

And then Tommy ran toward him, *under the wings of the machine*, screaming, No, Dad! No!

Seeing his son run right under the thing jolted Ray back to action and he raised the shovel but by then Tommy stood right in front of him, pleading, arms up, palms out.

It's scared, Dad! Stop!

The confusion which Raymond Peyne experienced at this particular moment was unlike any other he had experienced in his forty-nine years. It was so great, in fact, that he just dropped his shovel and reached out to for his son. But Tommy slipped from his reach, incredibly running back to the hovering craft.

At the approach of the boy, the drone pulled a little higher into the air.

Tommy raised his arms in the air, palms upward like a prophet. It's okay, he said, it's okay boy!

How do you know it's a boy?

I just do, Mom! It's okay, boy, nobody's going to hurt you. Come here, it's okay.

Maybe you shouldn't do that, Tommy.

It's alright, Mom! Come on, boy- come on down- nobody's going to hurt you.

No words were forming on Ray's lips. The confusion which he'd felt only a moment before had not, like so many moments of confusion, given way to clarity. In fact, when the craft began descending slowly toward his son's outstretched arms, he found himself perceiving reality in segments. Thoughts were jumbled on top of one another, not playing out. At some point, Lydia had made her way over to him and was gripping his arm tightly. He wasn't sure when or how. He only realized when it began to hurt. *I could have- where did it- my god, Tommy- propeller is going to mangle my rhodo- still time to have more children- what can I- need to piss-* It was a strange manner of existence for a man who had always prided himself in making informed decisions and staying cool under pressure. Until this moment, as a killing machine landed in front of his son, Raymond Peyne had been in complete control of the events of his life, which was all he really wanted.

With the drone on the ground now, Tommy could, on tiptoe, barely touch the edge of the wide lens camera, mounted on a dome swivel below the nose of the silver helmeted head of the thing. The camera was pointed directly down at the boy. The propeller ceased to whirl. Just in front of the V tail wing, a small satellite dish swiveled back and forth in a hundred eighty-degree arc and, for one ridiculous moment, it reminded Raymond Peyne of a wagging tail.

Lydia, putting words to his thoughts as she so often did, said, My God, Ray, I think it likes him.

Ray's mouth hung open. No thoughts could overcome the sight of his seven-year-old boy petting the surveillance camera of a military drone and speaking to it in soothing tones.

The boy turned to his father, his eyes bulging with excitement. Can I keep him, Dad?

Ray's lower jaw moved up and down, but it was a meaningless muscular exercise as it occurred without a tongue and without breathing of any sort. He moved his head, trying to shake out words that didn't exist, realizing too late that his son took the gesture as an acquiescence and the boy began jumping up and down.

What'd you do that for? asked Lydia.

I'm going to name him Buddy!

None of this was lost on the neighborhood. Just down the road at the first, gentle bend, the nearest neighbors had crowded closely together, sensing safety in numbers, murmuring excitedly amongst each other as the scene developed, Sherm and his wife, the Douglas's, Jerry and his wife, the Feins, even Pete, who would have had a much better vantage point from his own front yard, chose the safety of the flock, forgetting his wife, apparently, who peeked out from behind her living room curtains.

Adjustments had to be made, of course. Buddy went everywhere with the boy, from morning until night. During school it stayed out of sight, but in the mornings, on the way to the bus stop, or evenings, playing in the yard or in the park, it was always there, playfully hovering and dashing, or watchfully sitting. They engaged in spirited games of tag. Hide-and-go-seek was another favorite and always ended the same, with a giggling Tommy being exposed in his hiding place.

Once she had deduced Buddy's favorite landing spots, Lydia re-landscaped the front yard and laid down the law. Now, Buddy, *this* is your spot, here and over there! She pointed and the wide lens surveillance camera followed her motions. Buddy had ruined several shrubberies and two flowerbeds and she was determined to make him go in the right spots. Buddy learned quickly.

Other than that, care for the new pet proved to be much simpler than she expected it to be. There was no feeding to speak of, though when and where Buddy got his fuel remained a mystery.

Ray's calls to the nearest Air Force base some 75 miles away were fruitless. They claimed not to have lost a drone. The phone calls to various law enforcement agencies led to several different explanations of how there were no stray drone laws and how each level of public safety had its own unique deficiencies in regards to procedure in that area. No one seemed to want to claim it, and since the Peynes had no idea how to begin getting rid of it they did what human beings have always done. They adapted. They adopted.

Now, when the neighbors saw Tommy pedaling down the sidewalk toward them, he was accompanied by Buddy, who, despite his friendly name, could still remind people of an angry, metallic dinosaur, a flesh-eating titanium pterodactyl. It's to be certain that Tommy's voluminous questions received much more thoughtful replies.

The board of the homeowner's association met in secret. When it was revealed that they each had already made the same calls to the same government institutions with the same replies, the decision was unanimous. This one exotic pet would be tolerated.

I'm telling you, said Pete, out in his driveway, sitting on his new Husqvarna. There's somebody somewhere that's driving that thing, somebody sitting in a room somewhere, watching everything that goes on around here.

Jerry Nelson, a shrewd real-estate investor and a college professor, said, No, I'm pretty sure that's one of those new automated drones, programmed for law enforcement.

Automated! What the hell do you know about drones? asked Pete.

I'm telling you, I read it somewhere, online, or something.

There is no such thing.

Sure there is! said Jerry. And I'll bet we're all a lot safer having it around, too.

Safer, my ass. I see that thing hovering outside the kid's window at night. There's some pervert somewhere driving it, watching the kid undress and shit. You should hear the noises that come out of it.

Noises? Like pervert noises?

Yeah! If a machine could make those. Just weird-ass noises

It is sounding the deeps of its nature.

The voice came from behind them. Jerry, Pete, and Sherm all turned like syncopated dancers.

A nearly naked old man grabbed Pete by the shirt and pulled him close, hissing urgently in his ear. And of the parts of its nature that are deeper than it- *do you hear?*

Carl! How'd you get out here?

Japs, he said, squinting and waving off the unimportant details. Nazis.

Lydia Peyne's father was a World War II veteran, no one ever asked in what capacity. He was clad simply in blue-striped boxer shorts and brown slippers. All parts of him appeared in danger of sliding off. Pete could see Lydia, coming out her front door, headed their way.

Watch it, boys. Watch it! said the old man. It ain't right.

It isn't right, said Jerry, automatically, hypnotized by the hairless sagging skin gathered around two sticks which comprised the veteran's legs.

Thank you for your service, said Sherm, holding out his hand. Living a couple houses down, just around the first gentle bend of Laurel Lane, he'd managed to never see Carl before today. Carl looked at him like he was crazy as Lydia wrapped an arm around his shoulder.

Sorry! she said. Lydia was her bright, gay self as usual, and all of the driveway contingent felt, for a moment, their own privately held slice of jealousy toward Ray for his younger, voluptuous wife, shortly followed by their own quick fantasy about seducing her, except Sherm, of course, whose fantasy was to be seduced by her.

The home care worker called off today, she said, and I was caught up in cleaning. Come on, Dad.

The three men all took another moment to enjoy the luxury of Ray's absence and the near-holy spectacle of Lydia Peyne's ass in yoga pants, while displaying an obvious concern for the escorting of the old soldier back to safety. Then they each realized, in turn, and with private embarrassment, that no one had said a word to her.

The old guy's really out there, isn't he?

Oh, I don't know, said Pete. I told you. I don't trust that thing and you damn-well better believe I wouldn't even be saying that if it was anywhere nearby right now.

Yeah, well, you know, these are all pretty nice houses here. First time a drug dealer comes in here looking to rob us, you're going to be glad it's here.

Hmm.

The debate was over for the day, obviously. All three men were distracted. Sherm was already glancing off toward home. I gotta go, fellas, he said, and started wandering in that direction. He thought about drug dealers that wanted his stuff, his mind fell to his collection of old coins, and then he was pinned up against the wall by Lydia Peyne and she yanked at his belt. He briefly thought it odd that the drone be there watching, in his fantasy, but then he just went with it.

Yeah, me too, said Jerry, giving Pete a skeptical squint. The argument wasn't over yet as far as he was concerned. He was sure he'd read about the automated drones somewhere, loaded with behavioral recognition software. It had piqued his curiosity as a sociologist. As he crossed the street, Jerry was working on a theory, something big, something incredibly relevant and revolutionary. He could feel it brewing in the back of his mind.

Nothing was brewing to change Pete's mind on this, certainly not internet rumors. He'd heard it out there, at night, moving around. It might have been designed for minimum noise, an unobtrusive noise, the kind that could easily blend into the background, but at the same time, it was a suspicious sound, and suspicious sounds bothered Pete. He'd heard it out there at night, and once, when he watched it from his bedroom window and whispered to himself, what the fuck is it doing, it had turned and looked at him.

Boy and drone were inseparable. They were often seen at the park, sitting on a gentle hillside in the grass. The boy would be chatting away and Buddy's wide-lens camera would be fixed upon him, his satellite dish wagging. Did it talk to him, the neighborhood wondered? No one was brave enough to ask.

Sometimes on warm nights, Tommy would drape tarps over the drone's wings and camp underneath. From the porch, Ray could hear him talk to Buddy. The tarps were lit from within, red from the drone's running light on the underside of its belly. It was the only time Ray ever saw that light lit up. Something seemed wrong about it, that red. Something seemed wrong with everything these days. He was no longer the master of his household, the master of his life. Everything was out of control. Even sweet old Carl was on edge now all the time. A few nights earlier, at four in the morning, he woke the entire house when he began screeching, Tiny pilots! over and over, and laughing like a crazy person.

Events had cast Ray aside, made him irrelevant. A drone was raising his son. An anger was beginning to build in him.

Later, Lydia couldn't say why she bought the balls and Frisbees.

It just seemed like the natural thing to do, right? I mean they can't go on playing hide and seek all the time, can they? Ray? How was I to know?

Before they'd left the house, Tommy had shown Buddy the bag and said, I got something for you! By the time they got to the park, Buddy hovered close over the boy, turning this way and that, his little satellite dish spinning in full circles. Ray and

Lydia sat on the hillside as Tommy carried the bag out into the open grass, the drone close behind. They watched as Tommy dumped the toys out of the bag on the ground in front of him, a blue ball, a green ball, a red Frisbee, and a yellow Frisbee with a happy cartoon dog face on it.

And you bought two of each, why? asked Ray.

Oh I don't know, you never know which one Buddy will like.

Seriously? I mean really, how is he going to catch a ball or a Frisbee?

The answer to that question soon became all too apparent. Tommy chucked the blue ball as far as his eight-year old arm could throw. Fortunately, it was far enough.

Buddy the drone shot straight up into the air nearly two hundred feet and began to dive for the blue ball laying in the grass. As it descended, it released a small, laser-guided bomb and blew the hell out of that blue ball, leaving a ten-foot crater where the ball used to be. The force from the blast was enough to knock Tommy onto his rear thirty yards away and brought Ray and Lydia to their feet.

Tommy jumped up. Wow! Oh Wow! Buddy buzzed around over his head. A crowd of spectators was beginning to form.

Lydia's hand covered her open mouth. Oh, she said, the Homeowner's Association isn't going to like *that*.

No more balls, Tommy, yelled Ray.

Okay Dad! Wow!

Ray realized his mistake in specificity when Tommy picked up the red Frisbee and flung it. This time, Buddy swung out quickly to the right and launched a small air-to-air missile and blew the red Frisbee out of the air.

Wow! Oh, wow!

The crowd of spectators clapped.

Well, at least that didn't deface the grounds, said Lydia.

No more, Tommy! yelled Ray.

Just one more, Dad?

No!

Aw, please?

Everybody did seem to like the Frisbee thing, said Lydia.

Pleeeease?

Alright, yelled Ray, but not the ball, just the Frisbee!

Tommy picked up the yellow Frisbee with the happy cartoon dog face.

And throw that thing high!

Tommy launched the Frisbee. Buddy launched his other missile. At least, Ray thought, that is the last of his missiles.

This time however, the air-to-air missile shot past the yellow Frisbee with the happy cartoon dog face. Past the Frisbee, out of the park, and over the hill. Past the Frisbee, out of the park, over the hill, and straight into the bathroom window of Tony Cunningham of Cunningham Chevrolet Toyota Kia.

After the television crews left, the Laurel Lane Homeowner's Association board called another secret meeting. Tony Cunningham had been the neighborhood's most vocal opponent of the exotic pet exception made for the Peynes, but everyone knew that was because his application for an ostrich was denied.

Birds were filthy things, the board decided, and there were going to be no oversized chicken coops on Laurel Lane, backyard or not.

Still, it was rather disturbing to see the top of the Cunningham home blown off, and then there was the whole matter of the hole in the park. Some of the board members felt it was time to revisit the "Buddy" issue. Other members of the board loudly, and seemingly to the air and walls, announced that they would never ever have a bad thing to say about that darling Buddy.

In the end, it was decided that, as far as collateral damage went, Tony Cunningham was about as good as it got, and as far as the park went, a resolution was passed to approve the budget for more topsoil and sod. Several board members chipped in from their own pockets to avoid upsetting the books for the year.

For historical purposes, and for the comfort of his family, it should be noted that Tony Cunningham was not sitting on the toilet when he was killed, as was so cruelly suggested in the meeting minutes. He was in the shower, singing "Waltzing Matilda."

That night the news broadcasts, despite the fact that all of the camera crews had seen the drone, reported the explosion to be the result of a gas leak.

Raymond Peyne was not to be so easily assuaged as the homeowners. His son's pet had just killed someone. And somehow, the next morning Buddy had two brand new missiles and a bomb to replace the ones he'd used. If things weren't out of hand before, they damn well were now. For twenty-three years he had meticulously built his life, from his total dedication to his education, to his successful practice, to the perfect marriage to the perfect woman with the perfect son and the perfect house. One piece at a time, all under control. And now that was all being taken from him.

Sitting in front of the computer in his den, he searched for independent journalism websites. If it took a bunch of liberal writers to bring attention to the subject, then so be it. He perused the headlines he saw there.

US Inadvertently Lets Weapons Fall into Terrorist Hands
Invasive Communications Bill Passes

Following the Money: Corporate Ties to the War on Terror
More Americans Below Poverty Level Than Ever Before

Congress Hides Domestic Terrorism Budget in the School Lunch Bill

How had it ever gotten this bad? As Ray scanned for the website's contact information he slowly became aware of the noise to which he had grown so accustomed. He turned in his chair and saw the wide-lens surveillance camera, just outside the window. Ray pulled the blind, turned off the computer, and went to bed.

Laying there, he tossed back and forth, his anger rising. He was a prisoner inside his own home! Spying on him! What would he do if Buddy found out about his weekly tryst with Wendell Bichner's dental hygienist at the Super 8? It was all he had left. The damn thing wasn't going to take that too. He rose from bed with the intent of mortal harm.

Executing as much stealth as one inexperienced in stealthy activities could muster, he snuck through the house and into the garage where he most silently slipped the largest metal crescent wrench from its holder on the pegboard and crept out the backdoor. Through the black he glided, a wrench ninja, ready for violence. He would find the right bolt somehow, loosen the fuel line- god knows where it got its fuel anyway- or missiles- fucking missiles- got to be quick- fucking twig- why do I pay that guy to rake the yard anyway- wait- what-.

Buddy's internal mechanisms whirred to life with Ray still twenty yards away. There would be no slipping in now, curse it all. He couldn't even sneak up on the damn thing. When he realized that his legs had frozen with the sound, Ray could take no more.

He charged the drone at full oral surgeon velocity, emitting a primal scream to make the staunchest marine proud. Lights began to flicker on in houses as far down as Sherm's. The metal crescent wrench rained down on the fuselage with rhythmic fury, driven home by the power of his screams. BAD drone! BAD drone! BAD! BAD!

Unbeknownst to Ray in his blind wrath, Neighbors were on their front porches, Pete and his wife were watching from their living room window, and Lydia was trying to calm a wailing Tommy.

BAD drone! BAD drone! BAD! DRONE!

Then it seemed the drone had had enough, whined to life, and sprang into the air with a gust of wind that nearly knocked Ray to his knees. Buddy whirled around, facing him, and Ray heard the *clitch* and the hiss of escaping gas that he'd heard with the garden shovel in his hand. It occurred to him that he had chosen an even more pathetic weapon than the last time he'd been in this situation.

The floodlights on the outside of the house blasted to life, blinding Ray for a second and by the time he had adjusted he saw Carl at the edge of the front porch. He wore his helmet from the war and his infantry rain poncho with his M1 strapped across his back, army green from the waist up. Below that it was blue-striped boxer shorts and brown slippers. He waved his service revolver around in the air.

Fuck! Tiny Pilots! Nazi Shit! Damn the torpedoes, boys!

And then he began his charge, shooting as he came. Of course, Carl's charge was more of a high-stepped lurch, jerky, like a baby's first unsteady scuttle across the high-piled carpet. His first shot took out one of the beautiful round gas lamp globes which adorned Laurel Lane. Everyone with a direct line of sight of the scene ducked. Across the street, Pete and his wife had adopted a Kilroy pose, only the tops of their heads visible in the window.

Ray, too, dove for cover. The idea of Carl with live ammunition frightened him worse than the drone. He had no idea there was a live clip in that trunk.

Carl's second shot took a small branch from one of the young oaks. His third missed all solid objects. His fourth went straight into the ground as he struggled with his balance, mid-lurch. The fifth shot took out the stem in the middle of Buddy's satellite dish.

There's some apple for your pie, Adolf! Don't turn back now, boys!

The drone reared back into the air, a whip about to snap. Carl pursued it out into the middle of the yard, now shooting wildly overhead, unable to look up and lurch at the same time.

Ray saw the whole thing from where he took cover around the front corner of the house, saw Carl stop, shove in a fresh clip, grip the .45 with both hands, and spread those wobbly sagging legs to steady his aim, saw Buddy launch his deadly cargo, saw the rocket on its deadly course before he covered his head for the explosion.

So it was that Private Carl Reynolds left the world as a war hero and later Ray thought, if there is any sort of justice in existence, then he entered the afterlife to find his entire regiment, in dress uniform, saluting him.

Buddy flew off and disappeared beneath the stars.

When it was over, it was as if no one had paid any attention at all. Much like a few days earlier, the neighbors were all questioned, the damage was scrutinized. There was much standing with hands on hips, shaking of heads, and conferences of serious men replete with fingers occasionally pointing in different directions. At least this time there was no fire to put out. The end result of all this questioning, scrutinizing, and conferencing, was a generous portion of shoulder-shrugging and embarrassed confessions of powerlessness.

The television crews were again on the scene, but like before, no interview portions were aired and the cause of the explosion was blamed on more faulty gas lines. Ray felt dazed by the whole experience.

Lydia hated him now for getting her father killed. The irony was that Carl had just been diagnosed with cancer. Like Pete said later when Ray told him about the diagnosis, Well that was a much better way to go than cancer.

Tommy hated him now for driving Buddy away. The kid cried for days, walking around holding the piece of the satellite receiver that Carl had shot off. He'll never come back now, he screamed at Ray.

But, as Ray suspected, the boy was wrong. A week later Buddy alighted on the front lawn, a shiny new satellite receiver wagging near his tail-wing. Tommy's joy could not be contained and all the neighborhood smiled strangely stiff smiles and told him how happy they were for him.

Like most boys, as he grew, Tommy took Buddy increasingly for granted, and the drone would often follow him now at greater distances, forgotten. And like it does for all boys with beloved pets, the time came when he had to say goodbye.

One morning when Tommy was in middle school, Lydia reminded him to go out and pay some attention to Buddy, but this time, when Tommy came near, the drone's internal mechanisms failed to come to life.

Buddy? the boy said. Buddy? Wake up, Buddy!

Tommy began poking at the cold metal and tears began to fill his eyes. He was now tall enough to reach the wide lens surveillance camera and he grabbed both sides of it, peering intently into its inscrutable glass.

Buddy! Buddy!

By now, Ray and Lydia had heard the boy's cries of distress and came running out of the house. Pete, headed to an early golf game, saw the commotion and wandered over, watching from the fence. Ray went over to him as Lydia consoled their son.

I think it's dead.

Good, said Pete. What the hell are you going to do now, bury it?

I don't think I want to dig that hole.

It was a joke, but Tommy remained inconsolable. He wanted to bury Buddy, like Grandpa. Ray, though a believer in firm truths, refrained from telling the boy there really wasn't that much of Grandpa left to bury. Disposal logistics were a real problem and Ray discussed it with the driveway contingent that weekend.

Maybe if you brought in a backhoe.

I'm not bringing in a backhoe and digging a hole that big in my yard! Are you crazy Jerry?

Aren't pets *supposed* to be buried in the backyard?

That's beside the point. If I could figure out how to haul it, I'd take it to the junkyard or something. Any ideas? Anything would be helpful here guys.

At that moment, a white, thirty-foot flatbed truck turned onto Laurel Lane and came to a stop in front of the Peyne house. As the four men watched from Pete's driveway, two strangers in military fatigues got out of the cab, walked into the Peyne front yard and, each gripping a landing strut with one hand and a wing with the other, lifted Buddy's carcass and began carrying him off.

Tommy ran from the house. Wait! Wait! Where are you taking him? Dad! he yelled across the street. Where are they taking him?

Ray lifted his hands, palms up, in front of him and gave his best confused expression. He wasn't about to look a gift horse in the mouth. Pete, Jerry, and Sherm were all eerily silent, as if in respect of the beast that killed Carl.

Tommy followed the men right out onto the street, screaming at them. Where are you going? Where are you taking him?

The men never spoke as they tethered the landing gear and the tail wing to the bed of the truck and covered it with tarps that fastened to the sides of the bed with button snaps.

Right before getting back in the cab, the one riding shotgun turned to Tommy with a fathomless expression.

We're taking him to live on a farm.

As it turned out, there was enough of Buddy left to have a funeral in the backyard after all. Digging a small hole in the corner of the yard, they laid his old satellite dish stem to rest.

He was my best friend, said Tommy. There'll never be another one like him.

It was this moment that Jerry Nelson chose to share the insights that had been gathering form all these years, the insights which would have been a major work of sociological research had it not been for the computer virus that wiped out all of his research, notes, pictures, and documentation.

I think we have witnessed a significant moment here, he said. The first time a spontaneous bond was formed between man and machine. Buddy was that first wolf to come into the campfire light those forty thousand years ago, the beginning of an era of cooperation and codependence. Someday people will wonder where it began. And it all began right here.

Jerry, said Pete, sometimes I think you are a genius.

He turned and started walking back around the Peyne house toward home.

And then you spout crap like that.

Some years later, at his college graduation, the entire graduating class erupted in applause as Tommy stepped onto the stage to receive his diploma. Tommy was a campus legend, not only for his legendary performance on the college debate team but also for the peculiar best friend which accompanied him everywhere, including onto the stage for his graduation ceremony.

Tommy had discovered Buddy, as he named him, right after his debate team had annihilated the team from Yale in a debate about concentration of wealth in a free market system. Buddy was a small metallic dragonfly with a three-inch wingspan that sounded like the rustling of leaves when he flew.

Sitting in the restaurant after the graduation ceremony, Ray, long since divorced and remarried, said to Tommy, Why, son? Why do you tolerate that thing? Did you learn nothing the first time?

Aw, Dad, said Tommy, holding out his hand for the small flying machine and, as it landed, looking deep into its tiny fiber-optic lenses. Not all drones are bad. Some of them love us.

MYTHS OF REGULATION

Larry D. Thacker

Sure, I know we've been dealing in Buddha statuary for well over a year now, but change is inevitable. Change is painful, yes. Change is constant. Pain is constant.

We didn't like it when the Currency Committee switched from Elvis albums (pre-Vegas) to Buddhas either, but we adjusted, didn't we? We did what we had to do just like all the other times before. Nobody starved. Nobody did without for very long. We scoured the countryside and towns for what we needed, the baseline values were established pretty quick, and got the marketplace back on its feet in no time.

Anyway, I don't know about you all, but inflation's wearing me out. It was so much easier a year ago when a pocket full of clay Buddhas could feed your family for two or three days. When there were still temples to raid within a day's hike. Not anymore, right? Now a solid concrete, twenty-five pounder dug out from a yard won't buy shit. Probably couldn't buy a rotten can of PBR for that now.

See what we've done? We've saturated the market again, just when everybody went ape over the Elvis stuff for two years. It was too much of a good thing. At least you could carry a little Buddha in a pocket. Albums don't transport easy no matter how much you love the King. I'm tired of busting my ass loading up a wheelbarrow full of Buddha junk just to go shopping for the bare necessities.

So, the Committee's starting over. Again. It won't be the last time, so don't get comfortable. But guess what it is now? Just guess.

Ceramic, mid-century Japanese-made clowns? No, but I'm sure that'll happen sooner or later.

Hubcaps? Not a bad idea, though I think they'll be more specific, like only VWs or something. 8-track tapes? Another good idea, though there just ain't many good players left.

No, folks. It's unicorns.

Yeah, you heard me. Unicorns.

Statues. Music boxes. Books. Everything unicorns. Paintings and pictures. Brass ones. Carved wooden ones. Gold ones. Movies. Sky's the limit. Clothing. Shoes and hats. Necklaces. Bedding. Pajamas. Blow up floaties for pools. Unicorn furry outfits, for sure. Halloween masks, yes. T-shirts. All the t-shirts.

Oh, and don't forget the general standards: age, material, size, weight, aesthetic, origin. That early 21st century Trump-era Chinese-made junk ain't gonna cut it this go around. Won't be worth much. They want US-made stuff. Items from Taiwan, Japan, Korea, maybe Vietnam if we're lucky. Early China, but only if it's true vintage. Unless you find the brass goods. That's usually Indian, though, so no problem.

But this time, the faster and the more we hoard up and hold it back the more we'll control the currency values. We'll let out the unicorns as we need them this time. As hunger, shelter, alcohol, entertainment and other rationed requirements dictate. We'll have some say in the matter.

No more passive searching while we're out scavenging. Be intentional. Go into the wastelands. Check the houses, the new age stores. There'll no doubt be less unicorns than Buddhas to find. Maybe. We'll see. Goodwills and thrift stores, too.

What's that? No, I don't think you're going to find a real unicorn out there, though that would be like winning the lottery, wouldn't it? How could you ever spend a live unicorn? That's definitely a one time purchase of something. Something amazing.

Steaks? Unicorn steaks? Sure, but how long would those last? Imagine the taste!

I'd rather have the live unicorn, wouldn't you? Yeah, we could sell rides on it in exchange for little porcelain unicorn statues. Who wouldn't want to ride a unicorn when the world's gone to shit? One ride per statue. Step right up. Watch for the rainbow droppings.

I take it back. Maybe there is a real one out there. I hope one of you do find a damn unicorn out there! If you did find one, we'd take over this dump!

We'd set the rules. We'd be kings! Queens!

What are you standing around here for? Go find me a goddamned unicorn!

WHAT ARE FRIENDS FOR?

Larry D. Thacker

"Don't you leave me fucking bleeding, man," Carter ordered his buddies, Freemont and Shawn D. "You better have that iron ready to go, ya hear?"

"Don't you worry none, we'll burn it closed. Just don't run off hollering in the dark bleeding everywhere so we can't find you," one of them advised.

As happens with many interesting concepts turned bad ideas, what was about to happen involved too much alcohol and the blind trust of longtime friendships. You might suspect a dare was involved, but that just wasn't the case. What transpires herein occurred voluntarily and without the least provocation.

This isn't to say that Carter wasn't nervous. You'd be too if you were having to psych yourself up to willingly chop off your own left pinky.

It was the third, and last, night of these boys' annual camping trip on the banks of Clinch Lake. Carter, Freemont, and Shawn D were friends from all the way back in county grade school days. They'd traded conspiracy theories all their lives. Everything from UFO government cover-ups to Kennedy Assassination theories. No one was surprised when halfway through high school the boys started up the ETPS, short for the End of Times Prepper Society – membership three.

They weren't athletic, per se, but they were from farming families, so they had strong backs and arms. They went to work the summer between their sophomore and junior years digging what took until their sophomore years at the local community college to turn into quite the comfortable end of the world underground bunker. They called it "Calamity Clubhouse." They'd dug deep enough in a corner of Freemont's daddy's cornfield and hauled two metal dumpsters into the hole. Shawn D was the welder of the trio so he hitched the dumpsters together good and torched out a hatch and air vent on top. They plastered the walls with survival plans and articles and lined up stacks of canned goods for when the time came to close the hatch for the "long haul" as they liked calling it.

This was their seventh summer camping trip to the lake. They'd started them as a way of meeting up and getting away from the wives after college was over. They were all on the close side of thirty now. Never had all the long conversations about what might happen – what most definitely would happen, sooner or later, someday – been more important.

Each had downed a six-pack of their preferred beer with several shots from a shared fifth of Jack along the way. It was on around one in the morning when Carter broached the subject of sacrifice, commitment, and food stores.

"No, really. What comes of things when all the canned goods run out? When we come up from the shelter and all the food's been scavenged from all the houses?"

"We hunt. Duh," teased Shawn D.

"Not necessarily. What if the game is poisoned? Or it's run off or hunted out? Or we're just not that good at it?"

Freemont nodded. Carter had a good point.

"We need a contingency, boys," Carter pointed out.

"A contingency."

"Yep. I don't reckon anyone's got to starve during the apocalypse if they don't feel like it," Carter offered with drunken confidence.

Freemont frowned at Carter over the top of the camp flames. "How you figure?"

Shawn D wondered too. "Yeah."

"Man, y'all are so stupid sometimes."

"Hey!" Freemont yelled, tossing an empty Highwayman IPA can.

"After all the zombie films we've watched over the years and you fellas would sit around and wait to starve to death. Damn."

"We gonna eat zombies? Oooh. Yuk, man." Shawn D wasn't having it.

"Naw, dude," Freemont said. "I get it. That would be us basically. But as cannibals. Right, Carter? That what you getting at, man?"

Carter nodded. "Finally someone gets it. Why starve when there'd be meat everywhere?"

"I ain't murdering anyone to eat," Shawn D protested, draining one of his PBRs.

"No. No. We wouldn't have to, I don't think. Not with the rate of people dying off naturally. Think about it. People die all the time as it is. They'd be dying a hundred times faster in the end days. We'd have more meat than we could handle."

Freemont scrunched up his nose.

"I don't know if I could eat…human meat."

Carter shrugged. "You would if you were hungry enough."

Freemont shrugged back.

"I guaran-dang-tee it."

Shawn D shook his head no. "I bet it tastes a might different, y'all. The Lord wouldn't have made humans taste any good, would he? If that sort of meat tasted any count everybody'd been doing it a whole lot more and not just them head shrinkin' cannibals out on them isolated islands."

"Would y'all do it?" Carter wanted to know.

"How the hell are we supposed to know?" Shawn D asked, getting perturbed now.

"I guess we'd do it when we had to make the choice, huh?" Freemont added.

"But what if you couldn't when the time came? Shit…y'all'd starve sure as the world."

"Would not."

"Would to."

"Naw, man."

One of them crumpled another empty and tossed it in the fire along with another log.

It was quiet for a while. The fire popped and hissed. They chugged more beer. Passed what was left the Jack.

Freemont spoke up.

"What if one of us died and was out alone. I guess I'd consider it. Unless we were all diseased or something awful. At least we'd know where we'd been, right?" He stared into the fire, thinking it out. "Know what I mean?"

Carter nodded. "But what if…what if you were the last one…?"

"The last one?"

"Yeah…the last. What then?"

The alcohol and fatigue were really taking a toll.

"What if you had to eat your own body?"

One of the boys gasped at that. That was just too much to consider. Carter knew that as well.

"Just as an extreme measure, though? To make it just long enough?"

"Long enough for what the hell?" Freemont wanted to know.

"For whatever," Carter said. "Whatever."

"Yeah," one of them agreed, finally getting it. "For whatever."

Carter had the Jack bottle. Spun the last swallow around in the bottom. Was thinking hard. Harder than he'd thought for a long time on much of anything. Held the remainders of the Jack up to the firelight, watched the spinning amber, the dreggy hints of all their backwash congealed with the pretty dancing fire. Felt the brotherhood they'd shared for so long in a way he hadn't in years in that instant.

"I'll do it."

Freemont and Shawn D looked up confused. What had they missed in the conversation?

"Do what?" Shawn D asked.

Carter stared at the last shot in the bottle, swished it around, upended it and swallowed it down. He reached over near what was left of the wood pile and grabbed the hatchet and sat back down on his stump and looked at the boys seriously.

"Fellas, how we gonna ever eat the flesh of man if we've never partook of the flesh of man?" He was staring at his left hand, turning it over in the rippling firelight.

"…fuckin stupid mutha…" Shawn D mumbled.

Freemont got up and pulled a stump over to Carter.

"What are you thinking on doing, buddy? Huh?"

Carter kept talking, mostly to himself. "Now I'm right handed…so I wouldn't want to maim the right…and I'd need my left hand and thumb…most my fingers…"

"Right," Freemont agreed.

"And I'd want to use my right to do it. For accuracy."

Shawn D was sitting up close now, too.

"Right," Shawn D agreed.

"The pinky." Carter said it matter-of-factly. "The pinky," he repeated.

"The pinky?" one asked.

"The pinky," another repeated.

"Yeah, I don't need it. Who does, really? My hands are big and there's enough meat on it to give us all a decent enough taste." He held up his hand in the firelight with only his pinky stuck out and twisted it in the light like he was inspecting a BBQ wing. "Whatcha think?"

The boys were drunk enough to be equally disgusted and intrigued.

A few minutes later and they had it all planned out. Carter would lay out his pinky finger across a stump and take if off himself with the hatchet. The boys would have a red hot knife ready to cauterize the fresh wound. Freemont, the best cook of the trio would fry up the finger for the three of them with his grandmother's sixty-year-old cast iron skillet, the one they always used for camping. The story would be that Carter had accidently chopped his finger off cutting kindling for the campfire.

"So you're sure?"

"Yeah. Yeah."

"You don't want one of us to do it?"

"No. You'd miss. Take half my hand off."

"Here drink another beer."

"Too bad we don't have any more whisky for you to slug like in those Civil War movies."

"You gonna back out?"

"…"

"This is crazy, man."

"What if we change our minds?"

"Well, dude, we can't waste the man's finger."

"Yeah."

"True."

"Here we go…wrap the tourniquet around his palm…"

"That too tight…?"

"Ow. That's good…Let's to it."

All three inhaled briskly. Blinked hard.

Carter's on his knees by the stump. The boys are leaning on him, holding his arm. Wincing before anything even happens.

The hatchet flashes light as Carter raises it.

He yells out like they used to when they'd chase each other through the woods, like wild boys, crazed like starved wolves, and lets it fall.

The sound is a wet thump. A thump on wood.

Then chaos.

"Where'd it go…?"

There was a lot of blood. Suddenly. More than they anticipated.

Carter felt lightheaded, probably from holding his breath too much, not from any pain. His hand was mostly numb from the tourniquet.

"Get the knife, dumbass!"

Shawn D grabbed the glowing knife from the campfire's edge.

"You hurting yet?" Freemont asked.

"Find my finger, y'all. Not yet, but…"

"You're about to."

Which was worse they couldn't tell, the sound of blistering flesh or how loudly Carter screamed when Shawn D pressed the red tip of the three-inch knife to what little stump there was of Carter's pinky finger. He yelled, took a breath, yelled again. Cussed both his friends, yelled some more, swore it was never his idea, yelled, blamed them, threatened to cut off one each of their fingers to make it even. He had to sit down when he almost passed out, not from blood loss or shock, but from hyperventilating after screaming curse laced threats at his friends.

Once they were calmed down, the worst of the bleeding was staunched, Carter was over his screaming spell, most of the pain had turned to a pulsing numbness, the boys set about the curious, but gruesome task of finding Carter's pinky finger out in the campsite dark. The firelight only reached so far. It couldn't have shot off too awfully far from the stump where Carter had brought down the hatchet, but he'd flinched pretty good from nervousness and Freemont hadn't been holding on tight enough. For all they knew they'd already stepped on the thing and drove it into the mud like a cast off piece of gristle from supper.

"How far off did it go?"

"I saw it go plumb over the campfire, I'm pretty sure."

"Check those bushes."

But find it they did. Shawn D saw the fingernail glistening from the firelight. They rinsed it off. Or rather, Freemont, the appointed cook did, both full meaty knuckles of it.

"Um…we battering this thing?"

Carter was feeling better now. "Hell no. That would kill the real taste."

"True."

"Plain oil it is."

The cast iron skillet was on the grill screen. It sizzled when Freemont poured the oil.

"Don't forget to pull that nail off," Carter reminded.

"Lucky us you'd bit most of it off."

"What kind of oil you using?" Shawn D asked.

"What's it matter?" Carter barked.

"Just wondering's all."

"Canola. All we have."

"OK."

"I'd prefer olive oil usually, but canola works fine, I guess."

Carter huffed. "I hope we're all together when this goes down so I can remind you of this conversation one day."

Shawn D reached over when Freemont yanked the nail from Carter's paling finger.

"Gimme."

"What you need with that?"

"I'll need something to remind me what really happened tonight once I sober up, when Carter's telling everybody he lost his finger in the woods."

"All I know is, you better have sense enough to remember to clean out your pockets before Jess does laundry and finds that nail or we'll all be in a world of hurt."

"Can we go to jail for this shit?"

Carter was inspecting his own severed body part. He gave it a sniff, frowned, looked up and winked at Shawn D, leaned over and tossed it in the skillet. The appendage snapped and popped and hopped in the oil like a luscious slab of breakfast bacon.

Carter sniffed the air.

"Go to jail for what?"

THE SQUATTERS

C.M. Chapman

Norman Watkins usually walked in the early evening, out through the small field behind his house and into the woods until he reached the barbed-wire fence separating the woods from the back fields of the Pringle farm. Then he'd follow the fence along and out of the woods past the old Armistead place, now overgrown, though sparsely in the spot where the old man's truck used to sit. After passing the house off to his left, he crossed the dirt road and down into the woods again. The walk offered several natural lingering points and the little waterfall in the gulley next to the road was one of those places. It was also a natural rest before climbing the opposite hillside and into another field which would lead him back to Parkins Road. He'd follow the road home. A couple of the hilly parts were steep enough to make him wonder if it wasn't a bit much for a man of 59, but then he knew it was worth it.

The whole walk, at least in early spring as it was now, required him to leave by 6:30 if he wanted to be home before dark, but here he was, putting on his boots at 7:15, a direct result of a couple days earlier, when he'd gotten a late start. It occurred to him that if he'd left at his normal time, he might not have seen any of it. This was his reason to leave later tonight. Still his mind told him it could have been anything in that damnable flickering light, people moving furniture, statues maybe. Someone must be moving in, perhaps artists.

Norman didn't have a problem with artists. Back in '74, he'd lived in an artist colony in New York, on a farm near Batavia. Writing during the day, partying at night, driving into Greenwich Village on weekends. Whale Belly Farm was where he'd met Monica when she was a painter. They were married by a Unitarian minister with a Zappa mustache three years later, after his trip out west. That was back when he believed that everyone had a soulmate, that there was someone out there who completed you, before he'd completely understood that this search was inward, not outward, before he'd completely understood that Monica didn't love him nearly as much as she loved the familial notoriety of marrying a black man. That realization, along with the business in Philadelphia, is what drove him here, to Wetzel County. Old Moses Armistead had been his closest neighbor then, a man who'd made no secret that he'd never had a neighbor who looked like Norman.

No, there weren't many who looked like Norman for a few miles. Yes, it was West Virginia, but being so geographically near Pittsburgh, Cleveland, and Cincinnati, it just seemed unlikely, this white enclave right in the middle of the three. Overall, he hadn't run into too much trouble. His closest neighbors all seemed decent, the Pringles up the road, and Moses, maybe the one he'd learned most to appreciate over the years before the old guy had passed on. And now someone was moving into his house, artists with strange statues, perhaps, or squatters, meth-cookers. Maybe that was the cause of the flickering light, he thought. And maybe drug fumes were on the breeze, fueling arcane vision. Maybe he didn't see what he thought he saw.

The sun stole its last peeks from behind the hills to his west, the direction in which he set out, threading through the shin-high grass and the occasional clump of wild geranium. A couple small saplings, a white ash and a sumac, marked the woods' attempt to spread its loamy opulence beyond its current boundary. Norman had given up any attempt to mow this area. When he first moved in, he used to mow the whole thing, but thirty years had given him some perspective on landscaping. He cut a small patch behind the house now, but no more.

His pace was quicker than he'd anticipated, and he was soon winding through the woods along the fence. At this pace, he would be there too early, but hoped what remained of daylight might have some revelations. Strapped around his neck was a heavy pair of Jason Statesman binoculars that he'd had for many years. He would stay at the edge of the woods and not venture out into the open this time. At the end of the trees, he found a rock to sit on. Here he was inconspicuous and yet, with the binoculars, could see the house pretty well. In the circle of his enhanced vision, the house did not look so different. The old white paint was still cracked and peeling. The wooden screen door was still torn. The sheer curtains in the window were still yellowed from the sun, hanging straight and taut. Norman still remembered Armistead saying, "That way I get two windows for the price of one."

Old Moses had been beaten down by a lifetime of work. He'd labored for the chemical plants, driven a bread truck, been a farm laborer, and had even gone down in the mines briefly. "Don't have much love for the big dark," he used to say to Norman. When Norman had moved here, in '85, Armistead was living on his Social Security and a backyard garden. With the binoculars trained on the garden area to his left, he could see the splay of the old man's asparagus, now growing wild amongst the weeds. Cancer had taken the old guy, arguably Norman's best friend out here, nearly five years ago. He hadn't let his mind dwell on it too much up until now, but sitting here, waiting for the light to dwindle, he recalled moments which had escaped him.

Most times he thought of the day that Moses had shown him the small waterfall on his property and told him he was welcome to visit as often as he liked. Somehow Norman had felt compelled to confess his deeply spiritual thoughts about nature and, for the first time in his life, had been greeted with a look of total understanding and given a gift beyond measure. There was something about that spot.

But today, looking over at the overgrown patch of garden, he remembered that it was the first place he'd ever seen Moses Armistead. He'd been exploring his newly purchased three-acre property. The sight of the old man, looking the part of the quintessential hillbilly in his coveralls, with his hoe, had intimidated him at first and he stopped at the edge of the woods. The old man, looking up, rested his hands on the top of the hoe and said, "Don't often see a black fella looking at me from behind a tree while I'm gardenin'." Norman's embarrassment drove him into stepping out of the woods and into his first awkward conversation with his new neighbor.

He hadn't known then, how to articulate his reasons for moving there to the old hillbilly. He hadn't known how to paint him the big picture. Philadelphia was only the latest, if not most blatant example of the world he witnessed. Much of it he hadn't even realized until years later. Monica had given herself over to what struck Norman as an art beast. The new rising art brokers were like nothing he'd ever seen or imagined. He had been welcomed into this circle, of course, at first for being Monica's black writer husband, and then later for the book. A joke, that.

Catching his mind wandering reminded him to scan with the binoculars again. Still only the movement of weeds in the breeze, not so much as a ripple behind the curtains. It felt as if twilight would last forever.

It was the thought of his book which brought him back to the moment, mostly because that was the central theme of the piece. He really hadn't meant for *Speaking Tree* to go the direction that it did. He'd meant it to be a literary exploration of self-awareness as the key to a larger world, concepts he'd learned from various medicine men and women when he'd toured the reservations out west. But that was the dawn of the "New Age" publishing explosion and somehow those folks turned it into something he hadn't really meant for it to be.

Norman drove new-age festivals from his thoughts, chided himself for leaving the house too early, and scanned his surroundings. Crawling up a tree next to him, a brown caterpillar with a hairy white spine and spotted skin stopped to lift its head from the trunk and wave it side to side as if looking around. Norman wondered what it might be trying to tell him. The language of God usually only made sense in retrospect, and sometimes, he'd found not even then. Still, he raised the binoculars yet again, his mind still crossing the country, to those barren monuments of despair and strength, the reservations.

Ultimately it had been brother Malcolm's autobiography that had driven him there. Reading it as a young man, the idea of the white man being the embodiment of the devil had really stuck with him. It had led him to researching the concerted effort to wipe out indigenous populations worldwide, and then reading about these cultures, eventually volunteering to teach Creative Writing on the reservations for two years.

Monica hadn't wanted him to go. She felt her career was at a critical stage; she was starting to make connections. She'd sold a few pieces, sculptures.

"You know," she said, "with some artistic clout then we could really help those people. And you can always go volunteer later, after we get established in the city."

For a while, he thought the trip might end them. She became more distant on their phone calls, depressed. But then she landed her gallery job and things began to improve. As he figured out a few years later, it didn't hurt her reputation that she was married to a black writer who was volunteering on the Indian reservations. His absence deepened his mystery.

The shadows deepened his more immediate mystery.

At first, he was upset that time got away from him. He could now barely make out the outline of the house. There were no lights, no confusing silhouettes or movement. He now suspected meth-cookers, most likely just using the house for the cooking, not staying there. He now began to debate whether he ought to go in and look for evidence, something to tell the state police or the sheriff's department. But what if they came back while he was in there? It was likely that they were sneaking in at night. Still, if only in the spirit of his friend, he thought he should check it out. Old Moses wouldn't have approved of meth-heads using his house. Norman pulled himself up from the rock into a crouch, unfolding slowly and carefully to avoid straining something.

His hands gripped his lower back with his thumbs as he approached verticality and a flash of light birthed a flickering yellow from inside the house. The combination of the position change and his degree of startle came out louder than he expected, an "mmphh" which sounded like a muffled woof.

Within seconds there was movement. Norman ducked back down as he heard the front door open and two figures emerged. Though he couldn't see well in the darkness, Norman judged they stood still, just outside the drawn door. Norman held his breath and thrust his hearing sense through the thickness of the night. Finally, he was able to discern the rhythmic quiver of noses. They were sniffing, for crying out loud! And though he suspected it was some addict trait, he found himself to be relieved to be downwind. Movement in the window caught his eye and he had to suppress a cry. There it was, the statue he'd seen. Now he understood its familiarity. Monica had studied Egyptian Art. The form was Anubis, but its shape alone would not have been enough to nearly make him cry out. He'd seen pictures and statues of Egyptian gods before.

No, the movement threw him.

Statues don't move.

They don't turn their heads or raise their snouts and howl.

The shadows were too deep to distinguish either of the figures still outside the front door. All Norman could perceive was the subtle flash of motion in the dark when one of them moved... and the sniffing. All that motion seemed congregated in the space of the doorway so even though he didn't dare run, at least they weren't searching for him. He remained crouched when, rising from inside the house, the whining and growling became a twining vibration of dread, twisting around him, constricting, pressing in through his elbows, a current that, when it hit his spine, exploded as chills through his entire body. From the sorrow and repressed malice of the initial sound, rose the unholy barks, reeking of violence, the chase, the kill, becoming louder suddenly as the door opened and the two figures re-entered the house. Norman noticed from the silhouettes that they had on strange hats for the weather, then one shook his head and Norman could take no more.

He arose from behind his rock, and with a single crunching leap, made it back to the path. Keeping himself scrunched over, he walked as quickly and quietly as he could. He didn't dare turn on the flashlight, but he knew every root and stone on this path, and found himself almost jogging in places, pursued by the muffled canine chaos of whatever insanity was going on in that house. Howls occasionally soared above the din, probably the one he'd seen behind the curtain.

By the time he emerged into his field, it all sounded like a weird quivering tone, a perversion of singing, angry frog song, creeping into you, subtly, like growing resentment. He'd experienced nothing like that the first time. He'd experienced nothing like that, ever. Breathing heavily, he stopped, his own house lights just ahead. He bent over, his hands resting on his knees, his eyes unfocused on the ground, looking at moments ago, trying to find some other explanation to dispel his certainty that he had just seen dog-headed men at old Moses Armistead's place.

#

Who do you call when you think dog-headed men are squatting in your dead friend's house? This question, along with a state of high alert, kept Norman tossing and turning through the night. Every night sound, of which his place had an abundance, was scrutinized. Deer? Raccoon? Possum? Branch falling from tree into old leaves and new growth? Dog-headed man?

His preoccupying thought, upon getting back into the house that night, was to dismiss his first theory, werewolves, as a possibility. The idea of werewolves, with big floppy ears that flapped softly up and down when they shook their heads, just seemed too incongruous. If he hadn't been scared shitless at the thought of a dog's head on the body of a man, he might have found it better if they'd had jingly collars. The image, separated from the clothing, the walking on two legs, and manipulating doorknobs part, was all dog.

So, who do you call? The sheriff? The state police? The pound crossed his mind with a wry twist. It was one of the ways he dealt with problems that seemed unsolvable. He had developed quite a sense of gallows humor from the state of his country and the world. But the idea of explaining to the dogcatcher was no more ridiculous than the other choices. Where were the paranormal FBI investigators when you needed them? These were the things which allowed for only momentary fits of sleeping, separated by frozen moments of high alert and frantic thought. Was that sniffing? Surely, they didn't know he had been there. He quit looking at his clock around 3:30am.

But sleep remained elusive. Something about that noise stayed with him, a deeper rage with which he was familiar on some level. It stayed with him in the way you sometimes understand an animal's wishes. It took him back to 1985, after Philadelphia, when he decided he just needed to get away. He'd read "The Guidelines" by Brother Africa and found much of it had resonated within him, respect for non-human life, for the natural system. He craved these things, but not the company of humans. Put any group together and the original thought becomes corrupted, sooner or later, when faced by the realities of the world. Motivations become diffused and cloudy. Then the police firebomb your house. It was not the company of people that he sought when he moved. It was the company of the caterpillar he'd watched earlier. His friendship with Moses

Armistead surprised him, mostly with its brotherhood and acceptance and love.

This had been his biggest surprise. Other than this friendship, he'd found the world much the same from his new vantage point, worse in many ways with the passage of time. But at arm's length, it was easier to deal with on a daily basis, just harder long-term on the soul. A child shot in Ohio, an innocent woman dying in jail in Texas.

The only trouble Norman had ever encountered while living here that he could have deemed racially inspired, apart from a couple slur-shouting drunken teenager drive-bys, was deputy Cole Snyder. Snyder had seen him at the grocery store in the early days and had given him the eye. He pulled Norman over on a flimsy excuse when he left. Whatever Norman had said to him that day, and Norman couldn't really remember anything other than addressing him respectfully, had cemented the deputy's hard feelings. He pulled Norman over a few times over the years, for any slight reason. In that time, he only issued two citations.

But now light filled the sky. Norman wasn't sure he'd reached any real sleep. He rose with the image of dog-headed men. He still could not make his mind up what to do. The Sheriff's department was out. The more he thought about the conversations, they were all out. He supposed not having his throat ripped out in the night was one reason to breathe easier, so he quietly came to the decision to keep his mouth shut, for now.

This was part of how he chose to live when he moved here. The main idea was to get away from the noise, pay attention to the seemingly mundane, quiet the mind. In and of itself, this lifestyle showed him many miracles which he always wanted to relate to other folks and learned not to. Keeping quiet about his current conundrum was a whole other level, but not that different ultimately. As the day progressed, he tried to keep it from his mind, to avoid seeking an explanation, like he had tried so many times before. It was human nature to seek that explanation, to understand the cause and effect of seemingly random events that felt deeper somehow.

This felt deeper, deeper than a tale of werewolves. Something about the noise still haunted his, something vague, but familiar, which he could not pinpoint.

So, he began looking for the explanation on the computer. It took him only five minutes to find some validation, a web page devoted to the first eyewitness reports out of Africa from the ancient Greeks. The Cynocephali, the dog-headed men.

Sometime after his limited enlightenment and his Campbell's Soup lunch, he stepped through the sliding glass doors onto the small back patio and braved the April outdoors. The sun was strong on this day and the morning chill in the air dispersed quickly. Norman saw some movement at the back of his property, just inside the wood line.

It captured his attention entirely and he stared hard at the spot from whence it came. Was someone behind a tree? Yes, he saw a leg and a foot. Someone was spying. There was a hand around the trunk of the tree. And then the face.

The face.

They knew about him. He fled back into his dining room, his breath now in short gasps as he stepped through the doorway toward the kitchen to the right and then stopped immediately, peeking back from around from the side. So, they knew about him. What was this now? Were they letting him know? It seemed a non-hostile act.

Leading the evidence for this was the face, unmistakably canine, perched on flannel-covered human shoulders. For the purposes of instilling fear, they might have sent someone less spaniel-like. Norman couldn't stop himself from peeking out the windows and, on second and third sightings, past the initial jolt of recognition, found the face appealing. It was one of those permanently friendly dog faces.

When he came to the realization that he was unable to pull himself from his watch, he forced himself away from his kitchen window and turned back to his computer. The machine had been the source of many unproductive distractions. Perhaps it could distract him now. He wanted no more about the warlike Cynocephali. He opened Facebook. It was hard to concentrate on his friends' problems, their successes, ...their dogs. The first picture he saw of a dog in a hat, he laughed and exclaimed, "Oh! You think that's something, do ya?" As soon as he said it, he recognized it as one of Moses' common phrases, stuck with him. Still, as he scrolled, he kept musing over the possibility of sharing his dog story. Too bad he didn't have a picture. Could he get one? He tried to put it out of his mind. The thought of blabbing his plight on Facebook dissipated with his imagining of the responses. He imagined a "you're crazy" emoji. A picture could be faked easily with Photoshop.

Still, he kept wandering to the kitchen and shuffling toward the window. Any movement now? The answer always came quickly, a glimpse of a khakied leg, a Niked foot, a friendly, furry face. By the end of the day, Norman had concluded that it was making itself known, only half-hiding. But, why? After sunset, he returned to his computer, to other people's lives, to the issues of the world. These days had brought a renewed assault on the environment, pipelines, mines, companies poisoning the water, trying to roll back environmental protections. This was hitting minority populations the hardest and it was only getting worse. Flint, Michigan had only been the beginning. The pressure grew within Norman daily.

But this was one of the reasons he'd moved out here, to hear the music of the earth, to learn faith in the magic of existence, to develop patience. The city only offered the music of man, only had faith in the tragedy of existence, and patience did not exist. He'd been trying hard to let go of his anger but here it was now, in its full glory and he felt it transferring to his overall situation. Trapped in his own home, afraid of the unknown. That furry face behind that tree wasn't going to intimidate him. He'd never in his life been afraid of any dog. He was going out there again. This was a puzzle that needed solving, and he'd be damned if he'd live in this place with fear bearing down on him. He could've stayed in New York for that.

By the time he arrived at the edge of his woods, the spy was gone. Perhaps the thing had seen him coming. It was dark so he couldn't be sure. Carefully, he stepped onto his well-worn path and began working his way toward Moses' house. The sound hit him almost as soon as he set foot upon the path. Howling, barking, whining, snarling, yipping, yelping, growling, muffled from the outside world by the walls of Moses' house. The combination made the effect especially disconcerting and Norman couldn't bring himself to approach as closely as he had the night before. He wasn't sure how he was adding to his understanding, but he felt he understood the noise at some basic level. As he listened, he found himself sympathizing, though he didn't know with what specifically. It just seemed to cement him into everything he was feeling.

And that was when the dog man stepped out from behind some dense vegetation.

He looked straight at Norman and cocked his head with the classic expectant dog expression. Norman had no treats, nor did he have any idea what the thing ate. It began vocalizing, a complex, shifting sound. The fur on its head ran down its neck and apparently under the collar of its flannel shirt. Aside from that, its form was utterly human. Human hands gestured as it spoke its strange language. Norman didn't know what to do, he only knew he wasn't afraid.

"Look," he said, "I'm sorry I stumbled onto you guys. I'm not going to tell anyone. You don't have to worry about me."

The creature seemed to recognize something he said and stepped toward Norman. Norman instinctively withdrew from it. This was all too much. Was it going to let him go? He turned to subtly flee when the hand grabbed his arm and held him there gently. He was now in arm's length, in the clutches of the beast. When he turned to look at it, it appeared to be smiling, that damn expectant dog look. Its tongue lolled lazily from its mouth.

"What?" asked Norman. "What do you want?"

At this, the dog man put its arms around him and laid its head on Norman's shoulder.

Norman didn't know what to do, had been in no way ready for this.

Wrapping his arms around the thing's shoulders, he reached up and did what felt natural. He began to scratch its head. The dog man emitted a long, contented breath. In the middle of this moment, Norman found himself wondering why he'd never owned a dog. This peaceful and warm, loving bubble formed within the cacophony which issued from inside the house. Norman, still in disbelief that he was petting this creature, felt this discord keenly. There it was, swirling all around him, a black boy shot in the park for the crime of being who he was, the poisoning of whole cities for profit, the lonely death of the creature who is the last of his kind. Like the howling and whining, it all weaved in and out of itself, making a horrendous ugliness. Norman felt it rising up within, injustice, taking him.

The dog man raised his head and scrutinized Norman in that dog way, looking at him from several angles, cocking his head gently, slightly puzzled, wanting. It came clear to Norman in a shining instant, what it wanted.

His eyes opened wide in horror. "No," he said. "No."

He pulled his arm from the dog man's gentle grasp and began to back away.

"No."

Nothing was going to stop Norman now. He was getting the hell out of here, albeit a different sort of exit. The dog man followed at a discreet distance. Any noises it might have made were subsumed by the house chaos, louder now, stretching deeper into the woods. Finally, he left the patch of trees, entering his extended back yard and the safety of home. He did not look to see if he was followed all the way. He just wanted his four walls around him, to protect himself from what he had so recently felt. He knew what the dogs wanted. He'd come close to giving it to them already.

But it wasn't who he wanted to be.

Once inside the house he seated himself in a meditative posture and began deep breathing exercises. He imagined a purple light covering his body and tried to calm himself. In his imagination, he conjured an image of Moses, in those old denim overalls and dirty t-shirt. His mind shifted as it was so wont to do at these moments, to a night when Moses had been dressed just like that and they'd shared a twelve-pack of beer. It was that night when Norman had confessed his real reasons for moving here.

"So you's just wanting to get away from all that stuff?" asked the old man.

"Yeah," said Norman. "It's getting bad out there, man."

"I understand," said Moses, "and I been divorced, too."

"Oh, it's not just that. It's people in general. It's government. It's values. It's all going downhill. I'm done with the city… with people."

"You know, when I moved out here twenty or so years back someone asked me if I was moving to the city. I told him 'no.' and he said 'Well, don't worry. It'll move to you.'"

Just the thought of that smile brought some calm to Norman's brain. He recognized as much as the old man did, the truth of it, though it would be several years before he would see evidence sprout a few miles down the road. The development was mostly private, a Home Depot, a Sheetz convenience store, a McDonalds, but still the city was not here yet.

And, out in the night, the voices of dog men rose above the walls of the house which used to be the home of his friend, Moses Armistead. The voices floated through the surrounding woods, howling and whining and growling for vengeance and blood and death and war.

THE UNIMAGINABLE

C.M. Chapman

The Unimaginable wakes in a dense purple dawn after an uneasy sleep. He sits up in the ancient oak bed, stained dark with an ivy engraving along the running board, and looks listlessly around the room, trying to recapture what has just come before. After a moment she understands that whatever answer was there is gone, yawns, rubs her eyes, and slides her legs to the floor. It rises and delicately cleans its fur, checking carefully for stars fallen during the night.

The Unimaginable has a distinct problem, which might seem obvious to a non-existent observer, but which, to him, is a mystery, a past which eludes him, a future which cleverly hides as if in ambush. Was there a traumatic amnesia? Will there be a crime? Perhaps she once killed a family of four in a Kansas farmhouse, or possibly drowned her own children. Or is there the possibility of some heinous act of genocide, today even? It ponders shooting a president from a grassy knoll, of exceeding the speed of light, or of destroying whole worlds with a word.

But no, none of these. He slides a slice of bread into a toaster in a red and pale-green art-deco kitchen with a checkered floor. The toast is a doom we cannot see from here.

She presses a button, it doesn't matter where. *Peer Gynt* spills into the air, in every room, music flowing like a wispy fog, out over the polar bear rug, the Louis XIV armoire, the lava lamp, the priceless tapestries of dead civilizations. The pastoral flute floats like delicate, yellow pollen on a spring breeze. Childhood drifts in those notes, cartoons and play, and it dreams of toys, of Rock 'Em Sock 'Em Robots, of jacks, and the Atari Asteroids video game, or could it have been a thermonuclear device in a tan, faux-leather briefcase etched with a reptilian pattern, or possibly in a giant silver suppository with a barometric fuse and an exploding bridgewire detonator made of shiny gold?

Maybe that was yesterday, he thinks, or maybe this is just the wrong music. She scours a billion songs. For now, The Unimaginable favors "Tomorrow Never Knows," by The Beatles.

In the afternoon, it ventures forth from impeccable oblivion, tentative, anonymous, crossing the street to the bench next to the schoolyard, where its view of the cavorting children through the weathered iron railing is best. Who knows why he does this or why he thinks of toys and cartoons? Perhaps she senses a shift in the polar axis or mourns loss of innocence. Then again, it might be a despicable peddler in human flesh, only scouting victims to keep in its basement dungeon for horrendous pleasures. But no. He understands enough to know this. She shakes her head at the insecurity of it all.

As it watches a game of red rover, The Unimaginable wants to know, more than anything, how to "come over," and yet it fears that knowledge like death, like utter extinction.

He is not in the newspaper or on television today, but he has been, or will be; he cannot remember which or tell the difference. Time is a crazed grasshopper, its mind rotted by radioactive decay, springing erratically through the quantum cornfields with no regard for linearity or certainty or nuclei, snapping a percussive ditty as it splits proton kernels with voracious teeth. Will I? Did I? Have I? Do I? Was I? Am I? She sighs and rises from the bench, looking around her at the totality of life- is it her? The totality of life? The children are gone, if they were ever there. There might have been a school shooting, possibly.

It turns its back on the playground and shambles up the street, a Lovecraftian abomination, a brilliant angel of the highest firmament. The cracks on the sidewalk yawn into chasms before him.

The Unimaginable cannot pray and knows no faith She knows no holiness. It knows no god or good or evil. There are only the walls of oblivion, the fog of ignorance, the milky cataract of hope that sometimes arises with the laughter of youth. The Unimaginable dines on shredded purple twilight.

He asks the question. She inquires about the opening. It queries the editor.

There is a story, after all. Architect of Armageddon. Long lost twin, miraculously found at an International House of Pancakes in Fairbanks, Alaska. Ambassador to All Possible Dimensions. Hydrogen salesman on Jupiter. No, not these.

He feels certain that he is running toward fate, to the fulfillment of his destiny.

The collapse of the food chain. Secret of Pi. One abrupt moment of complete, clear introspection for all humanity. For all gorillas. Sudden, certain elimination of greed. Of love. Carnivorous dinosaurs genetically altered to appreciate the finer points of city living.

At the same time, she suspects she is running away from the story, absolutely terrified.

Multi-dimensional aliens who swim through consciousness like wine, drunk on the very essence of being? The solution to all the world's suffering? No, no, none of these.

The Unimaginable waits. Always. It puts on Scooby-do pajamas.

He feels that maybe she has been imagined once, perhaps today, moments ago, or moments from now, but it isn't sure, and it isn't true.

In numerous studies of midwives and fiction writers, there is wide agreement that The Unimaginable deserves as much pity as we can lavish upon it.

Yes, of course you need to be told this.

Another troubled night ahead of him, The Unimaginable wonders if he will dream his way into existence. She smooths her fur, rubs her itchy snout with her stout paw, and climbs into the great oaken bed with ivy carvings and four posts which weren't there before. It waits for sleep, and for awakening, one eye watching out the window for falling stars.

MR. POPPER

Larry D. Thacker

Almost eight full days had passed. No sign of a strike. Had the culprit moved on? Changed his mind? Was he toying with us? The police weren't telling us anything and the community was more nervous than ever.

We were glued to our televisions for the six-o'clock evening news last Friday night. The streets were all but empty of traffic and pedestrians. Shops closed up early. If the police weren't going to help, maybe the news would ease tensions.

Channel 6 promised the "area's best coverage of the growing balloon crisis," Channel 8 countered with a promise of "inside information," and Channel 12 guaranteed their "usual up-to-date accuracy, with no funny business, especially these days."

Jane Willard, Channel 12's brightest star news anchor, broadcast live from an eleven-year-old's birthday party that evening, family and friends circled around the kitchen table, bright blue candles burning on white-iced cake. Everyone in the room accept Jane, who held her microphone, held a helium balloon on little strings. Some red, some yellow. One was orange. Another blue. They held them nervously in the background as Jane broadcast live.

"I'm here with the Simpson family at what would have once been a normal and calm affair, an innocent birthday party, in this case, Ernie Simpson's eleventh birthday." She motioned toward the young boy sitting behind the cake, candles burning down. He looked anxious.

"But these days a gathering such as this remains fraught with anxiety as surprise attacks on balloons continue across our region. We're celebrating this evening with the Simpsons in order to see if city officials' efforts at thwarting these attacks by the self-proclaimed, 'Mr. Popper,' have been successful, even as the culprit has threatened anew to extinguish every inflated balloon in the city today at exactly 6:16 PM, as a show of power. We've coincided Ernie blowing out the candles on his cake with that countdown. So what will it be? Restoration to life as we once enjoyed it, or continued fear and chaos?"

Jane glanced away from the camera.

"So here we go, ladies and gentlemen…10, 9…Simpson family, 8, …*Happy Birthday to you, Happy Birthday to you*, 7, 6…*Happy Birthday dear Ernie*, 5, 4…*Happy Birthday*, 3…*to*…2…*you*…"

Before Ernie could expel a puff of breath to blow out what was left of the candles, a great rush of air beat him to it. The wispy black bangs of his hair blew sideways. The room went dark. Everyone screamed in surprise though they knew what was probably coming.

All the balloons burst at once. Gone.

There was a rush of shuffling in the dark of the room. A loud grunt. Someone was on the floor. Had fallen. The lights came back up. The grandfather of the family was on the floor clutching his chest and breathing hard.

"Ladies and gentlemen," Jane Willard said, adjusting her attention back to the live camera, "it appears 'Mr. Popper' strikes again. And like before, there's always the possibility of casualties."

The camera panned down to a man performing CPR on the old man. A woman was in the background yelling, "Call 911, for God's sake!"

Little Ernie was still in his chair behind the table, a look of shock working across his face. A dab of frosting clung to his forehead. The boy would never be the same.

You don't realize how often balloons play a role in everyday life until they start popping when you need them most. A half-dozen balloons blowing up in front of a room full of three-year-olds, including the little guy having the birthday, is traumatic. A kid walking down the street with a shiny new balloon is a fine sight. That same kid holding the limp string to an exploded balloon laying on the sidewalk is depressing. And what about hot air balloons? Weather balloons? Condoms that were blown up on the assembly line for testing? No one wanted to think much about that, did they?

Someone ran the numbers and estimated that regional balloon sales were a $20,000 a year business. These days those numbers were plummeting. Only the most optimistic and defiant balloon users were buying them now. But it would get worse.

I was bullied my whole childhood. My early adulthood. Maybe I had a target on my back. On my front, too. On my head. My forehead, perhaps. On my ass. That's a funny image. I could never see the targets, but I imagined they were stuck all over me. "Easy Target."

It was the only explanation I could come up with as a kid for why I was given so much grief by so many. In class. On the playground. Walking down the damn street minding my own business. I must have looked inviting.

It's nice to realize there was a purpose for all that pain now. To focus that back out into the stinking world.

My father used to laugh his ass off popping balloons near my face. Those are some of my earliest memories, I think. Something about how my eyes flew open, that look of desperate surprise only a two-year-old can have when something unexpected happens. He was high on meth most of the time. It enhanced the comedic effect for him. He'd wake me up in the mornings that way sometimes. We had helium tanks all over the house. Some for his balloon business, some stolen where he could find them. Balloons were everywhere all the time. I grew up scared of them. Of him. Of loud noises. Of people. But I learned to giggle when he'd do it. Behind tears. Long before I could talk.

I was eight, I'm pretty sure, the first time I burst a balloon just by thinking. Of course, I didn't know it at the time. It was only looking back on it later that it made sense. My father was taunting me like he so often did, calling me one of his several nicknames. Either Farty Fred or Fat Head Freddy or Fred of the Dead. He was like a child in a parent's body. He'd go on so long that I'd eventually laugh, which made me even madder that he'd gotten me to laugh when it was me being made fun of. How cruel is that? It was the first time I told him I hated him.

I whispered it. *I hate you.*

He saw me, though. He knew I'd said something defiant.

"What was that, boy?" When he called me boy I knew I was in real trouble.

"Nothing."

"C'mon, boy. What now? You mad at your old man…Fat Head?" He laughed at that.

He was holding half-a-dozen balloon lines, readying an order.

I raged inside. I saw red, like a flash of fire in the middle of my vision. I looked him between the eyes.

"I hate you."

And just then, a yellow balloon floating right beside his head where he was standing, exploded, as if to punctuate what I'd just confessed to my father.

I said it again.

"I hate you."

Another popped. Down to four.

He jumped. I laughed at how it startled him. Oh, how his face looked.

He beat me unconscious.

It's like when you're watching a basketball game as a kid – or an adult, for that matter if you're really obsessed – and the rival team's shooting free throws. Ever concentrate through the TV trying to make the player miss? I mean really leaned in, believing you could make the guy screw up his shot? Sure you have. Did it ever work? Or, at least, feel like it did? Ever come to an intersection and use your Jedi mind trick on the stop light to your advantage and it end up timing just right, but it felt as if you actually made the light turn green? Sure you have. Ever wish someone would trip and they did? Sure you have.

The first time I exploded a balloon by thought, and realized what happened, was like this. I was playing, but it was real. I'd painted my father's screaming face on a white balloon with finger paint and tied it off to the door knob. I shot nerf arrows at it, at him, but kept missing, over and over.

I screamed at it, finally, "I hate you!" and it popped. I'd seen that same flash of light I'd experienced as a kid. Call it a flame. A strobe. A flicker or laser. Whatever it was, reached out of me like a hot and angry fist of needles, squeezing that mean painted face, destroying it.

Maybe it was a fluke, I thought, but after an afternoon of experiments, I knew something very strange was happening to me.

And for me.

It took most of my teenage years to perfect. I destroyed so many thousands of balloons. Who knows how many.

I had to be close to one at first. I had to see them. Be within arm's reach. I worked up to popping them from across a room. That took two years.

I was fifteen before I managed to pop one in another room, across the house. Sixteen before I popped all the balloons at a birthday party across the street.

I hadn't been invited to Frank Everson's party, as usual. I could tell he took great pride in knowing I could see the festivities around the backyard pool from my upstairs bedroom. Watch all of his guests showing up. Some of them I knew, but none considering me a friend. Did I have any friends then?

Where the balloons floated wasn't visible to me, but I could feel them from where I stood in my bedroom window. It was like I was standing there in that asshole's backyard. I knew I'd made a breakthrough. I waited until I heard everyone singing. Those bright happy voices ringing up from the backyard. Innocent. Glad. Unsuspecting. Deserving.

When the feeling hit, all I had to do was blink. Blink with a real hatred for what I knew was happening across the street and behind the house. Where I wasn't invited. At a party like I'd never have.

Fuck all of them.

I couldn't destroy balloons as often as I wanted. People might have suspected and we'd have been in the situation we are now a lot sooner. I honed my skills. Once a got really good at close range I'd practice by venturing out on the weekends with a tank of my father's helium and a box of balloons. I'd tie a balloon just off the main road, in the forest cover, every half mile or so. I'd set them for miles. I made a deal with myself that once I could pop them out to fifteen miles I'd feel confident I could remotely destroy a balloon out to just about anywhere. It took another five years. I was twenty-one.

It was the same year my father died in the house fire.

He had a habit of smoking while he worked. He had an order for 500 red, white, and blue balloons for the 4th of July. Being a "noble" gas, helium isn't really flammable, but the tanks are under pressure and if leaking enough, can displace oxygen and smother you. It seems there was just such a leak in the sealed room where my father liked watching TV into the early morning. The ceiling was filled with a whole evening's worth of balloons, at least two hundred of them. The gas didn't explode.

It made him sleepy. Slowly replacing all the oxygen in the room. In his lungs. In his grogginess he dropped a lit cigarette. And while what filled that many floating balloons wasn't flammable, that many latex balloons sure were.

They never found the burner phone I used to make the order for 500 balloons.

Is Mr. Popper my real name? No. But it's a good name for a villain, right? It might have been just too strange, even for me, had Popper been my real last name. I'd have taken on a different moniker, of course. Like, The Balloonator, or, Mr. Anti-Helium, or maybe, Dr. Imploder. All of those would have been fine, I suppose. Yet Mr. Popper, in all its simplicity, tells you all you need to know, doesn't it? Mr. Popper pops things. Things you probably like. Or even love.

I was in the audience on Graham Stallworth's opening night here in town. You've heard of him, maybe? He won the grand prize on *America's Got Panache!* His gig is intricate balloon shapes during his comedy act. His stand up was so-so. But man, could he tie off some balloons. His winning creation on the show was a rendition of the entire United States, in color, with Alaska and all of the Hawaiian Islands floating by way of helium. It practically filled the stage.

That night at the theater here in town he was fashioning a giant elephant, talking about how you couldn't eat one in a single bite, but one bite at a time, etcetera, etcetera. Some metaphor about approaching problems in life and laughing off your troubles. I hate it when comedy turns preachy. About the time he had this twelve-foot-tall balloon elephant blown up, twisted, and tied off, I'd had enough. I struck. I popped all the balloons necessary for only a few to remain there in his hand: the undeniable shape of gigantic cock and balls. He cancelled the rest of the month's shows and didn't perform again for a year.

After that I knew I could do what I wanted with them. The balloons were mine to control. Think of them as my army of suicidal minions. Finally something I was good at, I figured. Everyone loved balloons. Used them at one time or the other. I'd take them away at my leisure. For pleasure. In revenge. As Mr. Popper.

"A terrible tragedy struck the Annual Hot Air Balloon Festival yesterday when freak weather caused the crash of four balloons performing a synchronized demonstration for a crowd of thousands. Eleven balloon riders were sent to local hospitals with multiple injuries, two life threatening."

Hatred is my fuel. I imagine that kind of anger reaching and attacking that pleasant, loving emblem. The pretty balloon. The cute balloon. The innocent balloon. The gentle, floating, vulnerable, thin-skinned being, aloft for only a little time. The short life, like a summer insect. They die at my hands, and with them, your little hopes and dreams. Enjoy your inflatables, like so many binged and gorged egos, while you can. Mr. Popper will strike down your colorful little dreams. One sudden rupture at a time.

I spent days walking the streets. Newly aware. You don't notice things until you search for them. With new eyes. Balloons are literally everywhere. Not just strung from happy little children's wrists. Department store windows. By the bundle from a florist in the back of a van headed to a 50th wedding anniversary. Swinging up high over a car lot Labor Day blow out sale. All through a major Thanksgiving Day parade.

Gigantic inflated cartoon and movie characters. Dozens of them. Thousands of balloons held along the parade route by participates, along the sidewalks held by families. I was eating popcorn sitting in the driver's seat of my van in a pay and park lot on a knoll that gave me a good view down a parade avenue. I had to time it just right. The avenue was long and straight enough, the balloon characters massive enough, so that at least ten of them were visible at once: Charlie Brown. Snoopy. Hello Kitty. Spider Man. Ronald McDonald. SpongeBob. Pikachu. A nutcracker soldier. Garfield. The Monopoly guy.

I caught myself enjoying the moment. Two or three award-winning bands were playing at once. People in the street were dancing. For a mile. People marched. Skipped around. Kids played. And these larger than life animals – monsters, really – were coming. Controlled by the little people dragging the lines. Or was it the other way around, that the monsters were dragging the people by tiny leashes?

I waited until I was finished with my popcorn. Never let good, warm popcorn go to waste.

The act was over before my empty, wadded-up popcorn bag hit the floorboard.

Every. Single. Balloon.

Pop.

Gone.

I no longer needed such concentration. I simply willed it into being.

Individually, the pops would have proven inconsequential. But as one concerted, miraculous event? It was a deafening sound. Explosive from every direction, echoing off the skyscrapers, all that concrete. It was beautiful music.

People didn't know how to react. The noise came from everywhere. They ran in every direction. They ducked. They hid behind each other. They fell over one another. They passed out. They froze. Watched the giant monster balloons float flaccid to the road. Their ears rang. Babies cried. Parents huddled over their confused children. Old people held their chests.

Beautiful.

Mr. Popper was legit after that. No one could deny something weird was up. It was me. No freak incident of nature would account for my creativity. All the balloons in just a single town on one holiday. Balloons popping, for a solid week, only thirty seconds after being blown up. Only red balloons big as a basketball. I referred to myself in the third person more and more.

Spread the word. Mr. Popper lives.

But I'm bored. It was inevitable. Balloons just aren't enough.

I knew I was destined for bigger, more awful things. I was parked outside the condom factory just randomly popping condoms as their testing machines puffed air into each one as a test of the prophylactic's durability and airtightness. The machines could test hundreds a minute. I was trying to focus my concentration well enough to pop every tenth one. Every sixth. Every 100th.

Then. Three of the tires on the vehicle next to me exploded, the two on the car closest to me and the spare hanging off the back. It nearly deafened me.

Fifteen minutes later and my van casually exiting the lot is the only one left with inflated tires. It must have sounded like a warzone. I drove north from the industrial park, passing every imaginable emergency vehicle. I allowed half of them to make it. Let's just say a lot of tire shops in the city made their daily goals the next day thanks to city insurance policies propped up by the taxpayers. My boredom was over. I knew that when a firetruck skidded on its side through the intersection where I sat waiting. I'd popped only two of its tires, but it was going a good forty miles an hour. It slid a hundred yards.

I sent my first letter to the news stations the next morning. I'd start everyone out slowly. No demands. Just a quick hello.

Mr. Poppers lives.

I followed up with the loss of all launched weather balloons across three states. This sent national and private weather forecasters into a panic. I didn't let the balloons get up past a thousand feet. It took them until my second communication to attribute their fears to Mr. Popper.

Mr. Popper lives. No balloons for you.

And they believed. The random balloons on the street. The grand parade mystery. The condoms. The birthday parties. The mass tire losses.

Believe.

BOUND TO TRAVEL

Larry D. Thacker

The problem with leaving the county was all the spells. They'd up and break the instant a *carrier witch* stepped foot, one foot, even a little toe, over the county line of origin.

Things would have been just fine, but the smartass politicians just over in Lincoln County wanted to annex a little part of Labor County and that tiny section they coveted included the mountains where Sae Jean Mink's cabin set.

Labor County was about broke, so the money the crooked politicians on this side would acquire for selling the mountain chain off, added to the state park in Lincoln County, stood to make the government quite a bit of ready cash. The sewer plant was falling apart. The community pool was cracked. An election was coming up. The county would live off it for some years like any sort of soul-selling gets you. For a while.

Sea Jean's cabin was a hand-me-down heirloom from her great aunt, another carrier witch, the one that gave over all the spells to Sea Jean. She'd been known simply as Old Ruby. Old Ruby's spells were given her by her mother, Emelda-Ruth Hind. Back and back the spells went, back and back the promises necessary were secured and kept for holding the sacred words true and together, always the carrier witch prohibited from exiting over, under, or around the bounds of the promises. In this case it was the county line all the way back to its original settlement.

The potential brewing storm worried hell out of Sea (and some others once the math started adding up). For generations of spells to suddenly unravel would invite devastating consequences. Family fortunes would collapse. Marriages would go to ruin. Crops would fail. Political cliques would disrupt. Rotten bodies would roll in their graves enough to surface and walk from the cemeteries even. People would surely die. Many. Some deserving. Some not. There was no fairness to expect in what would come, only cause and effect.

There were technicalities to consider. For instance, unless the ink was sanctified by a true witch – and properly, with signatory blood – on the document establishing Labor County, then no paperwork of man or woman could rightly change the boundary. Witches, and their blood on parchment, had established the county way back in 1814 as it was. But as far as she knew by stories passed down, the boundaries *at this moment* fit the legal ones. If sanctified ink was used on these coming changes – with her full involvement – then the boundaries would change, of course, and all would remain calm. Someone way back when had laid down the lines of Labor County in salt and that's what held in her spells and every spell she'd inherited. She couldn't step foot over those lines, simple as that.

So it was blood and salt holding it all together. Life and earth.

She knew things were getting strange, though, that people were fretting, when gifts, bribes, started showing up on her porch and property. It was a few simple bouquets of wildflowers on the front porch at first. Then orders from the florist. Daisies, carnations. Then roses. Lots of white roses, which people new Sae Jean loved. The old road up to her cabin wasn't maintained well by the county, but it was drivable if the weather wasn't bad. It kept most undesirables off and packs of curious kids away on adventurous weekend dares.

But more people were making way up the mountain now. She'd hear a noise, a bump in the evening dusk, catch a glimpse of someone running back down the road, know there'd be something waiting on her out there, some gift, as if she possessed the ability to control what the damned politicians might soon do. To control the future even more than she might.

But those in charge, at the very top, weren't believers, were they? And she wasn't that powerful, was she? Or was she?

The three-century-old trunk was filled with spell pacts, some as old as two-hundred-years. The trunk chipped at the corners from too many layers of plain paint. Charred bits showed through from its surviving at least two house fires. It had traveled across and back over the Atlantic twice and over and back across the Pacific. She produced the skeleton key from the twine necklace around her neck where it always remained. The ancient padlock clanked free.

New and old paper fill the box. Everything from scrolls to single sheets. There were a few pieces of thin tree bark. Some cardboard. All if it written upon, finished with signatures. Shaky Xs. All bore spilled blood. These were spell pacts. Magical agreements. Favors. Deeds done for the desperate. The lonely. The angry. Those in terrible love. She was the protector of a deep box of secrets. All of these deals were sealed in blood. By anyone in on the agreements.

What would happen if it all suddenly fell apart? No one wanted to take that chance.

Sae Jean wasn't skilled enough to cast so strongly that county elected officials would change their minds, but she did possess the power to influence how others felt about her.

She craved vision. An answer to this impending crisis.

The formula was three days fasting, the dust of a raven's eye powered over her own before sleep, waking to seven self-baptisms in the cold creek before a full moon bath. Epiphany came, but at a cost. She felt the mini-stroke hit like a meteorite between the eyes, driving into her third eye, like a red hot railroad spike driven home by the hammer of an angry goddess. When she finally awoke she knew what to do. She would run for office. County Mayor, to be exact.

She had three months to make it happen; to become a politician. And win.

She'd hardly left the mountain for years, but most people knew of her. She had that going for her, at least. As County Mayor she'd have the most influence on wrecking the deal. Could she run a campaign that transparent? With that outward goal in mind?

She ran her fingers through all the pacts. These were as good as votes. The signatures. The influences over the lives affected by this deep box of seemingly endless secrets. It wasn't that she wanted to maintain any sense of power. Just the opposite, indeed. The chaos that would ensue from the instant breaking of all these trusts would cause such a domino-effect of terrible unraveling it would spell disaster for more than just those involved in the initial agreements.

Such pacts have a way of binding for generations. You don't even know that your grandfather only married your grandmother after asking Sae Jean's grandmother to conjure love craft in his favor for her hand. And while your existence down the line is owed to that bond, you very well might not suddenly drop dead if the pact is broken, but you might. Or you might come to a bad streak of luck and disappointment concerning that family line. You might not lose the land your father "acquired" through a pact, but your house might burn, or all the good timber on that land might fall mysteriously overnight in a freak storm. Imagine such things coming to pass all at once.

The gifts kept coming, but that would have to stop if politics was in Sae Jean's future. It looked like bribery. In this case it was. Please don't let the spell be broken, the gifts begged. Bags of groceries. More flowers. Fresh herbs and minerals from the town farmer's market. Firewood for her stove. It had to stop.

She nailed a sign to a porch bannister: *I'm running for County Mayor. The best thing you can do is spread the word and vote. Stop leaving things. Blessed Be. Thank you.*

It mostly worked.

The thought of spending all that time off the mountain filled her with dread. She stayed cloistered away not just because of people suspecting her or knowing her dealings and pointing fingers, she could handle all that. She liked it up there. Solitary. Quiet. She farmed a little. Had a cow, a horse, three goats, two twin black cats called Day and Night, but couldn't tell apart. She raised corn and tomatoes and squash and sweet potatoes and cabbage and pumpkins and gourds and pole beans. The inside of her cabin looked like you'd expect. Full of bottles and jars, some labeled, some not, some freshly filled, some quite ancient. Books, so many books. Many very old. Tables full of "work" in progress. Herbs hanging to dry. A pot belly stove for heat and cooking. The place was full of warm scents of constant experimentation with herbs and minerals dancing with wood smoke and mountain air.

If someone wanted to see her badly enough they had to make the effort to search her out. This was her paradise.

But for something this extreme she would venture off for a time. Whatever it took. So she went down into town that Saturday hoping her cousin Trula Mae was home.

"I dreamed about you last night, Cuz," the woman said, meeting her at the door before she managed to knock. "Come in, I've got spice tea a-brewin'."

It took a lot to get Sae Jean off Long Grace Mountain. There just wasn't that much down in town she needed. Until now, that was. If she was going to seriously run for County Mayor she not only had to get off the mountain and into town, but she also had to get out into the county, too.

"What'd you see?"

Trula Mae stilled herself for a moment. "You…standing up on a knoll…one tree…you singing out some old song with people trying to follow along. But they didn't know the words…the language, even…some terrible murder of crows circling over all y'all." Trula shook her head. "Why you here, girl?"

"You heard? The next county over's trying to annex a strip of Long Grace to expand the park."

Trula's face began flushing empty of color.

"They can't! No."

"Exactly."

"You're a carrier."

"Which is why I'm here, Trula. I need a campaign manager."

They brainstormed all afternoon.

The county was made up of all sorts of people they figured. Those who knew exactly who Sea Jean was because they or someone in their family had benefited from her or her line's "services." People who knew exactly who she was, but down right hated her for it. People who had heard the rumor but didn't believe it. People who were ignorant of her. On top of that, there were the unregistered, those who always voted, sometimes voted, or who had never voted, but might this time. There were so many variables.

They figured her best bet was to get those who stood to gain the most – those whose families were wrapped up in pacts – to talk her up to the other potential voters. Word of mouth. Not because of the guaranteed chaos that might damn the county. Sae Jean thought that the idea of a neighboring county being capable of reaching over and simply buying up a strip of land because a handful of people wanted it to happen was despicable, besides the potential catastrophe.

They ordered campaign cards.

Stop the Annex.
So Mote the Vote.
Elect Sae Jean!

They thought their use of "So Mote" was quite clever.

Sae Jean would broach other issues through the campaign, of course. She liked the state road up to her cabin being in too bad of shape for most to come see her, but it would make a good example to bring up on how roads get neglected. The homeless shelter was overcrowded, as usual. Education always needed improving. The pool lining was cracked. The community center's ceiling was leaking in four places, Trula reported.

"What are you going to do the first time some little do-gooder hops up during a town hall meeting, calls you a broom-riding devil's bride, and dares you to turn them into a toad?"

"Well, she'd better hope I didn't bring my grimoire with me, huh?"

They laughed and sipped the rest of their tea.

It didn't quite happen like that, but it was pretty close. She was running against Brenda Fordham, the incumbent County Mayor. Fordham was a career politician if there was such a thing around there. She was a high school senior class president. Student Government president at the local college. Interned at the state legislature for two years. Had served two terms on the city council. Three terms on the PTA, one on the hospital board. She'd won Mrs. Labor County back in 2012 at the 3rd Annual Rhododendron Festival. She was on her second term as County Mayor and was working this annex deal like it might be the prettiest feather in her political cap yet.

It ended up being Fordham's husband, Jason, who hopped up during a debate event trying to embarrass Sae Jean.

"And what happens if you're not elected, Ms. McCallister? You gonna curse the whole county? Bring a plague down upon us like you're some kind of lady Moses?" Mr. Fordham laughed, though with a strain of complete seriousness down somewhere within his voice. "Are you running a campaign of intimidation?"

Could it get as bad as a biblical plague? Sae Jean had wondered. *Remember the stock market crash? Rumor was that was a direct result of international broken pacts falling into place just right — or wrong.*

"The only intimidation I see happening, Mr. Fordham, is the sort requiring you speaking for your wife the County Mayor."

Some in the crowd giggled. That zinger shut him up. He huffed, turned red and sat down. His wife shot him a disappointed side-eye from up on the stage.

"If we want to win this election," Trula told Sae, "we've got to wear out a pair of shoes."

"You gonna let me sleep on your couch?"

"If you want. It'll be like old times when we had slumber parties all the time, remember? Before you were initiated?"

"I remember it like yesterday. Before I was anchored to the land. At least I can live vicariously through you, honey."

"Shoot. I ain't never gone anywhere special, even if I can cross the salt border, honey."

What held a carrier witch within the boundaries of an "assigned" county, or any region within which she or he was responsible for "carrying" the spell pacts? Salt. Not ordinary, mundane salt, of course, but a special mined salt from somewhere in the Old Country as the stories spoke, worked over by the tons by the Old Ones, brought over water early during the colonial settlements, blessed by the new world witches, distributed out to the settlements, into the mountains by the whiskey barrelfuls. And when the time came to establish a boundary — in this case

Labor County – the county line – all 47 miles of it – it was cast down in salt, just like casting a sacred and unbreakable circle. Blessed salt is a powerful tool.

Sae Jean would never intentionally step over the border, of course. What she suspected the neighboring county might be up to, however, was some magical finagling of their own. If a carrier witch was properly bound, the border encircling that witch could be amended. It all came down to how strong the craft work was of the one binding the carrier and that of the realigning. It was all very technical and that was why it very seldom happened.

Oh, and, of course, Sea Jean could die.

Death.

If she moved beyond this realm before handing over responsibility to another, preferably a close relative, the borderline was up for grabs. Again, quite technical. In that case all the pact wouldn't instantly fall apart, but gradually unravel. A strung out mass chaos. Still not something anyone wanted, whether they knew they didn't want it or not.

That was the problem, wasn't it. Everyone in the county and even people outside the county would be affected if things fell apart, like unseen dominoes falling like malicious tentacles stretching out into the world through time and space.

She had to win the County Mayoral race.

The ratio of "Well, hey, c'mon on in and have a seat. Y'all like coffee?" versus "Get the hell off my porch before I call the law," greetings ran about half and half at first, but once word got around that someone running for office was actually making house calls people got curious. When people get curious they're bound to listen a little.

"Nobody's ever come asking for our vote before," some complained. "You just see candidates at big to-dos or at town hall meetings or pass them on the street. Maybe they'll toss a card at you. So you don't think this mountain ridge annex is a good idea, huh?"

The Twin Oaks Baptist Women's League sent Sae Jean an invitation for a Sunday afternoon luncheon. She thought it might be a set up. Trula, as the ever-wary campaign manager, agreed.

"What if they gang up on you? Want to pray the witch out you?"

"I got two feet, don't I?"

Something was odd right off. The ladies were almost too nice, too accommodating.

Andrea Wallens, the league president, led the afternoon guests to the head of the table. She was most gracious.

"Now you may have noticed," Mrs. Wallens began as everyone sipped on coffee, tea, and chilled water, "not everyone is with us today. Our League of Baptist Women is larger than this usually, but we don't mind a smaller crowd occasionally."

Sae and Trula looked around, now wondering about the count. There were twelve in the room besides themselves.

"Seems like a fine turn out to us," Sae Jean offered with an encouraged smile. She smiled so much more these days.

"Our membership is forty-seven. Our average attendance is in the high thirties," Wallens offered sheepishly, staring at something at the bottom of her cup. "However…those of us here today…have something unique in common, you might say."

Now Wallens was looking Sae Jean in the eyes.

"Those of us choosing to attend today…*really* want you to win this election."

Her emphasis on the word really wasn't in the least subtle. It was suddenly clear how all in attendance had something to lose if the ridge was sold off. If Sae Jean lost the election.

"Ruth's mother knew your mother, Silvy," Wallens said, beginning a litany of secret hints. "Wilma's father owed your aunt, Old Rub. Annie and Sue there are sisters. They owe being born due to your aunt's doing."

The whole room was bound by blood pacts, to Sae Jean's aunt and her aunt's mother and so on.

"And you probably remember Jenny there?"

"I thought you looked familiar. How's that hand doing?"

Jenny was the best painter in the county. Made real money doing it. But only as long as her arthritis was kept at bay.

"It's great, ma'am. I'm real happy with it. I'd love to help fill out some postcards for you sometime." Jenny was a shy girl, she remembered, but she perked up with the thought of helping out. "My hand could write all day. I'd like to keep it that way." Then she winked at Sae Jean.

"We'd all like to help. If you don't mind. If you can use us, that is. We could serve as your election committee."

Trula subtly elbowed Sae Jean.

"Well, Trula here's my campaign manager, as you know. It's really up to her."

"You're hired," Truly blurted out with a giggle. "We're just not paying anything."

"Let's just win," Jenny answered back, "I don't need my ex-husband coming back to town and beating on me anymore."

Someone said Amen.

Sae Jean was well asleep when the first thud smacked the side of the cabin. She stirred. Listened, eyes wide in the black. Another thud. This time landing and scuttering across the cabin roof. Then voices moving out in the trees. Muffled laughter. Another thud. Against the front door. Pumpkins. They were throwing her own pumpkins at the cabin.

She had a little surprise for the lot of them, didn't she?

All they saw was her front door bang open with the highest piercing screech of a cackle they could have imagined followed by blinding green fire bursts streaking from her hands and landing with smoky explosions across her front yard. The soft voices turned to yells. Men tripped over each other in the dark. Ran into bushes and trees. Fell over fences. Into ditch lines. Tore through her potato vine mounds and corn stalks. Someone yelped in pain. Feared being left behind.

It was quiet finally. The smoke screen cleared.

There was a wooden sign they'd nailed to her porch: *Die Witch Bitch*

"Is what people say about you true? I mean...*really*?"

County Mayor Brenda Fordham had almost gotten hit by a car crossing the street trying to get Sae Jean's attention that morning.

"We've not had much of an opportunity to talk, have we?

What's she up to, Sae Jean wondered. "Would you like to grab a cup of coffee?"

"I'm barren," Brenda blurted out before the coffee even arrived.

Sae Jean had wondered how they'd start up the conversation, but it was obvious now where it was headed. She wanted something. Just like everyone else that came around wanting to talk *over coffee, or tea, a little lunch.*

"Tell me more," Sae Jean invited, knowing at this point she wasn't speaking with the County Mayor any longer. The person across the café table was a woman who wanted desperately to be a mother. Barren. What an archaic word to use. A woman who felt guilty for not already bearing children. Such a biblical term. As if she'd been punished.

"Please forgive how my husband acted before. He's hardheaded. Jason doesn't know I'm talking with you."

Sae Jean nodded.

"I know why you're running to preserve that tract of mountain ridge. I understand." She spoke quietly. As if the two had known each other for years. "Let me get right to my point. I need a baby, Sae Jean. I think you can help me. Can't you?"

Every time a stranger approached her with a desire for mystical favoritism, she played dumb at first to challenge their seriousness.

"I'm not sure what you mean, Mayor. I doubt I've got much of a chance of winning. I just don't want to see the government owning the land my family's lived on for so long. Can you blame me?"

"Now don't play coy, Sae Jean. Call me Brenda, please. I think you know what I'm talking about."

"Well, let's say I did know what you were talking about. How could I help?"

Brenda got quieter. "I need some magic, or a spell, or potion, or whatever you call it to help me get pregnant."

Sae Jean didn't blink at that. Just smiled.

"And if it works soon enough…" the County Mayor said, "I'll withdraw from the campaign."

Sae Jean and Trula had everything they needed spread out across the kitchen table. They'd need all weekend up on the mountain to manage this bit of spell work.

It had taken a week for Brenda to gather up the items for her end of the deal: first, small locks of hair from her and her husband; second, a special oil soaked linen belt Sae Jean had instructed Brenda to hide away under her mattress at night and to wear round her waist by day for a week; and third, a short secret message written by Brenda with her own menstrual blood to the child on parchment. And, of course, the pact scroll signed in fresh blood drawn from a finger by both Brenda and Sae Jean. There was lavender for scent. Ghost pepper for the heat of passion. Red rose petals for true love's hue. They worked all of this, and more, in a cast iron pot, by ways and means only they knew, in manners only a handful of women and men alive understood fully. They worked to a culminating hour under the full moon come Saturday night. They danced hand in hand around a small bonfire in celebration.

Brenda phoned two weeks later – six weeks before the election.

"Can we meet?" Brenda asked. Sae Jean sensed some excitement in Brenda's voice.

"Where?"

"How about the County Courthouse. My office? Let me give you a private tour?"

"What are you saying?"

"Yes."

"Whatever you did worked wonders, Sae Jean," Brenda whispered as they hugged. She closed the office door.

"Sometimes the body, mind, and heart just need realigned, honey. A kick start is all we done. Are you all happy about it?"

"Jason's proud as can be. I just can't believe it."

"Well, whatever you do, don't let on to him what we've been up to."

"True. He wouldn't understand this, would he? Even if it was making him happy."

But Brenda couldn't keep it to herself. She loved Jason and felt like she was lying to him by keeping the truth from him as to how, after trying so hard for two years, they'd suddenly conceived. He'd lost it. They'd argued for days. He'd threatened to force her into an abortion. Or short of that, to give it up. He wanted nothing to do with a child supposedly created with the help of the devil's hand. Brenda was devastated. Said she'd have the baby with or without him.

Jason moved out. Jason found himself suddenly with nothing to lose.

Trula called Sae Jean up. "Turn on Channel Four."

It looked as if Jason had managed to gather up as many news outlets as he could muster for some kind of press briefing, not that he had any more authority to do so than any other citizen.

"Yes, my wife plans to drop out of the race due our recent news of a baby on the way, you heard correct," Jason was repeating. "But don't worry, I'll be upholding her long years of work by conducting a vigorous write-in campaign."

"But what about reports that you *aren't endorsed by your wife, the County Mayor?*"

"I wouldn't believe everything you hear, folks. This pregnancy was so unexpected, Brenda's just so excited, she's not herself lately. I'm sure I have her full support."

"What about reports that you're separated at the moment, Jason?"

"Our relationship is fine, people. Believe that. I'm simply living with my mother for a bit due to her ailing health."

"What about your opponent in the race, Sae Jean Mink?"

"I'm not worried. I'll let the people decide. But I'll say this. That woman, that wanna-be witch, tried to bribe my wife out of the race by tricking her into thinking she could help her get pregnant with magic. She's evil, that Mink woman. Anyone voting for her I wouldn't want voting for me anyway."

"Will you be pressing charges for bribery?"

"Let's let the court of social opinion decide this one, shall we? The election's a month off. Don't forget to vote!"

And with that, Jason walked off down the street.

The news crews caught up with Sae Jean by the next day. All the questions had switched around on her. The journalists no longer wanted to know how she planned to improve the roads, bring new jobs to the county, how she planned to stop the land annexation.

They wanted to know how long she believed she'd been a witch. What she thought a witch actually was. Whether men could be witches, too. If there were other witches in town and out in the county. If she thought people were beholding to her and others in her family like the rumors reported. Whether she'd ever sacrificed an animal on a full moon.

"Not on a full moon, to my recollection," she'd shot back, half joking, trying to throw the nosey little shits off their game, not caring at that point if it made them a little uneasy.

It all backfired.

It wasn't amateurs sneaking up on Long Grace Mountain this time. No one would give away their position with whoops and hollers this time. With loud whispers. No one was there to harmlessly toss vegetables at her cabin walls and roof to wake her from sound sleep. No one would nail a silly warning on her porch.

Whoever these people were they weren't there to harass her. They meant to kill her.

Smoke and fumes woke her, but barely. She gagged and choke, dark and thick air already filling her lungs. Where was any light? The smoke blocked most of her vision. She crawled best she could, to where the bedroom door must be, found it, pushed it open. Most of the front room was on fire, all her working tools, her herbs and minerals. Her liquid potions. Dried goods. She couldn't breathe. She kept crawling. The heat was ferocious on her skin, through her nightgown. She called out best she could with dry lungs ever full of smoke. She called to the forest gods to come save her. For a little relief.

All Sae Jean saw an hour later when she was coming to was strobing light. Red and blue, then streaks of street lights, the obnoxious siren. She was on a gurney, tubes in both arms, blood pressure cuff on an arm, machines beeping and buzzing all around. The EMTs were surprised to see her eyes open.

"Whoa there, ma'am, take it easy. Bill, she's awake."

She tried sitting up.

"Ms. McCallister, you're safe now. Don't you worry none."

Just then the ambulance swerved and rocked.

The driver called out. "Watch it, lady!" Things fell to the floor in the cab.

"What's going on up there?"

"Some crazy woman jumped in the road trying to flag us down."

A mile down the road the driver spoke up again.

"Looks like an accident up at this intersection. A car's on fire sticking out the front of a house."

"Keep going," one of the EMTs working on Sae Jean told him.

"Where are we going?" Sae Jean's throat was on fire.

"We had to intubate you for a bit. You died for a little while there, ma'am. You sure are a lucky one."

Sae Jean blinked. "Where are we going?"

"Well, something's got town's ER full so we're having to take you over to Lincoln Central."

"No."

"What?"

"No!" Sae Jean screamed as loud as she could manage. "Turn around! We can't go there. No! I can't leave the county! No!" She was trying to get up, pulling at the tubes.

"We're almost there now, ma'am. We've been driving for twenty minutes already! Calm down, please!"

It was too late, wasn't it? Sae Jean was past the pact line. Past the line of blood. Of salt. Of promises and fate. She'd died, too. All bets were off for everyone involved.

But then she realized something. She was free.

She raised her hands. Her sight was blurred. She focused in on the lines of her palms.

"She's pulled her IV out, get it started again," one of the EMTs told the other.

The EMT turned to the metal cabinet, rummaged for a moment, and turned with a handful of material to start another line on Sae Jean's arm.

He hesitated. Stared at her arm. Back at the bag of clear saline. At the long tube. The butterfly needle. Back at her arm. At Sae Jean now looking him in the eyes waiting for his next move.

"Jamie, you ok?" the other EMT asked.

"…I don't know…"

"What's the matter?"

The man didn't answer for a moment. He was concentrating.

"I don't know what to do…"

"What?" the other man asked, obviously frustrated with is partner.

"I mean, I've forgotten how to…give an IV…I think…"

Sae Jean just leaned back with a long sigh and relaxed. Closed her eyes.

She knew exactly what was happening.

GERTRUDE'S WAR

C.M. Chapman

The Bedroom

As Gertrude gazed at Clay in his dress uniform on the dresser, grainy and dead, she thought of war. Vague armies clashed in her mind. She remembered a painting she'd seen once at the museum; Napoleon's horse reared, his red cape flowing like blood as he cried the charge. Trumpets sounded from the far reaches of her dreams, and Jericho fell, somewhere far away. She didn't look at the photograph often, though it was always there, beside the gold pocket watch hanging under a glass dome with a grooved wooden base. As soon as she'd opened her eyes some moments earlier, she'd known the date. It was June 1st, a Sunday, the same date and day of the week it had been sixty-seven years earlier when she married Clay Strickland, a year home from the war.

She never knew how to think of Clay in the war and still didn't. She'd seen all the fanfare footage in the movie theater when she was a girl. She'd seen all the movies that came later, Lord yes, the ones that had stars like John Wayne, the ones that were always on television somewhere, the ones that Clay would watch while screaming "Liars!" from his chair.

Maybe that was why she could never picture him there, in all that mud, smoke, and rubble, bombed out churches in the background. Clay's behavior had declared it all a falsehood, a lie which she decided she could never know, could never understand, and she shut out the bad things, as you have to when you've decided there's no understanding to be had there.

Today the look at the photograph was obligatory, a ritual of recognition, filled with random images of historical conflict, none of which she connected with, distant paintings behind a velvet rope. Her mind was already elsewhere. It might have been the anniversary of her marriage, but that seemed the ancient past. It was Sunday, and Sunday held its own anticipations for Gertrude since her discovery.

It took her some fifteen minutes to straighten the bed and change into her brown dress with the red, yellow, and white flower pattern. It was the easiest dress to get into that she owned, with its zipper on the left side, the easiest direction for her to stretch since she had pulled the muscle on the left side of her torso. The fronts of her thighs were in a state of perpetual ache from the hip to the knee. The doctor explained it to her once, but she'd forgotten and had been embarrassed to ask him about it again. She had a barrage of medication. She assumed the medicine for her legs was included in her array of tablets, capsules, and gel tabs. Still, it was a long journey, dragging the end of the faded blue and white afghan up each side of the bed, leaning over to tuck it beneath the pillows.

She dispensed with hose and dress shoes, slipping on her house shoes as she gripped the foot of the bed. The Lord would just have to understand. She stopped again at the mirrored dresser which supported Clay's photograph and timepiece, pulling a string of fake pearls from her three-drawered jewelry box. From a different drawer she pulled a set of clip-on earrings, white daisies that matched her dress, and put those on. She scrutinized herself in the mirror and marveled yet again at the image there. For the last few decades she had felt separate from it. Funny how the spirit doesn't match the body. Ever, really. When she was in her prime it always seemed too young, and now of course, if it weren't for the tether of pain, she wouldn't even recognize it at as her own self.

Another glance around the bedroom reminded her that it had been several weeks since she dusted. If only it didn't mean moving everything. The lace half-doilies that sat on the dresser and chest of drawers had taken on a yellowish tint. Perhaps she could find the energy to do it this week. She left the pang of guilt lingering there on the dresser, hiding behind the photographs of Clay, and Tanya, and Sam. It was seven AM. It was Sunday. It was not a day for thoughts of toil or war.

The Hall

The smell of lilac and gardenia wafted from the small bathroom across from Gertrude's bedroom. The hallway was only twelve feet long but it took her a couple minutes to complete her pilgrimage past the black and white family portrait taken in 1953 and the posed history of her progeny that lined the walls. Tanya had hung these up when they moved her into the apartment two years back, some of the photos of the grandchildren even now seemed old. She seemed to remember there were great-grandchildren now. There were no photos of Sam on the wall. Tanya was still bitter. Most likely she was bitter about the fact that he'd left her alone to take care of their mother. She was always selfish that way.

Tanya wanted nothing to do with her mother. This was clear from her visits. She wanted nothing to do with selling the house and getting her into the apartment. Nothing to do with the doctor visits or the retrieval and organization of prescriptions, or the grocery runs. Twice a month she came with refills and would fill Gertrude's pill organizer with the proper medicines in their proper slots. Sometimes she would clean, but she always seemed especially disgusted about that.

THE KITCHEN

Because it was the first Sunday of the month, Gertrude pulled a box of Wheat Thins from the cabinet and poured a few into a bowl, setting it on the counter next to the refrigerator. The plain wooden cabinets in this apartment were cheap. They looked fine, she supposed, modern, but they were just a veneer. There was no substance there. She missed her old cabinets despite their layers of paint. She toasted a couple slices of bread and spread some grape jelly on them. She had told Tanya on several occasions that she would like to have some strawberry preserves, but Tanya only brought grape jelly. At least the last time she'd brought the grape juice that Gertrude had asked her to get. Maybe grape was all she could remember. One fruit at a time for Tanya.

She ate the toast at her apartment-sized kitchen table, wooden to match the cabinets. It was of similar quality, but there had been no room here for her dining room table. It had to go in the auction, where so many of the things she loved had been sacrificed to the dowry of death that now dwindled slowly in the bank.

Tanya had forbidden any donations to the church more than ten dollars, had threatened to take power of attorney. She didn't know. Couldn't understand any more than she could fathom a genuine feeling of affection for Gertrude.

"Just because you send money doesn't mean you can buy your way out of a blind eye, Mother. You will have to deal with your conscience some other way."

Gertrude wasn't sure what her daughter had meant by that, but then she hadn't understood or much liked her daughter since she'd been a teenager. She knew the feeling was mutual. Were there great grandchildren? Hadn't it been the oldest one, Valerie, who'd married? Or had she dreamed that? There were no pictures to tell her. Gertrude finished her toast and made her way to the sink, where she filled the stainless-steel tea kettle with water and set it on the apartment sized stove. Everything here was small. She missed her old gas range with the touchy pilot light, the one that had almost killed her.

"You'll be safer here, Mother. I won't be accused of negligence."

No, of course not.

As the coils heated beneath the kettle, Gertrude turned her attention to cleaning her breakfast mess. When she finished and the cozy was back on the toaster she pulled her porcelain teapot and a cup from the cabinet, hanging three bags inside the rim of the pot. They were cheap, generic teabags that said Best Choice in red, block letters on the tags at the end of the strings. She considered adding a fourth bag and decided instead to conserve. She poured a glass of water and took the three pills from the clear plastic slot which said "Sunday AM."

Gertrude's apartment was an H. The kitchen and living room stood on opposite sides of the small hallway like the bedroom and bathroom. She shuffled past the front door with the teapot and cup, placing them on a TV tray that sat next to her recliner. Her recliner. She thought it funny that the only chair in which she could now find any comfort was the chair of the man who had caused her so much discomfort. Gertrude often looked for the word, irony, but she never quite found it. Though the chair's framework had lasted, the upholstery had worn years ago and she had draped a brown afghan over it. Another afghan, striped a crooked red and brown, hung across the back of the couch. Lace doilies on both of the end tables and the coffee table completed the picture of Gertrude's apartment as a complicated network of knotted strings.

The doilies protected the wood surfaces from the various objects she had placed on these tables, lamps, pictures, a radio. On the coffee table it served as a lacy altar for her King James Bible which she now retrieved and set on the arm of the recliner. The TV tray rested upon crisscrossed metal legs that had lost much their shiny gold painted finish to the dull gray of the aluminum beneath. The surface of the tray was dark with a picture of a cornucopia.

The portable radio was vintage sixties, a rectangular black box with a permanent handle affixed to the top. The bottom two thirds of the front was covered in a silver metal mesh which covered the two speakers. The top third was dark translucent plastic with painted scaled representations of the FM, AM, Weather, and shortwave frequency bands. Two large silver knobs sat at either side of the display. Four black push buttons were aligned on the top, extruding through the black leather case which allowed the listener to choose a frequency band. Gertrude never played with these buttons. The AM button was pressed and she kept the radio tuned to 960 MHz. She turned the dial on the left and the radio clicked to life with Sam Cooke's "Chain Gang." It was 7:56. Gertrude poured a cup of tea and settled back into her chair.

Her eyes fell upon the wheeled walker sitting in the corner, unused now for six months. She had needed it for some time after the accident but now she wished it was just gone.

"Just keep it, Mother. You may need it."

Now it sat there, like a buzzard, patiently waiting.

You are listening to spiritual Sunday morning programming. And now it's time for the American Ministry Gospel Hour on WFAK-AM, Pendleton.

And now the familiar music and Gertrude's excitement began to rise. It was the arrival of friends at the door, the anticipation of shared stories, and of course, the Other.

She had never been a religious person, but when she found herself laid up for so long she had discovered the Sunday morning shows and found a curious hope in them that she had never known before. Two of the shows were live broadcasts of local churches and she began to see her neighbors in those broadcasts, began to get to know them and look forward to their company. It wasn't until she had healed that she had discovered the Other, hidden beneath the airwaves, during the local Methodist service.

It was during a moment of silent prayer that she became aware of it for the first time. It had always been there, a sound beneath all the other sounds. At first she noticed the hiss, steady and unwavering. But as her attention was drawn toward it, she began to realize there was another part to it, a high whine. She thought perhaps a note on the musical scale. It pulled her in, even further, attuning her ear to the highest sensitivities, where she finally noticed the whistle. Oscillating as regularly as a sine wave, it was a tiny delicate sound, a melody to the background. Three sounds in one, she thought, the Father, the Son, and the Holy Ghost. There was something otherworldly about it. When heard as a whole, it sounded like entwining, repeating whispers that she could almost hear and she so focused on them that she didn't even hear the preacher call for the hymn.

… How sweet the sound…

The line hit Gertrude's stomach like the descent of a roller coaster, and she had recoiled, rising from her chair as fast as her recently invalid state would allow, snapping off the radio as quickly as possible. She had set to busying herself, cleaning her teapot, trying to put it out of her mind, but it wouldn't let her go. Over and over again, though she tried not to, she wondered if she might have heard the voice of God or the whispers of His angels.

Every Sunday from that day forward she listened, but she could only identify that particular sound during the Methodist ceremonies. And so she examined it, listening intently for it, trying to understand what it was saying to her. Then, during the silence of the communion service one Sunday, something remarkable happened. From out of the whirling vortex of whispers, one of them became suddenly clear.

"You will be forgiven. You too must forgive."

Again, she recoiled. She wanted to think that it sprang from the radio but could not shake the impression that it had arisen from deep within herself. It did not feel like her own voice and yet it felt like the cover had been removed from the well of her own soul, leaving an echo she never knew was there. It felt important. She began to weep. She didn't know why. She didn't understand what she needed to be forgiven for and yet she knew down to her very marrow that the voice was true.

That was when the donations to the church began.

And now here's our host, the Reverend Doctor Timothy Greenfield...

Gertrude did not care as much for the American Ministry Gospel Hour. It wasn't even a local show. It came out of Alabama. She thought it could sometimes be too mean-spirited, though it was easy to see what a learned man Reverend Greenfield was, what with his carefully prepared arguments and obvious knowledge of the scripture. He quoted different scriptures too fast, and most of the time she had trouble even keeping up with him as she flipped through her copy of the Good Book.

Last week I had occasion to read the book <u>Restoring My Faith</u>, by Pentecostal preacher Martin Miller and while it was a perfectly fine exploration of faith, I couldn't help but notice that in Chapter Three, Miller claims to have found his inspiration when he heard the voice of God speaking to him in the ruins of a run-down country house. Now, I do not wish to impugn the man's claims, but it started me wondering. Can anybody hear the voice of God?

Gertrude began to panic inside a little. She was familiar with this tone. It was easy to hear that he believed the answer was no. She tried to follow his logic as he began with John 14, 16-18, but soon his verses got ahead of her as he skipped back and forth through the Book of John like a bee unable to choose a blossom.

And so, as we can clearly see, only the apostles were qualified to hear the voice of the Holy Spirit.

Gertrude could not clearly see that at all, but this was her first religious argument and she felt helpless to Reverend Greenfield's judgment. He had just proven that she was a fraud but she was at a loss to explain how he had done that or why she didn't believe him. There was something screwy in that argument, she thought, but she couldn't say what.

The Holy Spirit can speak to all people, but ONLY through His Word, only through the scriptures.

She was relieved when it was over and the local Catholic service began. She would decide whether or not she heard the voice of God, not some firebrand from Birmingham.

During the Catholic service, she took comfort in the female singer's reliably sharp delivery. It was as it was every week, and even though the airwaves did not seem imbued with the same mystical frequency as the Methodist broadcast, she would listen for it nonetheless in the moments of silent prayer that fell between the rounds of musical pageantry. But here there was only hiss and whine, no wavering whistle, no swirling whispers or mystical third to elevate the silence into the divine. Still, she retrieved her bowl of Wheat Thins and a glass of grape juice and when the time came for the communion ceremony, Gertrude did her best with solo transubstantiation.

Behold the Lamb of God. Beholdeth him who taketh away the sins of the world.

"You will be forgiven. You too must forgive."

She'd pondered those words many times and did again now as the radio station began playing a half hour of instrumental hymns which would lead into the live broadcast from Pendleton United Methodist Church. She tried to shut the Reverend Greenfield from her mind, dismissing him as a close-minded, mean-spirited man, and moved her thoughts into an equally uncomfortable area as the air around her was filled with the soft sounds of forgiveness, floating on strings and piano notes.

Her mind drifted to Tanya. Such a disappointment the girl had turned out to be. Gertrude wondered if she could ever forgive her for all the hateful behavior, for selling off her life and leaving her in this box, alone, waiting for death. Such unjustified hatred her daughter had for her, and none of it was her fault. The girl should put the blame where it rightfully belongs. The anger swelled inside her again. Forgiveness would be difficult.

And Samuel, well, he had always been so sensitive. Could she forgive him his weakness? Lord knows it wasn't his fault either.

Perhaps she was being called upon to forgive herself for ever marrying a man like Clay Strickland. He would likely burn in hell for what he did to that boy in the name of making a man out of him.

Good Morning, church!

Reverend Tanner's voice brightened her mood instantly and she automatically said, "Good Morning!" along with the rest of the congregation, some seven or so miles away. She could still see the brilliant smile that had once greeted her at her door.

"I am so sorry to call unannounced," he had said, "but I told Carol at church that I just had to meet the wonderful woman who was making such generous donations to our radio broadcast."

Gertrude had blushed and invited him to come in. He visited for around twenty minutes and she tried more than once to tell him why she valued his church's broadcast.

"It's like- sometimes- I can feel the Lord- almost hear Him speaking to me- through the radio- I wish I could explain better."

"No need, sweet Gertrude, I understand completely. The power of our Savior's love knows no bounds and cannot be made small, no matter how it reaches you. I am so pleased that we can help bring you comfort."

"But- it's like He's-"

"I truly hope you can come in person to a service someday soon, Gertrude," he said, pulling his jacket off the couch as he stood. "And I want you to know how much your donations are appreciated. I'll try to make it back and see you again soon."

She hadn't seen him since, but he had mentioned her on the radio several times and sent his blessings.

Let us pray.

And now it came as the silence descended on the congregation, the sound of Grace, and Gertrude homed in with all her faculties. There again as always was the trinity of sound and the layers of whispers coiling around each other in an elaborate macramé. Somewhere inside there was an answer to her life. With all her attention she tried to pull one of the strings, to extricate one from all the others and, for a moment, she thought she was catching hold of something that was trying to emerge.

Lord, we know we are imperfect creatures in your sight...

She almost caught herself cursing Reverend Tanner for speaking too soon. That would be the only silent prayer. Now she could only wait on the communion ceremony. Sometimes she wished the organist would not play during the offering.

Reverend Tanner's sermon today left her more impatient than usual, but finally she readied her Wheat Thins and grape juice, taking part in communion for the second time that morning.

Gertrude tried to imagine the cracker and juice as the body and the blood, tried to feel it coursing through her body, giving her strength enough to hear the word of the Lord. And then she listened, we-you-we-you-we-you-we-you-shhhhhhhhhhh, and then there! Was that a word? Yes, yes, listen harder! Surely God will speak today- listen! Happy? was that the word she heard? She drifted to and fro with the sound, dancing with it, perilously close to the cliff of dreams. Happy. She had only to find it again and there it was like the tide, repeating like the patterns in her doilies, eternal. She could not make out the words which followed, but she had the rhythm now. Happy... happy... happy... Yes, she wanted to be happy. She followed, waiting for the rest to come clear.

Happy anniversary, Dollface.

Her entire body jerked and the teacup flew out of her hands, spilling mercifully cool tea into her lap and falling to the tightly piled beige carpet, the handle breaking off of the side. Gertrude, her eyes suddenly wide with a jolt of panic and confusion, pushed herself from the chair and looked down at herself.

"Oh," she said. And then, with more despair, "Oh, my cup."

She bent over slowly, retrieving the cup and handle. Now her set was no longer complete. She carried the broken cup into the kitchen, threw it away, and tried to wipe the shame from her dress.

INTERSECTION

Larry D. Thacker

You might claim Main Street in Buckhannon, West Virginia, reminds you of a ghost town, but at 5:30 on a Sunday morning that sounds like such a clichéd notion. What sleepy little mountain town's main drag isn't dead before the sun's all the way up, before even the most reverent of churchgoers stir? Amidst this apparent mundaneness you must remind yourself how Buckhannon is a special sort of abandoned before sunup, on any day. Holy, or not.

You're hesitating at a four-way stop on your way to find the day's first cup of decent coffee. No cars wait their turn at the other three stops to hurry you along. It's fine to just idle in the shadow trickery of pre-dawn twilight between the town's century-plus-old buildings, foot on the peddle, the glow of your brake lights looming on the walls behind you telling no one anything. Down left is a long two-block view to the county courthouse. To the right it's clear another two blocks down past the Dairy Queen stand to the usually busy City Hall intersection.

You remain on the spot. Waiting. Not sure for what to happen. Or not to happen. Maybe you're waiting to see how long *the nothing* lasts.

It's clear a strangeness is present on the road, as part of the road, as part of the clouded morning air burns off to daylight. A something will be gone, or hidden, that's it, by the time cars stream along here in a little while. By the time more revealing light arrives.

Revelation.

Not only do no cars meet you at the intersection, there are literally none to be seen, none parked along the street. Ahead of you down toward the tracks. None to the left. Or the right. In fact, the only movement you're able to sense is your own darting vision searching for movement, for life. There is a new sense of aloneness in this moment. You've not felt this before.

No birds cross the sky as it morphs from a light speckled black to dark blue, to that twilightish gold in the east that grows in the motionless clouds. No lights come on or off in second story condos, not headlights in unseen parts of town bounce off buildings like searchlights, no squirrels stir, no stray animals finding way back from wild feral nights. There is no wind to budge the red and white striped corners of flags hanging from light poles.

No people. You see no people. Anywhere.

All is motionless.

Anxiety wells up, a mix of abandonment and curiosity.

Have you stumbled upon an old movie set, with all the vintage vehicles stored out on the back lot during off hours, behind the expertly fashioned Hollywood facades? Are you struggling from a dreamscape, but safe back down the road in your bed at Fleming Hall on campus? You're tempted to get out and check if the potted street planters are actually filled with patriotic red, white, and blue plastic impatiens rather than the real ones you stopped and smelled yesterday afternoon.

There's a spell at work here. Obviously. As if the something slows the moment, arranging time for closer observation. You could sit here all day and nothing would happen. Or would it, finally?

There's movement to your right, light from the east, a whispered sliver at first, growing, revealing sky, a bright orb coming to life.

Your eyes fill with daylight.

Then where has the time gone? A half hour at an intersection? Who does that? *A half hour.* Who can just hang out at a four-way stop for that long and nothing, *nothing*, happen? Have you fallen asleep at the wheel? You never did manage to get that cup of coffee, after all.

You notice later in the day how sunrise was precisely 6:03 and 25 seconds that morning. Something clicks. Was that the instant the old woman startled you banging out the pan of leftovers into the trash bin near your car at the Happy Wok Diner? When the sheriff's deputy emerged into view down at the courthouse, barked the tires up to speed and flipped on the blue lights and siren, sped off to some sudden emergency in the opposite direction?

Or was it when you noticed the art theater manager loudly dragging his ladder out to replace a letter square that had fallen from the marquis. Why confuse anyone still deciding on celebrating the gathering this week, right? You'd watched him climb up and replace the number that had fallen off the sign last night. A "2" right by the word July.

That's tomorrow:

JULY 2nd

WORLD UFO DAY

ALIEN

C.M. Chapman

The alien is with me. I don't know how long it's been here. It's difficult to say, for sure, because it vanishes suddenly. I follow it around a corner, only to find the room empty. I'll turn away for a moment and poof! I never hear a sound, aside from the elusive humming that heralds its arrival, and I miss that ninety five percent of the time.

The alien touches my mind with its extraterrestrial energies. This is the only way I can hear its prophecies of doom, its universal truths, its message of hope. When it speaks to me this way, I feel like maybe it loves me. I don't know how long it's been here.

Maybe the alien is a 'he.' Sometimes, I think it might be. I can't be sure because it blends into the environment. The cloak that it wears bends the light, and it's easier to see it from the corner of my eye. In the dark I see it best, a shimmering shadow across the room, watching. The alien says watching eternally. The alien says it never ends, no matter what happens.

The alien speaks of catastrophe. It tells me of the fragility of the food chain and the thin facade of civilization, so easily frayed. The alien says we are meddlers, filled with the kind of false pride that demands answer. It asks me if I am prepared, but I don't know what to say.

The alien is on the street. It occupies the bodies of others, but only the ones who aren't there. It tells me about their empty lives from their own lips. But I am no one to judge. I am as empty as any of them, no matter what the alien says. We all are.

Mom watches *Jack Van Impe* and *Fox News*. She thinks the end of the world is soon, but she doesn't talk about it much. When I ask her about it, she says that Jesus will be coming, and we need to be ready. Dad just nods but he's never really all there. He has given up. On Sunday morning, Mom begs and pleads for my soul, but I'm pretty sure there's nothing there to pray for. I pull the covers more tightly over my head and tell her to go without me. She yells something about video games as she is leaving. The alien says maybe she should give me a religion at least as interesting as a video game. I don't know how long it's been here.

The alien moves like fluid through Jefferson High, flowing like a current of displaced time in and around the half-humans that move up and down the hall. I tell the alien that Tracy Donovan isn't like the rest. It says that maybe I should save her then. I think about this a lot, saving her from the end of the world, but she doesn't know I exist.

Maybe *it's* not the alien, says the alien. Maybe *I'm* the alien, it says.

The alien scoffs at the idea that the end of humanity equals the end of the world and points out that life will go on. It says I'm smarter than that. It asks me if I am prepared, but I don't know what to say.

In school, they tell me to prepare for my future. But what kind of future am I supposed to expect when the government seems intent on self-destruction? How can these leaders say my education is important with a straight face? Why do I need to learn math and science when they ignore math and science? The alien says they're all nihilists, committing passive suicide because of their emptiness. I know deep down that I am the same, but I tell myself it is only because I am powerless.

The alien says I have power. I don't know how long it's been here.

It shimmers in the darkness and touches my mind. It says that I have a part to play, that I will be important. The alien asks me if I am prepared, but I don't know what to say.

GRAY RIDGE

Larry D. Thacker

REGGIE FIELDMORE'S JOURNAL
OCTOBER, 2010

I couldn't hold out. I carved it out of my arm tonight.

I felt it in there stronger than usual today. All last night.

I could hear the thing in there under the skin, moving and humming.

I'd wondered how long before it would start telling me things.

It was half-an-inch into my forearm. Near the bone I guess. It's still bleeding.

It looks like a chunk of smooth iron. It's sitting on the kitchen table. It shines in the light. About the size of a pencil eraser.

My arm stopped vibrating as soon as I had it out.

Maybe I'll get some sleep tonight.

PEPSI BAKER

Reggie was prone to blackout drinking. There, I said it, man. Happy now?

You'd think with all the cops and those FBI-looking ass-hats poking around somebody would have let them in on that little hint. It might be important to remember.

He was a damned drunk. Sunup to sundown he stunk from the drink, man. I'm surprised he had a brain cell left, or a liver, so if he was screaming he was on fire and dying I would have paused first before hauling water toward the sound of his voice. As far as being abducted by aliens goes, I think he was full of Grade-A horseshit, man.

I bet what happened was, he went on a three-day bender, like he'd do, got lost up there on the mountain, and finally wandered back into town. I put fifty on it with the boys. Can't ever collect now, though. Too bad about him and all, but he didn't get beamed up. No way. Not him. He wouldn't have merited that. Damn drunk.

LEANN FIELDMORE

Reginald Fieldmore. God love his heart. We were high school sweethearts all the way back to middle school days. Never really dated no one else, neither one of us. Not that I know of. We got married our sophomore year of college together.

Lasted almost two whole years.

After how he turned out I'm surprised we lasted that long. That man wasn't who I thought he was. He turned strange once we were legally bound. I got afraid to leave him.

But Reginald was the sweetest thing when he wanted to be. That interfered with my commonsense. He had a jealous streak back in school, but what man didn't, I figured. He'd see me talking to some another boy and he'd start up an argument over nothing. He'd fight someone at a club. Out in town. I thought that's how guys worked things out. I was stupid to think that. I was young. But when we got more serious, after we were married, it was worse than just jealousy. It was outright scary paranoia. He was a scary man.

I couldn't glance at a guy. He'd worry to death I was leaving him. It wasn't like he'd threaten me outright. He'd never hurt me for the world. But he'd have these meltdowns and cry like a kid. Beg me never to leave him. I felt so sorry for him it was about impossible to get away. He'd check my phone. My email. Go through my mail. Call my family looking for me in the middle of the night if I didn't answer the phone.

When I found the camera in our bedroom I packed my things and was gone by the time he got home from work. He'd hidden it in the base of the cake topper from our wedding. We kept it on a shelf. A little pretty reminder of the best day of our marriage. It must have taken him forever to carve the plastic out just right to fit the pinhole camera in there right where the two figures were holding hands.

I've never bothered to change my last name, but I think it's time now. Especially after all this. I don't need the association anymore. People ask too many questions.

REGGIE FIELDMORE'S JOURNAL
OCTOBER, 2011

I stayed up on Gray Ridge last night. I was too tired to drive back down. Now that's tired when you're too sleepy to drive off that place. There's a shed up there I sleep in. My daddy and the men built it for tools and warming up in the winter. I noticed a lot of them up there in it even when no work was going on.

Getting away from their families probably. It's got a potbelly coal stove and a cot. Some shelves. That old clock. All the tools are gone but what I've toted back up. I've had to run off all them that come around to target shoot and just hang out to drink. I don't have time for all that no more. I don't have much time left to get things done.

Deputy Williams

That wildcat mine the Fieldmore family had is the same as a hundred others spread out all over the hills and hollows through here. Some are growing back slow, a few are covered with four-wheeler trails. That Greenup Coal property's used as a Halloween trail every year. People drive through two miles of trail on their four-wheelers and get spooked the whole way. It's so loud you have to wear earplugs all night.

Most are pretty bare since they weren't legal to begin with and no regulations could force them to reclaim what they dug up. It's hard enough dealing with legal mines that never get around to it, let alone all the forgotten sites dotting the mountains. In the winter you can see a lot of them from down here in town. The Fieldmore property's up there on Gray Ridge, that high flatter spot you can see along the western mountains along there.

That's where we found Reggie. Even the buzzards weren't bothering him.

Reggie Fieldmore's Journal
December 31, 2011 / January 1, 2012

Happy New Year.

Will there be anything happy come from The Year 2012?

They're coming.

I have work to do.

PS: 479 days sober.

Mr. Fieldmore wasn't like my other neighbors. No, he was a might nicer than most. He was a polite and intelligent young man. He so reminded me of my grandson, Shane, out in Missouri who never bothers calling anymore. Mr. Fieldmore would mow my yard occasionally and trimmed my rose bushes. He was good at it. That time I broke my foot he walked my dog, Sampson, twice a day for a month. A fine young man.

His mail accumulated so much it fell out of his mailbox one day. I saw the mailman struggling to get it back in. It donned on me then that I hadn't seen Mr. Fieldmore in at least a week, which I found strange. That's when I called the police.

He was always out doing something in his yard. He whistled a lot. Show tunes, mostly. *Phantom of the Opera*, and the like. Boy, he could get up there with them high notes. Made the dogs bark down the street.

What's that? Oh, yes, he'd occasionally just stand there. Staring up. I never thought much about it. Figured he saw something interesting. Maybe he was praying, I don't know.

But the aluminum foil stuffed in the ears was very odd, come to think of it. He said he was doing some loud work and he'd run out of cotton, but I figured a tiny piece of cloth or even a trip to the market would've taken care of it better than foil. Looked like it was awfully uncomfortable.

After I called the authorities, first one police vehicle showed up and they knocked on his door then they came and asked me about the same thing I'd already said on the phone. Then another vehicle came. The officers walked around and looked in the windows. They said they were all covered with aluminum foil.

What's that? No, no, he never had any falling out with the neighbors. None that I knew of, no.

The police said a man was entitled to go on vacation they reckoned, but that if he didn't come back in a few days to let them know. I reckon some family had missed him by then I heard, so they was back and breaking in the front door and blocking the place off with that yellow cautionary tape. I felt like I was watching a filming of a crime show. They were there a long time. Took a bunch of stuff out in bags and boxes. A computer. His two cats in crates. No telling what they'd been living on. I never saw no body rolled out by a coroner, so I was glad he wasn't in there deceased.

I asked, but they never would tell me what they found so interesting in all that.

REGGIE FIELDMORE'S JOURNAL
FEBRUARY, 2012

I hate the cold. Never liked it. I hate digging up here. I hate sleeping up here. I hate being awake up here. I hate waiting. I hate this place. I hate carrying the rocks and the coal. I hate dragging all of it. I hate the voices.

That's what I hate the most – the voices – the message.

I wouldn't bother doing all this in the middle of the winter if there wasn't something to it. They laugh at me when I talk about it. Say I'm nuts. No. I'm not. I know what I hear in my own head. I know what's coming. They're coming. I need to let them know where to come. Show them. It's worth freezing up here. It ain't easy being chosen. 2012 is here.

Copy of Notebook, Title: *2012 Manifesto*

Copy of Book: *So You Think You're Being Abducted*

Box of Misc items / clothing constructed of aluminum foil:

Foil helmet-like hat (one inch thick)

Foil shoes and gloves

Foil underwear (boxer style)

Foil overalls (with suspenders)

Foil sleeping bag (wrap style)

Shooting ear muffs covered in foil

Foil plates, bowls, cups, and eating utensils

Select quotes from Fieldmore's *2012 Manifesto*:

"The Second Coming isn't what they thought."

"They need our energy stores. I'm only one among so many of the chosen throughout the region."

"They want the black rock."

"I've started sleeping in the closet."

"The messages are just too much to take all at once. I hope they forgive me for disrupting it some with the aluminum foil."

"Foil in the ears really works. What a relief."

"Taken. Taken. So many times. I can't count. Soon will be the last. I know that."

"I will go up to the mountain and not be back."

REGGIE FIELDMORE'S JOURNAL
MARCH, 2012

The bad tooth is out. Sure as hell wasn't going to a dentist. They'd have asked questions about what they found in the x-ray. Teeth are easy spots to put implants.

It got so bad it was making my skull ache. My jaw swoll up. My head hurt so bad I couldn't concentrate enough to watch TV.

I remembered how our father used to pull our teeth for us with needle nose plyers. That's what worked. The tooth cracked and I had to get it out in pieces. The socket bled a bunch. I spit out those tiny metal implants all night. Kept them in a glass baby food jar. They looked just like what I pulled out of my arm that time only smaller. They glowed a little in that jar when I turned the light out. Pulsed with my heartbeat even out of my body.

Preston Gibbs, owner
The Chrome & Foam (Biker Diver Bar)

Nobody paid him much attention. He'd come down off the hill, not talking much, covered in coal dust and mud, hungry as hell. Digging coal for the Grays is what he claimed. I figured he'd started that old spot his daddy'd give him back up and had an order to fill for the Gray clan.

He came in that one night and he looked different. He just walked in, sat in a booth and never looked up. Bailey finally went over to ask him if he wanted to order something. She said he looked like he wasn't in there, ya know. Like he'd vacated behind his eyes. We used to call that the "thousand yard stare." He had it. He claimed he wasn't hungry. Wanted a shot of Jim. Now we all knew he'd been quit from drinking for over a year, so something was up. Bailey wondered if we really ought to give it to him. But before we could decide, he jumped up and was headed out the door. Shoulder checked his buddy Harris on the way out like he'd never met him. Later that night we noticed Fieldmore's truck still out in the parking lot. No Fieldmore. Later's when I heard he'd gone really missing.

Daryl

He was half naked when he fell into the street. He'd come out of the alley beside Jenkin's Hardware.

Barefoot. No shirt. Tore up pant legs. Unshaven. Muddy hands and feet. Scratched all to hell. Smelled of dried piss. No alcohol, though. I would have noticed that.

They tell me I look bad. He looked worse and I'm homeless. I was napping on a park bench when he stumbled out and collapsed. At first I figured, great, more competition. Another one of me showing up. But no, I knew Reggie once I walked over and got closer.

I don't think he knew who he was. He could barely talk. Had that look like he was staring through you, ya know? Like he'd checked out. I figured maybe meth, or some bad synthetic trip. But this was different. He was sick, sad looking. Just staring.

I went into the hardware and told them what was going on. They called an ambulance.

He was stumbling down the middle of the street when we went back out. Kept looking up. He'd whisper to himself, but I couldn't understand anything he was talking about. We used to know each other. He'd say hey to me when he saw me, give me a dollar or two. Reggie didn't act like he knew me from Adam that day.

[…]

LS: Ronnie, they tell me you went missing for a bit. Is that right?

RF: (no answer, staring down at table, leg bouncing with psycho-agitation)

LS: Ronnie, we want to help. We do. But we need you to talk to us.

RF: (looks up, blinks several times, looks at hands)

LS: What do you see? On your hands?

RF: In them. They hurt…shocked.

LS: Were you injured, Ronnie? Working? Or did someone attack you?

RF: Shocked me when we touched…hurts…up my arms…

(physically shakes, face grimaces, voice stutters)

LS: Who shocked you, Ronnie, when you touched? Who?

RF: …the grays…

LS: (looks to notes) Who are the Grays, Ronnie. Are these people giving you troubles? Did they attack you?

RF: …abducted…for years…years…

LS: These people kidnapped you and tortured you…

RF: …yes….no! No…not people…

LS: What do you mean, Ronnie? Tell me.

RF: Damn…(sighs long)…aliens, woman! The grays are aliens!

I've dug the coal. Like I was supposed to. The best I can without the equipment to do better. I've gained an appreciation for how Granddaddy Earl mined when he was younger. I don't see why anyone would call all that the good old days. My backs about done. My hands are just big blisters. Digging with a pick and shovel is body breaking work. At least they had a mule and a ton car back then. I got nothing but a wheelbarrow to roll it out of the holes with. But I've made headway. All winter and spring. The Grays gave me a drawing. It was in a vision. How they need the fuel set up. I was surprised aliens use coal, but who am I to question an advanced civilization? The setup has to do with gravity beams and sacred geometry. All the coal has to be just right on the flat top of this old hill, in a fancy design for when they arrive. It reminds me of the crop circles I keep finding in the research. I'm supposed to be in the middle of the design. Waiting. Waiting for them. When all this is done it'll be my last abduction. Over.

Target date: December 21st, 2012 (My birthday of all days. Go figure.)

ROBERT CLERK
WRITER

It was only a matter of time before I happened across all the talk about Fieldmore. I'm surprised it took as long as it did. As a collector of paranormal stories I, of course, wish I'd succeeded in speaking with him, but by the time I'd run him down he was much too paranoid. Believe it or not, I'd overheard Preacher Henry at church talking with a deacon and the church secretary about getting Reggie on the prayer list, which wasn't all that out-of-the-ordinary a thing until I heard him whisper, "Let's not mention anything Sunday morning about his issues with little green men and all, ok?"

Oh, how they all just laughed and laughed.

I drove up to the mine site in early October. I'd have never made it without a four-wheel drive. He ran me off no sooner than I got up there. He met me at a makeshift gate of sawhorses made of two-by-fours he had blocking the way in. He didn't say much, but he didn't have to. I managed a pretty good look at what he was up to. He was crazy. I could see it in his eyes.

It appeared he was living permanently up there. There were clothes drying on a line. A tent set up. A table with cooking utensils. Tools laying around with fresh mud and coal chunks all over. He was digging and processing coal for sure, not off the surface, but back into little tunnels he'd started into the thin seams. The dark seam he was working was about knee level, maybe two-feet thick. There were two tunnels. The openings were secured with cut timbers. He was a hard working guy if he'd accomplished all this on his own.

None of that was impressive compared to what he had out in the flattened part of the property. From the entrance I could just enough of a downhill view to see what he'd been up to. He'd arranged a wild labyrinthine design with all that coal he was digging out from the side of the hill. He'd dumped long lines of it two feet high, creating circles within circles, with zig-zags and geometric connections all over. The whole thing was half the size of a football field, I'm sure of it.

He was dead only a few months later. I didn't want to judge him one way or the other. I only wanted to hear what he had to say.

Deputy Abrams

Williams and I got up there first. Fieldmore was dead. He was sprawled out in the center of big formations of coal that were burning. I can't help but think it looked planned out to me, though the autopsy was inconclusive as to whether he'd intentionally overdosed on all those mushrooms. The stroke actually killed him. The drugs might have caused the stroke. Or something else.

Here's the photos the State Police took from their chopper. He had a purpose, obviously, in how he'd arranged all the coal he'd dug from the mountain. All his journals were in the warming building, tied up like they were waiting for us to find them.

For someone who'd lost his mind, was waiting on aliens to come get him, he seemed pretty clear-headed.

Happy birthday to me. 38.

This is it. Their lights were all over the mountain last night so I know they're here like they said they'd be. Tonight's the night. I hope tonight is the night. For the first time in how long? I don't know. I'm not hearing them. It's got to be tonight.

. . .

I started with a small batch of the mushrooms I ordered. All they did was make me puke and see colors. I took the rest of the bag

just now.

I can feel them I can feel

---------------puked again---------------lights,

Lights...........

I'm going   to the center of   the Codex.   This is it.

It's time. I see lights

across the valley. I see

I'd wave at the boy when he come by haulin ass on that mountain road. I don't guess he was after a girl. Sometimes he was a-comin. Sometimes a-goin. Up or down, always in a hurry, I guessed. I'd wave. He'd honk his horn and toss up a hand. Never knew his name. Never met the fella, but after a while you get feelin like you know an old boy, right?

We knew where he was goin. He was the one so hard at work up on Old Man Fieldmore's site near the top of the hill. He usually smiled as he passed. I never thought the boy'd end up as crazy as they say he was. Course them lights they claim was drivin him nuts have been up here in the mountains long as I've been around and longer.

I knew something bad was up when I come out to smoke my pipe and the mountain side look liked it was on fire. Glowin all red. Pulsin. I yelled in to Maggie to call the law. Looked like the whole mountain was on fire again.

A WALK IN THE PARK

C.M. Chapman

Science and Mysticism sat together on a bench in the park.

Science, a lean muscular man, around thirty years of age, drank from a bottle of spring water. Mysticism, the older of the two, and larger in height and girth, sipped low-fat cafe mocha from a Styrofoam cup.

"This time, no bullshit." said Science.

"I seem to recall you saying it would be a cold day in hell before you'd work with me again."

"Don't remind me. I'm only here because the old woman insisted. Said you have good instincts… pfft!"

"Like *you* could ever improvise," said Mysticism, laughing.

"Fuck you," said Science, "like *you* could ever follow a fucking plan."

"Show me any one of your plans that ever accounted for all the variables. I dare you."

"Oh, here we go again. The ritual."

"Simmer down, now. We wouldn't want that sphincter of yours to implode. We might lose the whole solar system. And anyway, I love seeing you and the old woman getting closer."

Science gritted his teeth as a young jogger in a purple t-shirt walked past them onto the grass behind the bench. The two waited until he passed before continuing.

"It's not like I ever really have a choice."

"Look," said Mysticism, "I'm not happy about this either, but the old woman gets what she wants, so here we are… once again, just like old times. Why don't you just tell me the plan and let's accept what we can't control."

"That'll be the day," said Science, reaching into his inside jacket pocket and pulling out a folded map of the downtown business district. "The target is here, on Higgs Avenue, inside the corporate offices of General Unified Technologies."

"Do you have a blueprint?"

"Of course, I've got a blueprint." Science unfolded the paper, pointing to a spot in the center. "We go in through the roof."

"Any chance to use the gear, eh?"

"You have a better plan?"

"You're the one with all the plans."

"That's right, so shut up." said Science.

"What's the policy on witnesses?"

"Same as usual. No witnesses. The old woman was very specific about that."

"Any guards?"

"Two."

"Very well, then." Mysticism raised his hands to his face as if in prayer.

"Oh, don't start that samurai shit, please."

"Honestly, I don't really care if it makes you uncomfortable. I don't take life as lightly as you do."

"You do what you have to do to get the job done. It's that simple."

"With no thought about how it might end up biting you in the ass."

"Oh bullshit," said Science. "We've been down this road before. Can't we skip it this time?"

"I didn't start it." Mysticism held his hand out for the blueprints. Science handed them to him and leaned over, pointing at the document.

"Guards are here… and… here."

"Very good." said Mysticism.

"Why?"

"Just a figure of speech. I mean, I understand."

"Whatever- anyway we will go in… here… which should give us the drop on the guards."

"And what are we after?"

"What we're after is in… here."

"And… it… is…"

Science looked away. "I don't know. The old woman wouldn't tell me."

Mysticism laughed. "Oh, that must be killing you!"

"She called it the ultimate prize, and that we'll know it when we see it."

"Well, well, how are you dealing with *that?*"

"Shove it."

Mysticism chuckled again and stood, turning toward Science. "So, when does all this happ—hold on—did you see that guy back there?"

"What guy?" asked Science, looking over his shoulder in time to see the jogger passing the tree line, into the grassy mall area beyond.

"He was sitting right there under that tree."

"*That* tree?"

"Yes, he was closer to your line of sight, why didn't you see him?"

"He must have heard everything." said Science. "Shit."

"Whatever we're going to do, we better decide. He's getting pretty far away."

"We've got to eliminate him."

"Agreed." said Mysticism, "but let's see what he's up to first."

They set off together toward the trees.

#

The heart condition which led to Perry Nickels getting a pacemaker at 25 was genetic. Just a decade earlier, it likely would have gone unnoticed and he would have died suddenly and inexplicably at a young age. But the miracle of science had saved him, and that fact was not lost on Perry. He liked to think that God had a purpose for him. Two weeks into rehab with his new pacemaker, it was clear that he would be able to live a normal, active life for a long time.

"Eventually we'll have to replace the pacemaker," said the cardiologist during his last hospital consultation, "but in the grand scheme of things, that's an easy procedure and well down the road."

"So, I can do anything I want? Basketball? Jogging?" asked Perry.

"Well, I don't see why not, but why don't you start with walking first and build yourself up that way, okay? You've been down for a little while. I'd rather you didn't over-exert right away."

"Okay." Perry paused. "And no more meds, right?"

"We're going to gradually decrease your meds over the next six to eight months. When we're finished, you shouldn't have to take any more."

"Awesome."

"Now Perry, there's one more thing I have to address before you go."

"Uh-huh?"

"Now, I'm not advising you one way or another here, but the hospital's parent company, Halco, has put out a search for human test subjects who fall into a very narrow category. And, as it happens, you fall into that group. So, I'm obligated to tell you about it and, if necessary, garner your permission for a company rep to come talk to you."

"Huh. What kind of test are we talking about here?"

"Honestly, Perry, I couldn't tell you. They want young, healthy subjects who have pacemakers. That's the criteria and there just aren't many of them around. And it's for one of Halco's tech subsidiaries, that's all I know. It's all been very hush-hush. I'm told that I will be briefed if you choose to participate, but not before. These are the forms. One is an authorization to release your medical records and the other is a non-disclosure agreement.

Perry's eyes widened. "Wow."

"I told you it was all hush-hush," said the doctor. "Now, you be careful, Perry. I won't get to know anything until *after* you've signed up for it, so I won't be there to give you advice… *if* you even decide to talk to them."

Perry couldn't resist the opportunity to learn a secret. He signed the papers.

#

"Well?" said Attorney Walton Dobbmeier. "What do you think, Mr. Nickels?"

"I won't lie to you, Mr. Dobbmeier. I'm intrigued."

"Good, good."

"Nobody else has this?" Perry held up the paper with the product description.

"No one, Mr. Nickels. You would be the first. One out of what, seven billion?" Dobbmeier laughed. "You'd be like Neil Armstrong."

"Who?"

"First man on the moon."

"Oh."

"So, what do you think? Are you in?"

"Well, I don't know. It says here you've already finished the primate research. Did any of the test monkeys die?"

"Well, yes," said Attorney Walton Dobbmeier, looking nonchalant, "but not from any physical problems associated with the device, and it was just two out of hundreds. I assure you, neither was a direct result of the device. We have had 100% success with the implant."

"But I'll have to go under the knife again, I don't know that I'm crazy about that."

"You should only have to be hospitalized a few more days and the operation itself is minimally invasive. Believe me, you already went through the hard part when you got your pacemaker. This will be a walk in the park compared to that."

"A walk in the park, huh?"

"A walk in the park. What do you think, Mr. Nickels? I have the forms to fill out right here."

"My doctor can be involved?"

"Certainly! He will have to sign a non-disclosure, of course."

"You guys sure are secretive."

"Well, honestly," said Attorney Walton Dobbmeier, "we don't want the competition to know we've reached human trials. We should, in all probability, be the first to market, but we don't want them knowing how close we are. In fact, we'll run you through a primer on recognizing industrial spies, before you head back out into the world. You understand."

"I suppose so…"

"So, what do you say, Mr. Nickels? Perry? If I may?"

Perry stopped and thought about those people he knew who were always so full of themselves because they had the latest phone or tablet. He thought it might be fun to be in that position for once. Except *nobody* else would have this. Ha! A notion occurred to him.

"There's not going to be a huge market for this."

"Oh, you'd be surprised." Attorney Walton Dobbmeier raised his hands as if he were framing a future into which he could peer. "Once everything is perfected and streamlined, we'll have the entire senior market. We intend to add cell phone functionality at some point as well. And it's our goal to be able to offer this as an option right at the pacemaker installation phase, so for every new pacemaker…" He waved his hand across the table like a magician's reveal.

"Still…"

"Two million new pacemakers installed every year."

"Oh."

"And eventually, R&D will find an alternative power source that's not so invasive and then we won't be limited to customers with pacemakers. Then the sky's the limit, so, you see, those stock options we're offering you are going to be worth a fortune."

"I see." Perry imagined what he could do with large amounts of money.

"So what do you think?"

"I think I'll do it."

"That's great, Mr. Nickels! Just great! Now, this form is our agreement to absorb all your medical costs up to a period of six months after installation. Now after that time period…"

It quickly turned into a long sequence of contract-speak, during most of which Perry nodded without really understanding what it meant at all. He signed the papers and shook hands with Attorney Walton Dobbmeier.

Within a few weeks, Perry Nickels became the first human test subject for the Genaux Personal Sound System™.

"Do you see him?" asked Mysticism.

"Yeah, I see him," answered Science, "Purple t-shirt, right?"

"That's him."

"He's down there, see? On the other side of the duck pond?"

"Okay, yeah, that's definitely him. It doesn't look like he's worried we might be following him, does it?"

"No," said Science. "Remind me again why we can't just kill him?"

"Because I want to know what he's up to," said Mysticism. "He heard everything we said and didn't go straight for the cops. He doesn't show any sign of being afraid of us. I'm wondering who he might be working for. After all, the old woman *did* just give us a job that she described as the 'ultimate prize' and then… this guy."

"Just a coincidence."

"No, I have a hunch about this guy."

"Let's just kill him and get it over with."

"No."

"This is why I hate working with you."

"Blame the old woman."

The two followed at a discreet distance. When the purple t-shirt broke into a jog, Science glared at his partner and then took off after him.

#

The first thirty days were filled with such a barrage of malfunctions that Perry was forced to quit his job at Harris & Sons. It was hard to sell clothing when he couldn't hear the customers.

"It's in your *head?*" asked old Mr. Harris.

"Yeah!" said Perry, "It's the only one in the world! See this is the controller."

"I don't believe it!" exclaimed Mr. Harris in an offended tone. "I don't believe you Perry. I think you've not been getting enough rest. In your head, bah! It's in your head alright. Perry, I need employees that can focus on my customers, not their... inventor fantasies!"

Perry was offended, but, according to the contract, he had already said too much. Frustrated, and recognizing that this conversation would be happening again, Perry told Mr. Harris to shove it. One day, he would see.

As per the contract, Genaux provided him with a regular consultant fee, so he was able to pay the bills.

Most of the malfunctions he suffered occurred in the pocket unit which looked like a coin and operated on a similar frequency to automatic car locks. Indeed, one Saturday night, a Volvo owner, unlocking his car, inadvertently locked up the device, which resulted in Perry listening to Ricky Nelson's, "Garden Party" over and over, until he was able to get hold of a techie on Monday. They taught him how to do a hard reboot on the device, but not before a close bout with insanity and a realization about what might have happened to at least one of those monkeys.

#

"I thought he spotted us there for a second," said Mysticism, still huffing and puffing from the jog.

Science gave him a disgusted look. "You know, you're really out of shape. You need a better exercise regime."

"I don't recall asking your opinion." Mysticism put his hands on his knees, still looking down the concrete path where the man stood, fidgeting with something like a cell phone. "It looks like he's texting or something… shit."

"We *could* have killed him back there in the wooded section, you know. His path was pretty easy to predict. He circled the park *twice* for Christ's sake. We could have cut across and caught him there. Now he's out in the open and sending a text." Science was glaring. "Why can't you ever follow the rules? We should have just killed him, like I said from the beginning."

"We're collecting evidence," said Mysticism. "There. See? You can get behind that, right?"

"The most ridiculous evidence ever. What does any of this prove?"

"Well, nothing, but it suggests a lot."

"Do you even have a theory?"

"Several, actually."

"Great."

"And then," said Mysticism, with a note of delight in his voice, "something happens to dash those theories."

Down the path, the man in the purple t-shirt stood in the grass, unaware of their gaze, doing a little dance.

#

Pink Floyd's, Dark Side of the Moon *is a seminal work of art. Nothing like it had ever been heard before when it came out in 19- in the seventies. The album explores the themes of madness and isolation, from the opening heartbeat, through the- something something- of "Breathe," the album pulls you into another world...*

Perry composed his first "Music from the Inside" review in the park as he power-walked to the driving synthesizers of Pink Floyd's, "On the Run."

Now that the kinks had been ironed out of his new device, he marveled at how he had never really *heard* music before. Now, it was as if he were inside, enveloped by the whirling electronics, swimming in the music, like it was tangible all around him, like the sound had textures, even. He could feel it in his skin. It was awesome.

Tonight, he would see Karen. One of the volume malfunctions, early on, had inadvertently taught him that he could easily and surreptitiously drown her incessant chatter about her idiot friends. Considering it was her most irritating trait, he found it to be extremely handy.

So later, as Karen droned on about Jessica's miserable experience at the dress store, Perry was listening to Thom Yorke sing "He buzzes like a fridge/he's like a detuned radio."

Radiohead's, OK Computer *is a seminal work of art. When it came out in 19- in the nineties, nothing like it had ever been heard before. The album explores the themes of madness, death, and the isolation of the modern world...*

At the end of the evening Karen broke up with him, but he never heard. He nodded and smiled. He assumed her sympathetic look, used many times during her hospital visits, was for his health and rest.

"Are you serious?" asked Science. "I mean he's got some kind of mental disorder, right?"

"Oh, he's only more interesting at this point. I think maybe he's playing with us."

"What!"

"Or he truly has a song in his heart." Mysticism was smiling a little dreamily.

"Oh, for crying out loud… You know the longer this goes on, the longer I'm not preparing for the job."

"The job is already compromised. You know that. The plan is going to have to change."

"What-! But-!" Science spit and fumed, turning red in the face. "Damn it! I worked on that plan all night last night!"

"Well now, I can't rightly help that you let this guy sneak up behind us, can I?"

"I'd like to kill you right now."

"There he goes," said Mysticism. "Try to keep up, would ya?"

Purple t-shirt started power-walking toward the north end of the park. Science and Mysticism followed at a discreet distance. At the northern end of the park, instead of turning around as he had the last two times, he headed across the street and into a coffee shop called, The High Road.

"That's where he'll meet his contact," said Mysticism. "Let's move in."

"We'll never be able to kill him in there," said Science.

Mysticism looked at his partner like he was stupid. "No, but you think we might want to kill his accomplice too?"

"Right."

Science and Mysticism crossed the street to The High Road.

#

Thriller by Michael Jackson is a landmark album. Its release in 19- in the eighties, marked a new artistic high point for Jackson. From its beginning with the ripping "Wanna Be Startin' Something," it is clear Jackson is out to take no prisoners...

The "Music from the Inside" album reviews weren't going so well. Maybe if he wrote them down, Perry thought, or did a little research. He found himself wishing that his little contraption had an optical interface with which he could access the internet. How cool would that be? The techies had promised him cell-phone functionality within the next year. It would require another small implant.

The jobless life was beginning to wear on him and he'd been thinking about trying to get another one if his music reviews didn't pan out. Karen hadn't been around for days now and he was wondering about that too. In the meantime, he tried to keep as busy as possible, which included his mid-morning exercise routine.

He entered the park listening to Michael Jackson's, *Thriller.* As usual, he headed for the top of the hill overlooking the big lawn. He passed two men talking on a bench and did his stretches under the same oak tree that he always did. Then he headed down across the lawn, pausing at the duck pond to see if he could spot any of the bigger fish that sometimes could be seen in the shallows.

After giving up on the fish, he began his running route, twice around the park, once at a jog, and once at a power walk, ending back around on the south side of the park where he cooled down under a group of sycamores, a cool spot that he liked. "Billie Jean" came on as the title track ended, and Perry couldn't help himself. Like most music through the Genaux device, it got right into him, the beat moving him from within. He couldn't help but boogie a little before he headed to The High Road for his decaf cafe mocha.

When he entered the coffee house, he turned off *Thriller*. It was fun at the beginning, but then he didn't really know the last three songs. He considered some classical for his journey back through the park, perhaps some Beethoven.

He sat at his favorite table, sipping his drink, when the older man approached and sat down across from him.

"I've seen you here before, haven't I?" the man asked.

"Could be," said Perry. "I come here most days this time."

"Nice place," the man said, looking around. Perry thought he was a little strange, like he wasn't all there, like when he looked around, he was still scrutinizing Perry somehow.

"I couldn't help but notice that you seem to be a fellow with a song in his heart."

"Yeah," said Perry, grinning. If only the guy knew.

"I saw you over in the park…"

A neuron fired in Perry's brain. This guy seemed oddly familiar.

"On the hill," said the man, "*by the bench…*"

Suddenly, Perry remembered the two men he'd passed on the bench. This guy had been watching him *that* long? His mind immediately recalled Attorney Walton Dobbmeier, warning him about the possibility of tech spies. He looked around the coffee shop and saw the other guy skulking just outside the shop, casting furtive glances toward them. This didn't look good.

"Well," said Perry, standing, "nice to meet you."

The man stood and held out his hand. "I consider it my good fortune to run into a man who takes joy in his life. I feel like we were brought together by the cosmos." His smile was disarming.

"Well, everything happens for a reason, right?" said Perry, shaking his hand, immediately hoping the guy wasn't gay and that the statement wasn't misconstrued.

"Indeed!" said the man, his eyebrows raising and his visage visibly brightening.

The other man, outside, looked agitated by all of this.

He was either the object of nefarious attention or he was being drawn into a gay drama. Either way, Perry didn't want any part of it. He nodded to the old guy, headed for the door, and trotted across the street to the park. Normally, he would do two more laps of the park, the first walking, the second jogging. Today he would just jog, and straight home.

Once into the park, Perry turned around. The men were nowhere to be seen. Maybe he was wrong, he thought. Maybe it was nothing. He would do his laps. He stopped to pick out some music.

#

"Did you *see* that?" asked Science. "The guy was spooked! You saw him!"

"He doesn't know anything." Mysticism wasn't sure if he believed his own words. The way the man had grinned at him, like he knew something Mysticism didn't, was weighing on him.

"Oh, screw that! The guy was guilty as shit! Any first year new-fucking-born could see that! I'm going after him."

"Okay, okay."

They ran into the park, but the guy in the purple t-shirt had taken off quickly. They sprinted in the last direction they'd seen him and, finally, caught up to where he was walking leisurely, conducting an invisible symphony in the air.

Mysticism wondered about this man, marveled, even. "Everything happens for a reason," he had said. There was something deep and mysterious going on here.

Science pulled out his gun. "I'm cutting across and killing him now. Enough of this weird-ass shit."

"No," said Mysticism, "and put that gun away. We're on the main walkway."

"Well, I'm going *this* way," said Science. "You stay here if you like. It won't take long."

"I said no."

"What?" Science held his arms out to the side, gun dangling from his hand, his shoulders shrugged, a crazy look in his eye.

"No, you're not going to kill him."

"Aaaaaa!" Science dismissed him with a wave and started to walk away. Mysticism grabbed his shoulder from behind.

Science whirled, fury in his eyes. "I TOLD YOU NEVER TO TOUCH ME!"

He raised the pistol and shot Mysticism three times in the chest. In his rage, he didn't notice that a woman jogger had come around the bend and stood right behind him.

She screamed.

Science spun back around, but she already had the pepper spray in her hand and let loose full in his face. As he grabbed his eyes, she tazed him.

A mounted policeman came galloping up over the grass. He dismounted and drew his sidearm, pointing it at a convulsing Science.

"Freeze!" he yelled.

#

Beethoven's Piano Concerto No. 5 is one kick-ass piece of classical music. In the beginning, it's like the piano winds you up really tight, and then the orchestra comes in, like boom(!), and you go charging forward! Wasn't Beethoven blind or something? It's great music to jog to…

Perry had never listened to Beethoven of his own volition before now. Near the end of the piano concerto's first movement, Science shot Mysticism just 200 yards behind where Perry walked and enjoyed the dynamic interplay of the piano and the orchestra. He had decided to go home and was heading back toward the southern end of the park.

Several times, Perry thought the first movement was coming to an end, but the music fooled him. Right before the last crescendo, the music quieted to such a degree that he felt sucked in like the water recession before a tsunami. When the last note crested, Perry was so stretched, so absorbed, that he didn't notice the curb. He stepped on it awkwardly and lurched, off balance, tipping forward toward the street. If not for a stone, he might have recovered his balance, but the left foot that should have provided his counter-momentum landed on the deadly geologic remnant and continued to slide outward. Thinking he would regain his balance, he hadn't put out his hands to break his fall and so the side of his face collided with the corner of the back bumper of a parked Dodge Ram, a pretty burgundy, he noticed as he fell.

Dazed, head swimming, Perry lay face-down on the street, behind and partially beneath the truck. A high ringing inside his ears harmonized strangely with the Beethoven, and seemed to make him float, like a puffy cloud, up and away.

The second movement of Beethoven's Piano Concerto No. 5 is great music to die to. It is very peaceful and reflective and makes you think of the good things that have happened to you...

As the second movement neared its close, he was gone.

But the ending of Perry's life was not the end of his pacemaker's life, and though Perry no longer heard it, the great, inner-audio experience of the Genaux Personal Sound System™ continued in his lifeless body. As the lonely bassoon gave way to the first rousing rondo of the third movement, Science was in a cell, awaiting bail, and Mysticism was dead, awaiting resurrection.

On a park bench nearby, a bent, old woman watched the comings and goings of the emergency personnel. She raised herself from the bench with the help of a three-footed cane, looked over to where the body of Mysticism still lay, shrouded in plastic and turned to walk away, shaking her head, muttering something that to a distant observer might have looked like, "Brothers..."

The piano concerto in dead Perry's head came to a triumphant conclusion... and began over again.

THE SHORTAGE

Larry D. Thacker

The storefront's pane glass was missing but for some deadly looking stalactites of angular shards managing to hang on all night. Tawny was so deeply curious by the wash of glass sparkle on the sidewalk and the dimness behind where the seven-by-five pane was usually nested by a metal frame, she was tempted to just step through into the mass of the shop's darkness. She took a step closer, but the crunch under her feet snapped the silliness out of her.

They could still be in there, she realized. *At least go in through the door. Make some noise.*

She stepped away and tip-toed nearer the front double-doors. They were secure just as she'd left them locked up Saturday afternoon. Tawny stared at her reflection from the glass. They would see her, before she'd see them. The few track lights she always left on wouldn't do much good. The bells hanging on the door would sing out, alert them. Yes. Give them time to get out the back maybe.

She keyed the bolt and turned it with force, letting the metal bolt pop loudly, pushing in on the door and making sure the leather strap of bells jangled through the store.

"I'm coming in and calling the police!"

She was yelling out and punching numbers on her cell at the same time, looking around cautiously as her eyes adjusted. She held up at the check-out counter, listening, glanced over and noticed the register was intact. It was an old one. If they'd wanted to they could have carried it off. She leaned over the counter. Clear. She flipped the light switches. Her eyes rebelled from the sudden trip of light, causing her to squint.

911 answered. "I need the police at Tawny's Antiques. Someone broke in last night. They might still be here."

Tawny walked the aisles with the officer. Any prowlers were gone. Only the broken window seemed out of place. That is, until they reached Tawny's personal collection of prized clowns.

They were gone. Every. Single. One. The booth raided.

Cleaned out as if she'd ordered the move herself. Upstairs, perhaps, to a better spot, where visitors could enjoy seeing the two-hundred plus figurines in the brilliance of the second-floor stained glass window light. But no, someone had specifically taken all her freaking clowns. Left cash money alone. Left vastly more expensive antiques sitting everywhere.

Fifteen years of hard work. Combing all the estate and yard sales, the Goodwill and thrift stores. The money — a few thousand dollars by now — was beside the point. It was a one of kind collection. Many of her pieces went well beyond the definition of vintage into the hundred-year-old and older definition of antique. It was a stand-alone museum of clown art history.

The new replacement glass in the damaged window wasn't old enough to have dust on it yet when news of another break-in made its rounds. It was a shop across town, Sam's Bargain Barn. It was an even stranger scene over at Sam's apparently.

The thief had only partially vandalized and stolen at Sam's, ripping the heads off of a dozen porcelain-headed clown dolls. He was no avid collector like Tawny, but he did like the dolls and enjoyed finding and selling them. Now he was left with a dozen good-for-nothing funny dressed decapitated dolls. Creepily enough, the culprit had left the bodies right where they lay before the beheadings, all shoulder to shoulder, organized and comfy looking.

Mr. Reynolds, who insisted on being called Jimmy Boy, though he surely was old enough to be Tawny's great-grandfather, visited the store like clockwork at the end of the first week of every month. He was a collector of clowns. An avid collector. An aficionado. Childlike in his obsession. So much so that when he saw what had happened to Tawny's personal collection, she noticed a tear making way down his dry and wrinkled cheek.

"Those bastards," he hissed under his breath, taking in the scene, the booth still squared off with police crime scene plastic tape, not a single figurine remaining. "The awful, awful bastards."

After another moment of standing and shaking his head in disbelief, he turned and walked out without even a goodbye to Tawny. She figured he must have just been really upset. Last she'd heard Jimmy Boy was up to over four-hundred clowns in his own collection. He'd never explained where such an obvious obsession originated, but she appreciated what he was amassing for posterity. He had no immediate family that she knew of which made her wonder what would happen to the collection in time. She couldn't help but feel a little jealous of what he still had and what she'd lost, but it was only natural.

A week later the Jacobs family jewelry shop was targeted, the thieves making off with five mid-century clown wrist watches. At the largest antique mall in town — Village Green Antiques — when venders started missing clowns of all fashions in ones and twos, anyone not already having been thieved from simply removed their clown inventories. Clowns from thrift stores and Goodwills dried up overnight. After a few more weeks people wouldn't bother even setting them out in yard sales. They'd just vanish without getting paid for no matter how cheap.

Of course, while clown collecting is enjoyed by an extremely small percentage of the population, it's still enough that when something this strange happened there was talk and worry and speculation. The *Eldon County Register* ran a story on the strangeness: "Bandits Continue Odd Clown Crime Spree." Anyone not in the know probably ignored the news. What in the world would this have to do with most people? Especially after so many people started hating clowns after last year's clown scares. It would be a relief to many.

The end of the first week of October had come and gone. Jimmy Boy hadn't showed up like usual. This was odd. Even if he wasn't in the mood to buy any clowns for his collection, he'd still visit and look around Tawny's shop. A second week passed. No visit. Tawny got worried. Maybe since all the clowns had gone missing Jimmy Boy was depressed. Maybe he felt like there was no reason to get out like usual, he was getting up in age after all. She still worried.

Another week and she contacted the police, convinced them to conduct a safety check on the old guy. She met the officers at his house. She'd been there before to see his collection. He loved showing it off. Had he showed it off to the wrong person?

They could hardly push the front door in. Something was in the way.

Tawny called out. "Jimmy Boy! You home?"

"Mr. Reynolds! Sheriff's Department! We're here to check on you!"

An officer called from the back.

"Looks clear from back here!"

It didn't seem as though he used the front door at all. A week's worth of mail bulged from the mailbox.

The back porch door screen was unlocked. They went on in, but slowly. It was the kitchen. It stunk. A rotting meal grew mold and buzzed with gnats on the kitchen table. A full glass of milk was clabbered solid. The sink was full of dishes. The trashcan ran over with garbage. The kitchen looked mostly unused.

"Mr. Reynolds? You here, sir?"

Books. Books everywhere.

"Jimmy Boy! It's Tawny! From the shop?"

They listened.

Shelves of old books, like a huge personal library. Down the long hall.

A bedroom on the left. Trains. Electric trains. Antique trains. A miniature world laid out across the room's center.

Tiny trees. Roads and houses. A baseball field. A courthouse. A college. A sign reading, *Welcome to Buckhannon.* Cars. A lumberyard. Railroad tracks crisscrossing the town. Multiple trains loaded down with graphitized cargo and logs. But the faces of the little people. Clowns. Almost everyone was painted up as clowns. Almost. Some of the bodies were solid black. The walls were stacked with train collector gear. Unopened boxes. More track. Modeling material. Everywhere. Glue. Little hammers and saws. Raw materials for creating the town. The little world. A work table covered with incomplete projects.

Moving on, each room was like this. Packed full like a hoarder's house. A maniacal packing together of miscellaneous items. Yet it seemed obviously organized. There was no rule against orderly hoarding.

"He's usually a neat man," Tawny whispered to the officer, "Always dresses nicely." The mood of the house was definitely feeling eerie by now. "Jimmy Boy?"

Postal boxes filled the next large bedroom. It stunk. Empty boxes of all sizes. Some yet used. Some obviously arrived at the house and the contents emptied. Thick brown postal wrapping paper. Packing tape. The finished boxes were heavy. Address for different destinations in West Virginia. The readied ones covered the room's antique four-poster bed. Neat stacks. Pre-stamped. Ready to go. A batch never sent.

Then the smell of death.

At the end of the hallway. The living room. The doorway closed off with thick strips of hanging plastic.

"We might have a crime scene, y'all," one of the officers whispered, curling his nose against the growing stench.

They all duck through the plastic into the living room. What they saw halted them in their tracks. It had been converted into some sort of processing room. A choking dust hung in the air. Was the old man cutting coke? That's exactly what it looked like.

They cleared their throats, coughed. There was a long table in the center of the room covered with light pink to whitish mounds. The closest mound the consistency of talcum powder. The one before, rough chalk. The mound before, however, was chunkier, with shards, with color, almost ceramic. And at the end of the table was the damnedest thing any of them was expecting. A pile of ceramic clown heads, hands, and feet, torn from the doll bodies piled by the processing table.

"What the hell?"

And then they saw Jimmy Boy.

"Now we know why the door wouldn't budge."

His slumped body looked like a rag covered pile of bones. The head was straining up, like he was straining for air. The dress shirt chest was stained with the brown of dead blood. His slacks were soiled. The man's thinned out face was sunless, covered with the same powdered substance from the table, hardened by spittle, especially around the nose and mouth. His eyes remained open but were rolled all the way back. It didn't look like he'd gone out without suffering and it looked like he hadn't been well for a long time before that. He was laying on more piles of headless, handless, footless clown dolls. Hundreds of them.

"Tawny, we shouldn't let you stay here like this," an officer told her.

"Please. I know him…knew him, I guess, as well as anyone. Let me try to help. I've got a strong stomach."

"I reckon if you haven't lost your lunch yet, you aren't going to. Don't touch a thing, you hear me? This could be a murder investigation for all we know."

Tawny nodded. Sure, she knew Jimmy pretty well. As well as anyone, she guessed. But more than anything, she was curious about what was really going on with this seemingly charming elderly gentleman now drying up in the corner of his living room powdered in what appeared to be ground up clown dust.

It appeared Jimmy Boy had quite the enterprise underway. Remove the porcelain heads, arms, and legs from vintage clown dolls. Crush the material with hammers to break everything down into workable pieces, then with an industrial powder pulverizer, create the fine pinkish-bluish powder that was packaged up in gallon sized sandwich bags before being boxed and shipped off to West Virginia.

West Virginia. Little places Tawny had never heard of, like Elkins, Raybar, and Buckhannon. Seymourtown. Westbank and Eller.

And, of course, the burn pit in the back yard. Don't forget the burn pit. That's where all the bodies went. The clown bodies. There was a pile of burnt leftovers of what must have been thousands of stuffed clown bodies. Since so many were filled with foam and other stuffing, some didn't burn so easily, leaving much of the pile only partially destroyed. It was just a pile of half-melted, charred, headless, armless, legless, once colorful clown bodies. There was a burn barrel as well, a thick, tarry mess in the black bottom. Jugs of gasoline and lighter fluid sitting around. Newspapers. Fast food bags and wrappers. Boxes of yet tossed clown bodies.

And Jimmy Boy. What was this complete insanity?

She could hear the Coroner talking: powder coated membranes coated solid, blocking the nasal passage. Probably solid in the sinuses. Lips and mouth region covered. Teeth caked up. Gums white and drained of good blood. Tongue dried and withdrawn. Throat coated with a good quarter inch of the powder. All of his exposed skin hard with powder. Desiccated. Mummy like.

The curtains rained it down if disturbed. The furniture appeared dusted white. It was like a concrete factory run amuck, or drywall residue from construction work. Suffocating.

The floor was slick with the stuff. A scratchy handwriting could just be made out: *No more.*

"Look at this. Oh, Jesus," the Coroner said, a little too loudly. He'd been chipping away gritty chunks from Jimmy Boy's front teeth.

Tawny made her way over with the rest, leaned down for a look.

She saw the coroner lifting Jimmy Boy's upper lip, crusted, stiff, and colorless as it was, with his trusty First National ball point pen. Exposed, there was a set of perfect teeth, though crusted and damaged from the powder, with the addition of pointed inch-long canines.

"…the hell?" someone said.

"Those fake? Those his false teeth or something?" another voice piped up.

Tawny spoke up. "He did have false ones. Didn't have any of his original teeth left, he told me more than once. Said it was real convenient."

The coroner's pen raked loudly over both rows of nasty teeth. Smacked on the tips of the canines. "Y'all. These are real."

"Fangs?" Tawny asked, pulling back from the old man's face, the retracted lips holding in place from the stubborn rigor mortis.

"Fangs."

TOO TALL

Larry D. Thacker

If I was cutting off part of a man's leg, I mean with the intent of shortening someone, post-mortem, I'd have done it closer to the knee, not half way down the shin. That's plumb lazy if you ask me. Why not take advantage of the naturally bendable knee joint snapping loose easier rather than having to saw through four whole stubborn bones somewhere between the ankle and the knee on two legs?

Jacob claimed it was due to his determined exactitude, a family trait perhaps, that he insisted on sawing the legs as precisely sized as he possible. If he were committing to such a horrid act against a dead man (or woman occasionally), against humanity, he'd do it his own way, on his own terms. It was his funeral parlor, after all. A second-generation business inheritance. I was only an assistant. Who was I to question a gentleman with thirty-two year's experience in the same town?

If a man's head was prescribed by business standard to rest three inches from the head wall of the casket then that's how it was going to be. If a body's feet were supposed to rest closer than two inches from the toe wall, but less as determined by shorter heights, then that's how it would be. He sure as hell wasn't just going to bend the legs sideways at the knees, which would twist the torso, or break the ankles, just to puzzle a body into its final resting repose.

"They deserve to stand straight as possible. The Great Physician can put 'em back together, but I'm not bending them out of shape down here on this end. I nice cut is respectful, in my opinion, don't you reckon?"

I'd only nod. I needed the work.

I wondered how Jacob could be committed to the deceased's promise of meeting their maker standing tall on one hand, but on the other hand, willing to save money in such a dastardly fashion. He'd display the very tall dead to their family in the single extra tall casket the funeral home owned, but then would lay the sawed off portion of legs beside the remaining portion of legs in a standard, less costly casket which was used for burial at the grave. Money saved.

Before you judge too harshly, just remember it wasn't like we did this every week. At first. Before I joined on with the DeFusque Funeral Home, Jacob probably averaged one incident a month. That's one out of ten or so funerals. Not that many people are so tall as to need the tallish caskets.

But when Jacob bought out the next door funeral parlor things got to hopping. I wouldn't say he'd been competing with the Reynold's Funeral family over the years, but Jacob would definitely get in a bad mood when attendees of a service would park in his lot for overflow when nothing was happening at his place.

"Man's gotta park his car, I guess," he'd say eventually, flipping a cigarette out into an empty spot. "Wish someone'd go ahead and bring us some business, too, Jimmy," he'd say.

Timing is everything in most things. It sure was in this scam. He'd tried showing the body in a long casket with the body intact then *after the service* conducting the hatchet job on the legs and switching out the body and casket before the graveside service, but that became too complicated. He found that cutting on the bodies beforehand saved time. The problem, for me, at least, was standing among the bereaved, knowing, shaking hands, hugging, welcoming family, praying with them, helping them, doing my job, all the while under the realization that the deceased was laying there a few feet away in pieces. Right there.

Accidents happened in the funeral business.

One accident. One slip. The gig was up.

One topple of the casket. One weak pallbearer.

He never had me do the deed, but I was close enough to it to be guilty by association. I knew what he was doing behind the scenes. I might could have denied it. But he could have blamed me, even said it was all me.

I was really up against it when Jacob came to me with the travel trunks.

It seems rather than bothering with embalming the severed portions, Jacob had elected to not include them at all. The trunks were full of leather wrapped leg parts – half shins and down, feet only from the ankle. A few were taken off at the knees, too. Seeing that, it appeared he'd taken my advice on a few instances. By that time, I wish I'd kept my beginner's mouth shut. I'd been so anxious to contribute. There were two fully loaded steamer trunks.

"What in tarnation do you want me to do with these?" I asked him. I tried lifting the side of one. They had to weight over a hundred pounds each.

"You're going to take these to the Lincoln Society School of Medicine in Knoxville. I know a guy. He's a foot doctor and a professor. He lectures and practices."

"What's he want with all this?"

"He's also a collector, of sorts. And, the school needs skeletal demonstration material as well."

"And you want me to deliver?"

"Don't look a gift horse in the mouth, son."

"Or a big box full of feet," I responded, not sure if I should laugh.

"Especially when it pays your Christmas bonus."

"Well, where's the keys to the Saratoga?" I asked him. "I'm losing daylight."

My delivery two hours later lacked the ceremony I'd built up in my imagination during the drive down to Knoxville.

I'd imagined they'd tell me to wait until the sun went down.

Maybe I'd be told to back in behind a non-descript campus building, down a dirty alleyway.

Or would I get there and be told to meet someone far off campus for the transfer.

Would I get a check or cash? How many people would meet me?

But no, Jacob told me to pull up in front of Building 18 and wait. That simple.

So I did just that.

I found Building 18, pulled up and parked, but left the engine running. It took a while before anyone came out. A tallish guy in a white lab coat exited the double doors, gave me a look over the top of his round spectacles and approached the passenger side.

"DeFusque send you, buddy?"

He sounded like he hailed from New York or Chicago.

"Yeah."

"Let's unload." He was already stepping to back of the car.

All that imagining on the drive and he wanted to unload in front of a building in the light of day? This guy either didn't know what was getting delivered or didn't give a hoot.

We hefted the trunks from out of the back. The man grunted approval.

"Pretty heavy. That's alright, this'll do."

I asked if he was going to check out what was inside.

"No need," he said. "Jacob wouldn't send us empty boxes of ones filled with gravel, would he?" The guy talked to me like I'd been doing this for a long time.

"No. No. Never," I agreed with what I hoped was a relaxed laugh.

There was a flat roller just inside the double doors and we set the trunks on it and rolled them down the marble foyer of the building.

"Room three," he said, guiding the wheels. "Always room three, alright?"

But we stopped just short. He pounded on the wooden door. I heard muffled voices, the beat of music. The air smelled of cleaner and formaldehyde.

An older woman half opened the door and peered out, some jazzy honkytonk tune came beating out behind her, someone inside was whistling up a storm. She nodded to the guy, he nodded with a grunt, she opened the door just enough to pull everything through on the roller. I must have been invisible. She never looked at me. She closed the door with a slam and I heard a bolt lock.

The tall guy gestured as if cleaning his hands of the task.

"There we go. All taken care of. Let's finish up, shall we?"

I thought he meant getting the money.

In a small windowless room with only the minimum furniture necessary to qualify it as an office, the guy handed me an envelope, nothing on it. I could see the corners of bills popping out it was so stuffed with cash.

"Not bad for a box of discarded flesh, huh?" I joked.

He grinned, acknowledging my humor, but quickly turned grim.

"Sir, we respect our donors. Always."

I cleared my throat apologetically. "Yes. Of course."

"Besides," he continued, "that's not just for what you brought, it's for on the way back as well."

We'd walked right by it on the way in. Another trunk, theirs, for me to take back home to Jacob. I wasn't going to argue. I was going back anyway, wasn't I? Besides, I figured, maybe it was empty and what Jacob would use for filling up for the next trip.

It wasn't empty.

We lifted it onto another flat roller. It was heavy. Heavier than first delivery. It rattled of glass containers. They had a fullness to the sounds chiming through the old wood.

Now I understood.

A lab. A controlled environment. An obvious veil of secrecy. Plenty of cash. Far enough from town. A trunk full of liquid-filled glass.

I was about to make my first bootleg run.

I winked at the guy and shook his hand.

"See ya again soon, sir."

"You be careful, buddy. Don't you be speeding now." He waved me off. The sun was going down.

I'm surprise I lasted as long as I did. I was tempted to pull over a few blocks away from the school and check out the box, but I managed some self-control.

I made it as far as the south side of the Norton Lake steel bridge and pulled over on the shoulder away from prying headlights. I opened up the back. I was dying to look in the trunk. I wanted to see what I was hauling. Whether my hunch was right. I opened the trunk and all I saw was gleaming Mason jar glass and lids, liquid shimmering in the little moonlight. It was packed full.

I was suddenly even more paranoid. I had better reason now. Before I'd pulled over I had at least some deniability. I didn't know what was in the trunk. Now I knew.

I reached down into the trunk and gripped a jar. It was cold to the touch. I pushed my fingers between the jars, blindly, touching ice. The wind whipped the cold of the trunk against my face. I felt along the edges of the box. It was lined. Like a cooler.

I grabbed a jar and weighed it in my hands, gave it a little shake, thought about the last time I'd drank any moonshine. How strong it was, how it burned all the way down, coating my belly, warming with a hot sting. I'd always wondered how something so clean and crisp looking, like mountain stream water, could be so potent. So poisonous. So intoxicating.

I lifted the jar high, holding it between my vision and the moon's white sliver. It didn't shine through. The contents were dark. That confused me. I put it back and lifted another. As it came up into the moon's glow I noticed a red tint glaring through. I tilted it. Whatever was in the jars was red, not clear like regular "shine." The red was dark, a scarlet. It sloshed more thickly than pure, watery alcohol.

I had one open before thinking about it. The lid gave with the pop of a canning seal.

Then I smelled it. In the air. The unmistakable strength of pure grain alcohol, yes. But I also knew the scent of blood when it was in my nose, too. I'd been in enough downtown fights, tasted blood in my own mouth, to know it when I tasted it in the air.

I'd drunk some good apple pie moonshine before. Some cherry. But never this. Alcohol and blood? It was a beautiful thing. The scent. The look.

The taste.

Good Lord.

The taste.

QUIRKS, QUARKS, AND QUATRAINS

C. M. Chapman

I

Let's dispense with the formalities. It was the toaster.

"The toaster!" you say, in disbelief, but I kid you not.

Think about it. Dorothy was hit in the head with flying debris during a tornado. Alice tumbled head-first into a hole. And those poor kids in the wardrobe, well let's just say that it's my personal belief that their wealthy uncle was starving them in there. The point is that it's tempting to believe all such stories begin with a trauma of some sort.

For Dave, it was sticking a fork in the toaster, furthering that school of thought.

You are correct. It wasn't the brightest move, but no one ever said that Dave was really all that bright. Sure, he was good with numbers, and there *was* that one, shining moment when he saved all of reality, but still, not all that bright. Given his general lack of creativity, it's hard to believe that Dave's story was a fabrication. Obviously, it was very real to him, and I'm not of the opinion that he possessed the ability to invent a story like this.

Dave had wanted to replace that toaster for ten years. The problem was that he only thought about it when he wanted toast, which wasn't very often, and usually at times when he had on his pajamas.

Such was the case on the night in question. True to form, Dave's pajamas oozed tedium and regularity, off white with paired dark-blue pinstripes, one thicker than the other. You see what I mean? They were probably the first pajamas he saw in the store, and if I know Dave, they were on sale… cheap. So that's how he was dressed as he watched *Dancing with the Stars* and that odd craving for toast and jelly hit him.

Since his living room and kitchen were basically one room, he could see the television while he waited on the toast. Of course, the bread stuck, like it always did, and was beginning to burn. As he inserted a fork to free the slice, one of the dancers on the television stumbled and fell during a mambo, eliciting a large gasp from the audience. Dave turned to look and that, as they say, was that.

He felt what he later related to me as a "damn snakebite," and then total paralysis. Oddly, he felt himself starting to stretch, "like I was being sucked through a straw." He couldn't have said how long the whole process took because, as it was happening, he was completely distracted by what his eyes were seeing.

That can't be possible, he was thinking as he stretched into infinity.

In front of him, his toaster was smiling at him. Smiling and waving.

***

He awoke on his back, opened his eyes, and was struck by three things immediately. It was daylight, he was looking at open sky, and he was lying in soft grass, none of which made any sense whatsoever.

A small, helium-tinged voice, flavored with large, helium-tinged uncertainty, said, "Easy, big guy, easy!"

Dave jumped to his feet.

"Easy now! Don't freak out!" came the voice from behind and below him. Dave wheeled, only to come face to face, as it were, with his toaster, standing there with an uneasy smile. Though he was in no state of mind to elucidate the thought, the face reminded him of the train in the children's books. The handle that depressed the bread was its nose.

"You okay, big guy?" it said.

Dave shrieked twice; first, right before he kicked the toaster, sending it flying through the air with a tiny, alto scream, and second, when he realized he had neglected to put on his slippers.

The toaster landed upside down about ten feet away. "It's okay!" it called out, swinging its little legs back and forth in an attempt to right itself, "I'm alright!"

Dave plopped back to the ground, grabbing his foot and looking around, breathing in short, rapid gasps. He was outdoors, but even if the electrical shock had sent him flying from his window, he should have been seeing buildings and sitting on concrete, not sitting in the grass, looking at trees and blue sky. And what was with these trees? There was something wrong about the whole thing.

Well within the "something wrong" parameters that he had just established, the toaster finally managed to right itself with a tinny clank and approached him with caution, careful to stay out of kicking range.

"You okay, big guy?" it said, "Getting your bearings?"

Dave wasn't about to talk to a toaster. He jumped up again and began running, looking for something, anything, familiar.

From well behind came the toaster's voice, "You don't have to run! I'm not mad!"

He ignored it.

"It's not like I'm gonna kill ya or anything!"

Then, from even further back, "Hey come on! Wait up!" As he crested the nearest hill, he stopped dead in his tracks. This, most assuredly, was not his world. Oh, the sky was blue, and the grass was green, but in his world, people carved shapes into shrubbery, not trees. And yet here, stretched in front of him were hundreds of trees, stretching a mile or more, each trimmed into different shapes, not haphazardly or unnaturally, mind you, but as if the interior spirits of the trees had been brought out into physical form. Here was a rocket, there a bear, a snail, a basket, a guitar, none of them the same.

Definitely not his world.

As if to confirm that thought, he could hear *thunk-plink-ponk-rattle, thunk-plink-ponk-rattle* approaching him from behind, soon accompanied by little huffs and puffs. In his world, toasters couldn't walk and talk, either. Was this some sort of electrocution Disney flashback? Was he dying on the floor, pulling images from old movies out of his childhood?

"It's ooookay," came the tiny voice from behind, in the soothing tone of a miniature police officer, talking someone off the ledge, "Everything's ooookay, just relax…"

Dave whirled on the appliance. The toaster, looking alarmed, backed away quickly.

"Oh, I don't think everything's okay," said Dave, "I don't think anything's okay at all here."

The toaster backed away a few more steps, holding out his plastic hands palm down and moving them up and down. "Look," he said, "I know how you feel…"

Dave advanced, speaking through clenched teeth. "I don't think you *do* know how I feel, and you want to know why? Because you're a toaster, that's why! And don't think I don't recognize you, either, after all the toast you burned! Don't back away! If I wanted to kick you again, I could catch you!" He paused, looking around at his surroundings and muttered, "I ought to… just for the toast."

"Sorry about the toast, big guy. It was necessary."

"Yeah, well… what?"

"It was the only way we could get you."

"We… what- What are y-."

"We needed you, Dave."

"We-."

"We've been trying to get you here for a while."

"Who's we?" Dave finally managed, "Toasters? Is this the toaster planet or something?"

"No, but as I understand it, this is more than just a matter of one planet anyway." The toaster glanced around. "My two friends and I were given the job of bringing you here"

Dave looked around. "Your two friends?"

"Yes."

"So where are they, these two friends of yours? Do I know them too?" He laughed, a tad high-pitched.

"Come on out guys," said the toaster, "I think he's calmed down now."

They stepped out cautiously from behind a large stone… and he *did* know them.

***

First came the pig, dressed in a suit and bow tie, walking on his hind legs. He was significantly larger than the porcelain version of him that sat on Dave's kitchen shelf, above the toaster. Next came the little plastic Jesus that he'd gotten from his grandmother's house when she died. Unlike the pig, who seemed to be flesh and blood, little plastic Jesus seemed exactly the same, about six or seven inches tall, in a blue robe with white undergarment, arms held out slightly from his sides, palm outward, in the international gesture for "give me a hug." In order to ambulate, his plastic base was split down the middle and the extra surface area under his feet made his steps jerky and exaggerated. "Hi Dave," he said.

Great, thought Dave, another helium voice. He supposed the pig spoke in helium as well.

"Hi Dave," said the pig, confirming it.

"You're all-- from my kitchen?"

"Yes," said the pig, "and no."

The toaster gestured for the pig to shut up.

"Hey!" said the pig, "*he* asked."

"It's hard to explain, Dave. Let's just say we all came here together."

241

"How did we get here?" asked Dave.

The toaster looked at little plastic Jesus as if looking for an answer.

"Slippery slope, toaster," said little plastic Jesus.

"Look, Dave," the toaster said, "Have you ever studied physics?"

"No."

"Plasma Theory? Wormholes?"

"No."

"Ever heard of Heisenberg's uncertainty principle?"

"No."

"Wondered how your consciousness affects reality?"

"Not at all."

"Exactly. If you had, then you wouldn't be the guy we need."

"Uh-huh- wha-?"

The toaster appeared to gather its thoughts. "Don't bother yourself with all the hows, big guy. It just is. You're here- with us- and we need you."

"Okay, so where is *here*?"

The pig groaned.

"Again," the toaster said, "an exact answer to that question is not something you're going to understand."

"Jesus!" exclaimed Dave. Little plastic Jesus perked up. "Would somebody please tell me where the hell I am??"

The three kitchen-dwellers looked at each other.

"Well, different people call it different things," said the toaster, "But the three of us like to call it Quirky land."

"Quirky!!" cheered the pig and little plastic Jesus, throwing up their arms in celebration. Little plastic Jesus' arms seemed to move as one piece on a single axis and the effect was that he appeared to be signaling a touchdown.

Dave closed his eyes, clicked his bare ankles together hard enough to hurt, and chanted, "There's no place like home."

"Come on Dave," said the toaster, "Let's take a walk. There's someone you need to meet. He'll clear it all up for you."

"The Wizard?"

"The Prophet."

II

The road turned out to be stone, but there was enough moss growing on it that Dave wasn't uncomfortable in bare feet, though he was afraid of stepping on snakes or God knows what else. Little plastic Jesus rode in Dave's pajama breast pocket (yes, even pockets).

"So why do you need *me*, exactly?" Dave asked as they walked.

"Well, obviously not for your physics knowledge," snorted the pig.

"Don't mind him," said little plastic Jesus, "He thinks the suit makes him smarter than everyone else."

"Oh, don't whitewash it for him," said the pig.

Little plastic Jesus ignored him. "As to why it has to be you exactly, I couldn't speak to that. It just is. I know it seems like a strange thing to say, but we didn't pick you, you were picked for us. And until we found you, we didn't know it was you. The

Prophet foretold that you would save us, but not just us... the *whole* thing."

Dave stopped and assumed a resistant posture. "What do you mean by the whole thing?"

"You know," said the pig, "for a witless dullard, he sure has a lot of questions."

"Witless! Doll- what?"

The toaster piped up, "Big guy, you just worry about saving us from Berger, Green, and Schmidt. The rest will take care of itself."

"Burger, Green, and Smith?"

"Oh, please don't encourage him," said the pig, "It's like being around a two-year-old."

"Give him a break," said little plastic Jesus, "He's just the way he's supposed to be."

"Oh sure," said the pig, "always forgiving people's shortcomings. Admit it. He's a moron."

"And your point?" said the toaster.

"Hey," said Dave, "You guys know I'm here, right?"

"Sorry, Dave," said little plastic Jesus, "but I guess the moment is calling for some straight talk."

"Don't-" said the toaster.

Little plastic Jesus ignored him. "It's nothing personal, Dave. You are exactly as the prophecies foretold."

"And that is?

"Honestly, and no offense, but, well, you're a bit of a dull guy."

"And quite stupid," added the pig. The toaster groaned.

"I'm not stupid." said Dave, eliciting a sarcastic snort from the pig.

"Maybe stupid is the wrong word," said little plastic Jesus, giving the pig a distinctively un-Jesus-like look, "You've never cultivated your imagination which is a required element for intellectual curiosity. And of course, curiosity is a required element for learning new things. It's not all your fault, so don't see it as a value judgment. You're dull… dim. So, what? You're dull, dim Dave and that's just who the Prophet saw in his vision, so no worries. Everything is how it should be. Lots of dull people have done great things."

Dave's head hung in resignation. "I'm really that bad?"

"Don't worry about it, big guy," said the toaster.

"Put it this way, Einstein," said the pig, "up till this point in your life the most creative thing you ever did was buy a porcelain pig in a suit and bow tie." He rolled his eyes.

Funny, thought Dave, you'd think he would like a porcelain pig in a suit and bow tie.

"So, if I'm that bad, then how am I supposed to help anyone?"

"Don't ask me," said the pig, "I can't imagine it. You're like the Antichrist here."

Now it was little plastic Jesus' turn to roll his eyes.

"Buck up, big guy," said the toaster, "I like you just the way you are."

"It's best we're straight with you, Dave," said little plastic Jesus, "Honesty is always best amongst friends. The Prophet will ease your mind, you'll see."

Dave stopped walking again. "Okay," he said, "we'll see. It doesn't appear that I'm going home anytime soon-" he paused, distracted by a tree sculpted into the shape of a dancing couple, "but if I'm going on some adventure with guys who keep calling me stupid then I want to know what to call you. I mean, little plastic Jesus, I know, of course…"

"How about we go with LPJ instead, or better yet, LJ… yeah, LJ. I've always wanted to be called LJ."

"Ok, LJ," said Dave, "Now, how about you two?"

"We don't really have names, Dave." said the toaster, "You call us whatever you want. How's that?"

"Great, okay, well then I'm gonna call you Toaster and I'm gonna call you Pig. Toaster, Pig, and LJ."

"Atta boy Dave!" said Toaster.

"That's our man," said LJ.

Pig said nothing. He was currently occupied by a fit of hysterical laughter, laying on his side, beating the ground with his free hooves.

***

Passing beyond the sculpted orchard brought Dave a measure of relief. The countryside now seemed a little more like home, not that he was used to the country either. He was a creature of the city. Concrete and buildings were his natural habitat. So, while leaving the unnerving trees behind put him a little more at ease, the countryside itself was a source of underlying trepidation. What quirky monsters lurked in these hills, he wondered?

It wasn't long before he discovered one, though he was unsure, in the end, how monstrous it truly was. While relaxing with his feet on the cool moss, he was quite shocked to see the moss swell and envelop his feet, even passing up between his toes. Dave tried to pull his feet back, but the moss held on. His struggle ended ten seconds later when he experienced the best foot massage of his entire life, well, the only foot massage of his entire life. When the moss withdrew, his feet had been pedicured.

Even with the 'mossage' (as Toaster called it) and pedicure, Dave eventually expressed a desire to rest his bare feet. This was more exercise than they were used to, by far. They started looking for a place to settle for the night and eventually saw a promising sight off the road to their left. Silhouetted by the setting sun, a man stood at the top of a hill. Next to him were two large tents and a flag which hung limply on its pole.

"That'll work," said Toaster, "It's Colonel Standish. There'll be an extra cot there."

"How do you know?" asked Dave.

"Trust me."

As they approached the crest of the hill, Dave could see the man was wearing mountaineering gear. Carabiners, anchors, and ropes hung from his belt. Other than that, he was dressed for a safari. He turned as he heard them approaching. Toaster's plinking and clanking made it hard not to hear them.

"Ho! Fellow climbers!" he called out. "Welcome to the summit! Watch your step! We don't want any unfortunate tumbles from up here!"

Dave turned and looked at the gentle slope behind him.

"Come! Come!" said Colonel Standish. He had a big, gray, handlebar mustache. "You must be tired from the climb. I have water and trail mix."

"Colonel Standish sir," said the toaster, saluting, "Might we bivouac with you for the night?"

"Of course, of course! You have my utmost admiration for your ascent. A difficult climb, what? We had to set up camp halfway last night."

About halfway down the hill, maybe forty yards, Dave could easily see the remnants of the previous night's camp.

"So LJ," he whispered, "this guy's bonkers, right?"

"No, he just climbs slowly."

"Bonkers."

"Quirky."

"QUIRKY!" cheered Toaster and Pig, throwing their arms in the air. Dave hadn't realized they were listening.

Colonel Standish stood proud, looking out over his conquest. "Ah, nothing like it, lads. We're lucky men."

Dave thought the view was nice, but not what he would have called spectacular.

"So," said the colonel, "What peaks await you after the descent tomorrow?"

"No peaks, Colonel. We're taking Dave, here, to the Prophet." said Toaster.

"Ah," the colonel looked somber, "a long and difficult journey."

Dave looked at LJ, who shook his head as if to say, *No, no it isn't.*

"Tonight, you rest here, men. Take the tent that would have been for the rest of my expedition if they'd made it." He turned to look back out over his vista, "Such a shame- good men lost."

"He always waits, but they never make it," whispered LJ.

"'Cause they don't exist," Dave whispered back.

Little plastic Jesus shrugged. "I'm not willing to make that judgment."

"Don't worry," said Pig, "Dim, dull, dumb, Dave will do it for you."

Soon after, as Dave crawled onto the cot, not even the sound of the crickets, which would have normally unnerved him to the point of sleeplessness, was enough to keep him from falling asleep, not even the one cricket who was obviously chirping backwards.

Later he awoke in the middle of the night. Toaster was apparently keeping watch or maybe he just didn't sleep. Dave didn't ask. He looked out to see the colonel still standing in the glow of the firelight, looking for his lost expedition. Suddenly, a brilliant beam of light from above enveloped him in a cone of light. The colonel waved out into the night, as if his expedition were approaching, a look of relief on his face. Then he faded out, becoming more and more transparent until he was gone. The beam of light retracted upward, and Dave looked up to see a disc-shaped, metallic object whisk off into the night.

"Hmm," said Toaster, "*that's* new."

***

In the morning, the colonel was still gone.

"Well," said Toaster, "the Prophet's enclave is just a couple miles from here. We should probably get going."

Dave looked around at the tents and the flag. "What about the Colonel?"

"He's gone." said Pig.

"Yeah, but-."

"Let it go, big guy." said Toaster, "Don't try to get it."

"Yes, heaven forbid we suffer any more of your explanations." said Pig.

"It's just quirky," said little plastic Jesus, with a forgiving smile.

"QUIRKY!!!" the three cheered, throwing their arms in the air.

There was no use in fighting.

They did the quirky cheer at least six more times on the way to the Prophet's village. Dave was thinking he'd had quite enough of quirky for several lifetimes. It was becoming more difficult to even be impressed by any of it. You'd seen one quirky thing, he thought, you'd seen them all.

But that was before he saw the Prophet.

***

The colossal proboscis sat in a high-backed chair like it was growing from it. The words seemed to flutter out of it, like there were hundreds of tiny flesh flaps, vibrating at different pitches throughout the massive, rapidly flaring nostrils. The effect was that of an enunciating snore.

"A man of narrow vision comes today

Tomorrow brings us closer to the dawn

To Berger, Green, and Schmidt, he makes his way

His freaky friends are getting on his nerves.

Wipe."

A dozen acolytes, robed, hooded, and wielding towels, descended upon him quickly, wiping him from top to bottom. A general murmur had erupted in the onlookers behind them. The High Priest stood next to Dave.

"It has been many years," he said, as the adepts wiped, "since we were last graced with a quatrain from Nostrildamus. You are given a great honor, Dave."

Dave watched the intricate, worshipful cleaning with no words.

"Don't mind him," Pig said to the priest, "He sometimes has trouble processing, if you know what I mean." Pig pointed to his head.

"Ah," said the priest, "As it has been written."

"Man," said Dave, hanging his head, "I am sooo tired of being called stupid."

The twelve acolytes were reverently refolding the towels and laying them gently into an ornate hamper.

"Dave," snored Nostrildamus, "Do you understand why you are here?"

"No--sir-- no, I really do not. I must say, in fact that I don't get any of this, but even so, must *everyone* treat me like a nitwit? Please, just tell me what I'm supposed to do here."

The light dimmed.

The flow between the strands is out of sync

The multiverse is hanging on the edge

For Dave the job is bring the balance back

Or else for sure the multiverse is doomed.

Wipe."

This time the surrounding hubbub was louder.

"Two in one day!" exclaimed the High Priest, "A truly joyous occasion!"

None of this, though, was making Dave feel any better. A second set of towels was placed gingerly in the hamper.

"I see you are still uncomfortable, Dave." said the nose, "Okay then, I will give you the un-poetic truth. A plasma influx from the negative strand has permeated all the multiverse in the form of destructive inter-dimensional beings. This universe in which you now find yourself sprang into existence organically as a counterbalance to this influx. But now, these inter-dimensional beings have infiltrated *this* universe as well in the guise of Berger, Green, and Schmidt, threatening an inter-dimensional catastrophe which could end all reality… wait, let me think of a quatrain…"

The onlookers softly breathed a collective "Ooooo." The acolytes looked at each other in something akin to terror. One ran out of the building as fast as he could.

"Okay," said Dave with a tone of resignation, "maybe you should go back to treating me like I'm stupid."

Pig snickered.

"Oh, this is no good-" said Nostrildamus

Dave raised his finger. "That's what I'm say--"

"Inter-dimensional will just *not work* in iambic pentameter. Wait--" The great proboscis wrinkled up, pensive. If a giant nose can have a look of sudden realization, the Prophet did.

"The stupid man will see the light in time"

The acolytes truly panicked now.

"The king will lead his forces to the line

I know it's not my normal thing to rhyme"

He paused. The room was utterly silent.

"But chaos has a boon for Dave to find!

Wipe."

The murmur from behind the group now rose to frenetic levels. "Three!" Dave heard someone exclaim. The acolytes seemed frozen, glancing frantically toward the entrance.

"WIPE!"

The High Priest ran to the acolytes and spoke in hurried, hush tones. Then he, too, began watching the entrance like the others.

"WHY HAVE I NOT BEEN WIPED?!!"

The panic in the ranks of the acolytes had spread into the huge numbers of onlookers. Some were rushing forward, offering handkerchiefs, only to be refused. A woman in the back was emitting a moan that was slowly rising like an air raid siren.

"WHAT'S A NOSE GOT TO DO TO GET <u>WIPED</u> AROUND HERE, ANYWAY?!!"

Now, the panic let loose. The audience of devotees fell to the ground and began prostrating themselves, moaning like the woman in the back.

"Maybe we should go," said Toaster.

"That's fine with me," said Dave and the four of them turned and left. Walking out, Dave nearly collided with the acolyte who was running back with a fresh stack of twelve holy towels.

***

Dave was finished, mentally. At this point, he wanted the dream to be over. He supposed, not for the first time, that he was lying on his kitchen floor, dying. Wasn't your life supposed to flash before your eyes in such circumstances? What happened to Saturday afternoons at Grandma's house? Ice cream sandwiches and root beer? This seemed like a poor substitute.

Another day of travel brought the group to a hill looking out over a long valley. Just inside the ridge that enclosed the far end of the valley, Dave could see a city of tents.

"It's the King's army, ready to march on Berger, Green, And Schmidt," said Toaster, "That big tent in the middle there is the King's."

"And I suppose the king is a giant mouth, or an ear, or possibly a giant asshole who talks with farts?"

"I believe Dave is getting a little testy," said Toaster.

Pig harrumphed, "The usual reaction of idiots to what they don't understand."

Dave ignored him. "Let's just go and get it over with."

***

The King was surrounded by his court, which, you'd have to guess, was pretty quirky, but by now, Dave was no longer cataloging. It made him feel better to rebel against it, deny that any of it was out of the ordinary. The herald announced him. "Your Majesty, I present, Dave."

The king jumped from his throne, obviously excited. He was short and bald but dressed in festive robes and a crown that Dave refused to think about. "Oh! Dave! I've heard so much about you! I mean, I've read all the quatrains! What joy! We really must celebrate! Welcome! Welcome!"

"Thank you, your Highness." If there was one thing that you could count on from Dave, it was manners, at least.

"Highness!" the king said, as if mentally ascertaining the word's worth, "Highness? I've never heard that one before…"

"I'm sorry. Your Majesty, then."

"No, no, I think I like Highness… I do…" His eyes looked far away, as if he were posing for a campaign photograph. After a long moment, he looked back at Dave. "So, Dave, you are here to help us?"

"That's what I'm told," he said, "but honestly, I don't understand any of this or what I'm supposed to do."

The court erupted in laughter.

"Marvelous!" said the king, "Outstanding! Well, I see you are already in uniform so obviously you understand that- but wait-." He turned to look toward the side of the tent. "Sergeant! This man has lost part of his uniform. Help him out with that if you please."

The sergeant stepped out a moment later and handed him a pair of burgundy slippers, just like the pair he had at home. Dave gawked at the sergeant, dressed in the exact same pajamas and slippers.

As he knelt to don his slippers, he looked at Toaster, saying out of the side of his mouth, "Did you tell them what I was wearing?"

Toaster raised his hands in front of him as if to say, *Not me.* Dave stood up with slippers now on his feet.

"Ah! Much better, yes?"

Dave had to admit they felt as comfortable as his slippers back home.

"Yes, your Highness, much better, thank you."

"Perhaps you might wish to review the troops before you depart?"

"Uhh- sure," Dave said, wishing this guy didn't know more about what he was going to do than he did. "But before we go, may I ask a question?"

"A most gracious request. How may I help you?"

"I have been in your land for some time now and haven't been able to get any kind of straight answer on this from anyone. Since you're the King, could you please, please tell me the name of this place?"

A gasp came from the court. The king looked taken aback. "You mean," he said, "You don't know?"

"No, your Highness, I am sorry."

Everyone in the tent seemed to snap into some state of alert, and for a brief, terrifying moment, Dave wondered if they were going to do something horrible to him.

"This land," said the king, dropping his cloak behind him to reveal a shimmering silver suit and spreading his arms like a Vegas show announcer, "is *Mambo-land!*"

Dave hadn't even noticed the band before, but suddenly there they were, launching into an upbeat salsa rhythm as everyone in the court paired up and began dancing.

"Everybody mambo!!" cried the king, his arms still spread, looking into the heavens.

Dave looked at Toaster. "Is this the part where we leave?"

"Better not," said LJ.

"Yeah," Toaster said, "He *really* likes his mambos."

As quickly as it began, it was over, the court settling into a court once more. Then the king took Dave out to present the troops.

Thousands upon thousands of men stood in rank, armorless and weapon-less, dressed in off-white pajamas with paired dark-blue pinstripes, one thicker than the other, breast pockets, and burgundy slippers.

When the presentation was over, the king turned and pointed to the ridge of hills behind him. "Over that ridge," he said, "lies the enemy, Berger, Green, and Schmidt, led by my arch-nemesis, John Jacob Jingle Heimer Schmidt, the heart of all evil. Good luck, Dave. We're all counting on you. When we see your signal, we will launch the attack."

"What sig-" Dave began before Pig pushed him from behind.

"Don't worry about it, Einstein. We got it all figured out." Again, everyone knew more about the plan than he did.

There was a path that led up the side of the hill to the crest. When they topped the hill, Dave almost cried.

There, laid out before him, was home.

III

In front of them lay cityscape as far as the eye could see. Cars and buses dotted the scene like little moving ants. Maybe it wasn't home, Dave thought, but it sure looked like it.

"Oh man, I hope there's a McDonald's," Dave said, and began running toward it like a calf to the teat. Pig was able to keep up on all fours, but Toaster was left behind.

As they approached the gate to the city, LJ implored Dave to stop. "Please, wait so Toaster can catch up."

Standing there, waiting on Toaster's *plink-clank*, Dave examined the entrance to the city. To his delight, he saw the gate was guarded by supermodels in bikinis. He could tell already that this was going to be a great place. Finally, Toaster arrived, huffing and puffing and they all approached the gate together.

"Halt!" said the supermodel on the left, "Do you have an appointment?"

"Yes," said Dave, "I have an appointment with Berger, Green, and Schmidt."

The supermodel rolled her eyes. "All appointments are with Berger, Green, and Schmidt," she said, "Who is your appointment with?"

"John Jacob Jingle Heimer Schmidt."

"Oh!" She seemed impressed, "And what is your name?"

"Dave- uh, Smith."

"Very good, Mr. Smith," she said, checking her ledger. "I'm afraid your pets here are not allowed in the city until they've been quarantined." She plucked LJ from his breast pocket. "Brittany will take care of them for you. Here's your receipt."

"I have a bad feeling about this," said LJ, "Don't leave us."

But Dave was already walking into the city, arm in arm with a supermodel.

"Don't forget us, Dave!" yelled Toaster.

"Yeah," yelled Pig, "Put that brain to use for something, anyway!"

Dave turned and waved and saw his companions being led away in a different direction. "They'll be alright, won't they?" he asked the model.

"They'll be in a safe place," she said.

"Good," said Dave.

"First things first," she said, "If you're seeing the CEO, then we've got to get you into a proper suit."

"Oh, I don't have any money."

"Not to worry, sweetie. The company takes care of all that for job candidates."

"Well, in that case, is there any fast food nearby?"

"Sure," she said, "what do you like?"

"Chicken nuggets are good."

"No problem." she said demurely, sliding her finger under his chin and smiling, "I think we can manage a few nuggets."

The decision of whether to get barbecue or honey mustard sauce was the mental process that helped him to shut his three companions out of his mind, along with everything else from the last few days that he just wanted to forget.

***

"Sorry about the mix-up, Smith." The CEO himself, John Jacob Jingle Heimer Schmidt sat in front of Dave, scrutinizing him. "A lot of David Smiths out there."

"Oh, no problem sir, perfectly understandable."

When two men had shown up for the interview at the same time, Schmidt's secretary had gone through the roof, berating a human resources rep over the phone and slamming her appointment books around as she tried to track the source of the confusion. In the midst of the incident, Dave casually asked the secretary what kind of work Berger, Green, and Schmidt actually did.

She shot him a look of utter contempt. "You are in the media consulting division," she said, raising her eyebrows in a sarcastic expression. It was a good thing she was busy, because Dave thought she threw him a suspicious look afterward.

"Well," said Schmidt, pausing a moment, looking him up and down again and then chuckling, "You seem like a pretty agreeable fellow."

This prompted a spontaneous affection on Dave's part. Schmidt just seemed like the co-worker you could trust. "Yes, sir."

"What is it you do exactly, Smith?"

"Well, I've had a lot of experience in accounting."

"Ah, capital! Capital!" said the CEO, "You've said the magic word! That's what you're looking for then?"

"Yes sir, but I'm also interested in consulting work. I know I don't have any experience, but-."

"Well, Smith, maybe eventually, but with no experience in that field…"

"Do you consult for any other industries?"

Schmidt gave him an odd look, much like the secretary earlier. "We have divisions for everything, Smith! From television programming, to stone masonry, to babysitting services, to higher education. We do it all! There is no field of endeavor here in Big Town that we do not guide. We smooth out the problems, Smith… make sure everyone's happy and productive. Now," he looked back down at his papers, "I have accounting openings in every one of our divisions and subsidiaries. Any preferences?"

"I trust your judgment sir, wherever you think I'd fit best."

"I like you, Smith. I've got a feeling you could have a bright future here at Berger, Green, and Schmidt."

"Thank you, sir."

"I'm going to keep you near me, so I can keep an eye on you personally. You'll be working out of our financing department."

"Thank you very much sir," said Dave, "May I ask you a favor of sorts?'

"Certainly Smith, we want the recruits happy."

"My three friends that were with me when I came have been put in quarantine."

"Oh?"

"Yes, I was hoping someone might be able to help them find a job or something. I don't know what they can do exactly, but they're pretty entertaining and might make a good television act. Here's my receipt for them."

John Jacob Jingle Heimer Schmidt rubbed his immaculately shaven chin, looking at the paper. "A television act, you say. Well, we always need more of those! I'll have someone look into it, Smith. You can go now."

"Thank you, sir."

"And Smith-"

"Yes sir?"

"Welcome to the company."

***

And that's how Dave got home.

At first, anyway.

He was back in his comfort zone. Cubicle office. Decent apartment. There was even a version of his favorite TV sitcom. Alternate universe or not, the sitcom humor was the same.

There were, in fact, versions of every show that Dave liked, even if they were slightly different.

In the day, he crunched numbers and at night he watched TV, ate fast food, and minded his own business, just like at home. At times, he was even able to forget that he was no longer in his own universe. When the thought pursued him, he fled.

But a person can only run so far, and as weeks stretched into a month, Dave found himself headed out to the movies. At home he never would have paid outlandish theater prices. He would just rent a DVD. But on that particular night, he couldn't stay at home. For some inexplicable reason, the thought of being alone in the apartment drove him from it. He saw a superhero flick called *Captain Darkness 7: Revenge of the Dark*. The special effects were incredible, but even that couldn't hold his attention.

There was a churning in his gut that was getting worse, a restlessness he had never felt before, and each day after that, it got worse.

His thoughts kept returning to his travel companions, and in his mind, he began calling them the three musketeers, because of their all-for-one "quirky" cheers and, well, it also helped that there were three of them.

He kept hearing Pig's last words to him as he walked away.

Then, just when he'd get himself worked up enough to think he needed to go find those guys, another part of him would rise up and say things like, "Do you really want to start that kind of trouble?"

"You'll lose everything."

"Don't rock the boat."

"You'll get fired and then what will you do?"

At the end of this exchange he would feel exhausted and weak and resigned to the fact that you couldn't fight fate.

Then one evening, at the height of this spiritual conundrum, the supermodel who'd escorted him into the city showed up at his door.

"I haven't been able to stop thinking about you," she said, disrobing.

It took several more weeks before the churning gut made another appearance. Ultimately though, there was no better reminder for Dave that he was in another universe than making mad, passionate love to a supermodel.

"Smith," said Schmidt, holding aloft a manilla envelope "I've been looking over your report here and all these figures seem to be in order. Good work."

"Thank you, sir."

"Another issue has come up though."

"Oh?"

"Yes, I've been talking to the boys over in programming and they're pretty concerned about that act you brought in. Seems they've been trying them out in several different media and well, it's just not working out."

Dave tried not to display the alarm he was suddenly feeling.

"Yes, let's see here," Schmidt said, shuffling a stack of papers and looking down his nose through his glasses, "With test audiences we found that 70 percent were quote-*uncomfortable*-unquote, when presented with this act. 10 percent said they felt sorry for the mutants, and a whopping 74 percent did not understand the act at all. I'm afraid your friends just don't pass any of the parameters that define successful entertainment."

"What about the other 26 percent?"

"They loved it," said Schmidt, looking suddenly concerned, "But you and I know those figures are inconsequential."

"They sing pretty well- did they try them out on that?"

"In fact, they did, and the numbers are stunningly similar. You can't argue with the numbers, Smith. You know that."

"Yes, but-."

"The numbers don't lie."

"Well, what will happen to my friends, then?"

"Don't worry Smith, we'll dispose of them for you. It's one of your company benefits. We don't want you to have to deal with that inconvenience." Schmidt waved his hand as if it were all inconsequential. "So, anyway, back to work with you! There's still a half day of productivity ahead! Onward and upward, I always say!"

"Wait-," started Dave. His head was swimming. He'd never meant for the three musketeers to come to harm. He had to think fast.

"Wait!?" boomed John Jacob Jingle Heimer Schmidt, "What's there to wait for?"

"Perhaps-."

"Perhaps nothing Dave! I told you. The numbers don't lie! Now I don't care how attached to this project you've become. You've got to let it go!"

"Maybe the numbers do lie, sir."

The walls seemed to whisper in response to that statement.

"Numbers lie?" exclaimed Schmidt, "And just what do you mean by that, sir?"

Dave's mind raced for an answer. He reached and found something he could use, mathematics.

"Maybe there's a variable we missed, something intangible… difficult to quantify."

The whisper in the walls grew exponentially and suddenly there were dozens of men in suits, crowding around Schmidt as if shielding him from Dave's question. They seemed to materialize out of the walls, but Dave realized they'd been there all along, blending into the background. They whispered excitedly amongst themselves, the whispers melting together in some sort of squirrely hissing sound. Every few seconds Dave could make out bits and pieces.

"… intangible variables?"

"…incomplete data…"

"…seriously, what's the LCD here?"

"…what demo are we…"

"…is preposterous…"

The whispers intertwined like a clutch of snake babies. The men in suits were moving in much the same way. They were an organic whole, pressing Dave toward the door as if oblivious to his presence.

"Mr. Schmidt!" called Dave over the heads of the suits, "Mr. Schmidt!"

But John Jacob Jingle Heimer Schmidt was surrounded by men whispering in his ear. Dave would have to find his friends on his own. Before he knew it, he was in the hallway and the door slammed behind him.

***

In the hallway of Berger, Green, and Schmidt, the scene was not quite the cacophony of inside Schmidt's office, but there was still an air of agitation and all the workers moved with a sense of urgency. Schmidt's secretary looked at the clock, grabbed a pile of envelopes, and hurried down the hall.

Now, Dave had never done anything remotely disrespectful in the workplace, but he was beginning to really worry that his new friends were going to be lost in all this confusion. That damn toaster had burned every piece of toast for ten years, but he'd really gotten to like him. And Pig obviously hated him, but he was still awfully cute in his suit and bowtie. And LJ? Well, who would want little plastic Jesus to suffer? Not Dave. He had no idea what "dispose of them" meant, but he didn't want to find out.

As soon as the secretary rounded the corner out of sight, Dave began rifling her desk, looking for any communiques from the programming division. Finally, he found one. It was indeed about his friends. From the exasperated tone of the memo, it looked like it was one of many. Dave noted the division's address. It was just down the block. He tucked the memo in his pocket and ran for the elevator.

In the street, the agitation was spreading, and he found much the same scene as he approached the front desk of the programming division. Dave presented his company identification and the memo about his three musketeers.

"I'm running an accounting review of the disposal costs for non-viable acts." he said, "I need to see this act for proper identification and validation of the case study."

He wasn't sure if it would work, but the receptionist seemed distracted enough to not question him. She automatically turned to her appointment binder, flipped back a few dozen pages and said, "Sub-level B, Office number 223." She gave him a strange look and returned to her ringing phone.

Dave sprinted for the elevator. At Sub-level B he hopped off and looked both ways, up and down the hallway. These rooms were given office numbers but they were obviously cells. A desk at the end of the hallway was abandoned.

Glancing through the mesh windows on his way down the hall, he was shocked to see Colonel Standish in one of the cells, looking through the walls like he was still scanning the distance for his lost comrades.

Dave found *his* lost comrades in Office 223. When he opened the door, Toaster bounded out with a *plink* and a *clank*.

"You got 'em on the run, Dave! Now let's get out of here before they get mad!"

"It's about time, Einstein," said Pig.

"Wait," said Dave and ran down the hall, unlatching Colonel Standish's "office."

At first, Standish looked confused, but he soon regained whatever wits he had in the first place. "I knew you lads would get here!" he looked down the hallway at all the locked rooms, 'Go! I'll free as many as I can!"

***

The four made their way through the main lobby without a second look. No one was there. The entire population of the building was gone, and Dave imagined they'd been sucked back into the walls.

"You came in the nick of time, Dave," said little plastic Jesus, "We were about to break."

"They wanted me to snort," snorted Pig, "Thought it was funny. 'Oink!' they'd say! Morons!"

They burst out of the doors and into an empty street. It felt like low tide before a tsunami out there. Dave carried Toaster and LJ so they could make better time and ran for the gate through which they'd come into the city, months earlier.

As they passed the Berger, Green, and Schmidt Corporate Headquarters, the biggest building in Big Town, Toaster told Dave to stop. "Let me down," he said, "we have to go in there for a minute."

"Why?"

"You'll see."

They ran inside the building and Toaster led them down a side hall to a door marked "Supplies."

"Open it, Dave."

Toaster ran into the little room packed with cleaning supplies and promptly plugged himself into the wall. His insides began to glow and within moments he began vibrating and shaking.

As smoke began to rise from him, Dave cried out, "Toaster!"

"He knows what he's doing," said Pig.

Smoke rolled from him. Dave noted that his face had an orgasmic expression. Then, as quickly as it began, it was over. Toaster unplugged himself and turned to the others. "We've got to get out of here *now*."

Toaster took off toward the door and Dave had to run to keep up. The experience seemed to have supercharged him. His *thunk-plink-ponk-rattle* now had the cadence of a galloping horse. As they hit the street, Dave had to yell at Toaster to slow down.

"What was that all about?" he asked.

"We have to signal the Mambo King," said Toaster.

"And that was your signal?"

"No-."

A huge explosion shattered the building's doors behind them.

"*That* was the signal," said Toaster, "now let's go!"

"Holy- wait!" shouted Dave, taking off after Toaster, "How'd you do that?"

"I overloaded the wires in the wall behind the cleaning supplies." Toaster called back.

"But there were *people* in that building!… I think…"

"All of them little Eichmanns, big guy!"

Dave stopped dead for a moment then began chasing Toaster again, "Wha-?"

"Sorry," said little plastic Jesus from his suit pocket, "Toaster may have some repressed homicidal tendencies. We probably should have mentioned it."

"Well," said Pig, "you'd think ten years of trying to electrocute him might have clued him in."

"But he's so darn--" said Dave, struck dumb, "how--"

"Quirky isn't always pretty, Dave," said little plastic Jesus.

"QUIRKY!!!" they all cheered. Ahead was the gate, and the Mambo King's army was coming over the ridge. From behind them a dull roar was beginning to emerge from the bowels of Big Town.

***

Dave watched the battle unfold from the hillside with the Mambo King. "Someone get this man a uniform," he shouted to his guard. Soon, Dave was back in jammies and slippers.

Pig and Toaster chose to join the battle. Little plastic Jesus affirmed that he was, indeed, a pacifist.

"A sword!" yelled Toaster, still supercharged and running around like a wide-eyed maniac, "Someone give me a sword!"

The forces of Berger, Green, and Schmidt poured through the gate onto the field. The army was mostly made up of consultants in suits, looking as if they had all been cloned. The consultants advanced, hurling fart jokes and giggling about their private parts. The left flank of the Mambo King's army met them by dropping to the ground for a nap. The consultants stopped, confused, and began huddling together, discussing. Eventually one of them ran screaming from the huddle, "Ratings are down! Ratings are down! We'll all be fired!" and then he exploded. The BGS right flank fell to disarray.

The middle ranks were led by a phalanx of supermodels, advancing on the line in full runway strut. Many a quirky soldier stood transfixed, their jaws gaping as the beauties approached. That was when Dr. Chooly's robots were released. A whole history existed behind these controversial devices, much of which was related to Dave by the Mambo King as the battle raged (he seemed quite intrigued by them), but basically, they had one purpose, which they set to forthwith.

The robots zeroed in on the bikini-clad supermodels and once within range, a metal claw appendage shot out and snatched their bikini bottoms. The robots then ran off, chittering an ornery robot laugh, waving the bikini bottoms in the air. The supermodels, to a one, dropped into the same pose, legs crossed, right hand over crotch, left hand over pursed lips, and eyebrows raised in a look of innocent surprise.

If someone passing by had taken a picture, the supermodels might have played a more important role in the battle. As it was, no one did, and they stayed glued to their spots wondering why on earth this photo shoot was taking sooo long.

On the right flank, an immaculately groomed television reporter, oozing gravitas, led the advance of the BGS forces. He penetrated the quirky lines under the guise of interviewing soldiers for a human-interest piece. His last interview was Pig, who refused to be impressed by the cameras and gave only paradoxical answers to the reporter's questions, causing the correspondent's face to redden and his neck to throb. His lapel suddenly curled up and his top shirt button flew off. "CUT!" he yelled, "Wardrobe!"

Unfortunately for him, wardrobe was busy chasing Dr. Chooly's robots and the right flank stalled.

You might be tempted to say the end began when a consultant, singing lead for a boy band performing a ballad on the front lines, momentarily forgot to sing his part when he saw Toaster running at him with a sword he shouldn't have been able to carry, let alone swing around like that. You might be tempted to note that, when the consultant started laughing, he abandoned all the ideas of the mainstream, thus sowing the seeds for the ultimate dissolution of Berger, Green, and Schmidt.

But Toaster killed him, so that wouldn't be entirely accurate.

The boy band fled.

Confronted with so much incongruity at once was more than the consultant forces could take and they fell to confusion, some exploding right on the spot. A whirlwind rose from the middle of the battlefield, sucking all the consultants toward it and forming a giant heap of squirming consultancy. From this heaping mass emerged a massive head, and then a massive body, a monster of colossal proportions in the shape of John Jacob Jingle Heimer Schmidt.

"DAVE SMITH!" the colossus boomed, "REPORT TO YOUR BOSS!"

Dave almost ran off at that moment but managed to make himself step out in front of the King's Guard. "I apologize," Dave yelled up at the figure of Schmidt, "I know that was an awkward way to quit. Please consider this my notice."

A humongous fist descended toward him, extending a truly impressive index finger, and pointing at Dave.

"THERE IS NO INTANGIBLE VARIABLE! THE NUMBERS DON'T LIE!" the voice shook the hillside.

Dave was quaking, but managed to say, "Yes sir, I think there is."

"YOU CAN'T PROVE THAT! YOU CAN'T!"

"I think I can," he said. He reached over and took the arm of the sergeant beside him and began to mambo.

"STOP THAT!" boomed the giant John Jacob Jingle Heimer Schmidt.

"Everybody mambo!" yelled the Mambo King and the Latin music kicked in immediately. Once again, Dave hadn't even realized the band was there. From out of the city, which was beginning to crumble behind them, Colonel Standish and all the quirky POWs came spilling out.

Soon, the mega-consultant was surrounded. Something was clearly happening. John Jacob Jingle Heimer Schmidt was imploding, surrounded by soldiers doing the mambo in boring pajamas.

In a tortured voice, he screamed as he shrunk, "WHAT A UNIVERSE! WHAT A UNIVERSE!"

The process seemed to accelerate. He was rapidly shrinking now. "THIS DIMENSION SUCKS! YOU"RE ALL LOSERS!"

"BAH-" he scoffed, taking one last look at the dancers, "YOU CALL THAT ENTERTAINMENT?"

And then he winked out- with a fart sound.

One of the dancing soldiers giggled.

***

IV

They stayed with the King for a week or so after the battle. Before they left, Dave took one look back at the where Big Town had been. The buildings had all fallen, but the debris lay in such a way that, from the top of the hill, it resembled a huge game of tic tac toe. Quirkiness was already beginning to reclaim its space.

The journey led them back to Nostrildamus who happily explained to Dave about the strands and the influx of energy, and how Dave's own acts of creation had undone Berger, Green, and Schmidt. Dave still wasn't sure he understood any of it.

There were no quatrains.

The acolytes looked relieved, standing next to a truly large stack of towels.

They ran into Colonel Standish along the way too. They lingered with him for a couple of days, helping him climb a hill. For once anyway, his expedition arrived at the summit intact. Now, it was time to go home.

Another day, and they arrived back at the spot where Dave had first appeared.

Dave looked around and then down at little plastic Jesus, "So long LJ. It was nice getting to know you."

"Bless you, my son," he said, signaling a touchdown.

Dave turned to Pig. "Hope I didn't disappoint you, Pig."

"No, Dave," said Pig, "I may have been wrong about you after all. Good luck back in Dullsville."

Toaster stuck his hand out in front of him and Dave leaned down and shook it between his finger and thumb.

"Stick a fork in me anytime, Dave."

"I will. I'll come and visit someday."

"No- er, I mean, Good!" Toaster pointed to the ground. "I mean- well- now."

On the ground next to him lay the fork that he hadn't realized he'd dropped on that fateful day when he'd first encountered a walking, talking toaster.

As he began to stick the fork in Toaster, he said, "I hope we can still be friends after this."

"QUIRKY!!!!" cheered the three musketeers, and then Dave was gone.

***

Of course, I'm the one who found Dave, his hair all frizzed out, laying on the floor in his lackluster pajamas and slippers. I'd gotten worried when he didn't answer his phone because he never goes anywhere. He told me his story right then and there, wouldn't let me call an ambulance.

For a while I had my doubts, that's for sure, but as he went on, it dawned on me that inventing something like this was just way beyond anything one could expect from Dave.

When he finished, I said, "That's a wild tale, buddy. You should write it down."

"Are you kidding?" he asked, "write down a story about how stupid I am? Not likely."

"It's too bad something like that can't be proved," I said, humoring him, I thought.

"Oh, but I can," he said and walked out of the room for a moment. He returned with a pair of burgundy slippers in his hand that matched the ones he was wearing.

"Do I look like a guy who buys two pairs of matching red slippers?"

No, Dave looks and acts like a guy who buys one pair and wears them out. I started giving him more of the benefit of the doubt after that.

As for Dave, well, he certainly changed as a result of his "experience." He actually now watches and tries to understand documentaries about physics. He also reads more, and he's been known to refer to media consultants as "the lowest form of life on earth," that "ruin everything they touch." On more than one occasion I've heard him refer to his toaster as "that cute little terrorist."

Last I heard, he was dating. I guess the time with the extra-dimensional supermodel gave him a little more confidence. Good for him. I'd been trying to fix him up for years with no success.

I heard she was a quirky girl.

Imagine that.

WEST VIRGINIA'S VAMPIRE PROBLEM

Larry D. Thacker

Thank God clowns scare the hell out of northern West Virginian vampires.

Don't ask me why, I've not researched that deep into the mythology, but luckily enough for the MFA program I'm attending up in the sleepy little town of Buckhannon, West Virginia, the strain of nesting vampires there react to clowns like the Vatican was some sort of training school for Ringling Brothers.

I discovered this vital morsel of mortal empowerment one night early in my first residency. I hadn't slept well with the stress of being an older student and all the work they'd piled on us, but on this night I'd finally succumbed to some heavy rest after a hard day of poem-ing. It was winter and the old dorm rooms overheated, so I'd cracked my window. A mistake.

I was sleeping too soundly for my own good. Had I been struggling to sleep as usual I might have heard the long clawed fingertips landing on the sill, been chilled by the icy whirl of wind slipping in to fill the room, sensed the window inching higher, the bare and snow damp feet padding across the tile floor. None of that stirred me.

No, it was the beast's guttural gasp startling me awake. But I couldn't move, even as this *thing* constructed of menacing shadow, as if pulling darkness from the room, feeding from it, edged closer. Only the glow of my alarm clock glared in the monster's flaming red-orange eyes, off its perfectly pointed teeth, bared by twitching anxious lips.

I stared, helpless.

It stared. But not *at me*. It was distracted, it seemed, by the collection of porcelain clowns I'd picked up only that afternoon at the Buckhannon Goodwill. I had them prettily arranged on the bedside table. The creature seemed mesmerized, even frightened. I always purchased the creepiest ones I could find, of course. Lucky me.

This…*thing*…intruding on my mind must have lost some concentration and control, for I was then able to move in that instant, defending myself by snatching up the closest things worth weaponizing – of course, these heavy, vintage, Japanese-made, mid-century clowns.

The beast was frozen in its tracks, shadowy and wide-eyed now and I'm chucking clowns at it for all I'm worth, for my life. One bounces off its chest, doing no good, only pissing it off. But the next one careens off its forehead, crashing against the wall, my aim improving.

I smashed the head off a tall one like you'd do a beer bottle in a bar fight and flung it hard as I could, end-over-end, watching it plunge neck deep into the beast's eye socket like a dagger.

You'd have thought this innocent figurine was created of concretized garlic and holy water. It sparked and smoked like I'd broken hell open. The monster flooded the room with shrieks, like a stabbed overstuffed bag of rabbits, high-pitched and panicky, staggering about gripping its face, stomping and slipping on cheap Asian porcelain, the room strobing with fiery bursts from every orifice.

It was clear what I was facing. This was vampire country. You know a vampire when you're enthralled as prey, when a psychic link is established. My advantage had been the clowns' unexpected breaking of the spell, our strange uplink of sorts snapped away. And now the bastard knew that I knew what secret Buckhannon, even Wesleyan, harbored, as it turned and jumped headlong in retreat into the snowy night.

Who could I tell? *Where one is found, many lurk*, is the old saying. Trusting anyone was premature.

But I could do nothing if dead or myself turned. I had to preserve the innocents of the program and myself.

I had to replace my lost weaponry. I combed the town's stores for more clowns. I'd randomly position them throughout the dorm like little booby-traps in hopes of frustrating the creatures if they attacked.

In the meantime, it could serve as a joke for the living. I knew this group of writers. They'd cast equal blame throughout the group. I'd deny it like everyone else. Some would find the clowns cute, some creepy, some would harken back to an unexplained fear harbored from childhood, afraid to approach the little knick knacks as if the creepy smiles and unblinking eyes waited for sundown to animate and set out to find them in their sleep. It was that sort of near primordial fear I'd seen in the night visitor's one good eye as it leapt away.

I hid several around the building's perimeter, then more in plain sight inside: in the center of a random hallway, on the landing of the stairway, in the elevator. If these blood-starved Strigoi made it into the building, they'd have these sweet little hellos to deal with.

And I waited.

Nothing the first night. Or the second.

Were they waiting me out?

My fellow students moved the clowns around to play with each other's nerves. I denied having anything to do with them, just like everyone else. I lied. Writers are such good liars after all.

On the third night we were up watching movies. It was snowing hard. I fell asleep on the couch. A mistake. Perhaps everyone figured I was comfortable, so they left me. Alone. Vulnerable. Away from my room and my own supply of weaponry. I'd fashioned up what was a fabulous fighting tool. I'd stolen a mop handle from the custodial closet and attached an upside-down wooden cross, the end of which I'd whittled down to a fine piercing point. I'd taken a porcelain headed clown doll and crucified it on the wooden cross. It was my intention to shove a clown so far down the throat of one of these beasts that the whole nest would be burping clown paint for a week.

If only I'd kept proper vigil I might have detected 'ole One-Eye slinking up the building's back end, crawling vertically along the brownstone to avoid a fine little mime on a unicorn I'd stashed inside a snow covered holly tree, the fiend's shadowy infiltration of the main lobby, its tracking of my scent to the couch I snored upon.

I think my very obnoxious Insane Clown Posse hoodie caused it hesitation.

I was startled awake by the awfulest sounds of flailing and choking and of warm and wet splatting on my face. The creature had nearly gotten me, but was now halted, was vibrating violently, as if electrocuted, gurgling what I hoped was some last breaths, its one good eye locked on me in hatred and confusion as it fell to its knees and finally face first, motionless before the couch, revealing the sudden hero of the moment.

I noticed his huge, red floppy shoes first. The exaggerated striped baggy pants held up by blue suspenders over a white ruffled silk shirt dotted with blue. Blood splatters covered most of the outfit now. He brandished *my* crucifix pike, now gore-saturated, with his once white-gloved hands. The man's naturally red and curly hair flowed to his shoulders. The red foam nose set off the face, a serious stare squinting through a make-up job now melting off from sweat and blood.

But I recognized that smile under it all from class.

"It's about time someone showed up that can lend us a hand with these damn vampires," a winded, but familiar voice declared. The clown reached up and popped off his blood-splatted nose and tossed it to me.

"Here, catch," Dr. Allen ordered. This same man had lectured us on the pitfalls of the French Villanelle just that afternoon. "See how that fits. We'll fit you for your own soon."

ABOUT THE PRESS

Unsolicited Press is a small publishing house in Portland, Oregon and is dedicated to producing works of fiction, poetry, and nonfiction from a range of voices, but especially the underserved. Our team has published books that aren't afraid to take on topics of race, gender, identity, feminism, patriarchy, mental health, and more. The team is comprised of hardworking volunteers that are passionate about literature.

Learn more at www.unsolicitedpress.com.

ABOUT C.M. CHAPMAN

C.M. Chapman worked 25 years in radio production before pursuing his Master of Fine Arts degree at West Virginia Wesleyan College. He was awarded the Irene McKinney Teaching Fellowship and taught for four years at West Virginia Wesleyan. He was first published in the anthology, *So It Goes: A Tribute to Kurt Vonnegut*. Since then, he has published in many journals, including *Limestone*, *Cheat River Review*, *Dark Mountain* in the U.K., and *Unlikely Stories*. In 2017, his story "The Moth in the Stair" was nominated for a Pushcart Prize by *Still: The Journal*. He has published a fiction chapbook, *Music & Blood*, with Latham House Press, and a novel-in stories, *Suicidal Gods*, released in 2019 by Unsolicited Press.

ABOUT LARRY THACKER

Larry D. Thacker is a Kentuckian writer, artist, and educator now hailing from Johnson City, Tennessee. His stories can be found in past issues of *Still: The Journal*, *Pikeville Review*, *Fried Chicken and Coffee*, *Dime Show Review*, *Vandalia Journal*, *Grotesque Quarterly*, and *Story and Grit*. His poetry is in over 170 publications including *Spillway*, *Valparaiso Poetry Review*, *American Journal of Poetry*, and *Appalachian Heritage*. His books include the folk history, *Mountain Mysteries: The Mystic Traditions of Appalachia*, the poetry chapbooks *Drifting in Awe* and *Memory Train*, as well as the full collections *Drifting in Awe*, *Grave Robber Confessional*, *Feasts of Evasion*, and *Gateless Menagerie*. His short story collection, *Working it Off in Labor County*, is published with West Virginia University Press. His MFA in poetry and fiction is earned from West Virginia Wesleyan College. Visit his website at: www.larrydthacker.com